REMEMBER ME

Fay Weldon

BALLANTINE BOOKS • NEW YORK

All rights reserved under International and Pan-American Copyright Conventions. Published in the United States by Ballantine Books, a division of Random House, Inc., New York, and simultaneously in Canada by Ballantine Books of Canada, Ltd., Toronto, Canada. Originally published by Random House, Inc., 1976.

Library of Congress Catalog Card Number: 76-14165

ISBN 0-345-32976-7

Manufactured in the United States of America

First Ballantine Books Edition: November 1977
Third Printing: November 1985

1

Monday morning, six o'clock. Who's asleep?

The doctor, the doctor's wife, the doctor's children (alleged), but not the doctor's cat, who sits waiting on the bathroom windowsill for the family's awakening, and his own sliced oxliver, comfort and repose.

Two blocks away, in his tall terrace home, Jarvis the architect sleeps, and so does his second wife Lily beside him, and so does their small son Jonathan in the adjacent room. Do Jarvis and Lily dream sweet dreams or guilty dreams? Sweet dreams.

Jarvis Katkin is the doctor's patient. The doctor's wife is Jarvis's employee, and a little else besides. Who's asleep? Not Madeleine, Jarvis's first wife; not at all. Four blocks further on, in her sorry basement home, Madeleine lies awake on her lumpy mattress, as is her custom at this hour of the morning, and curses Jarvis, his second wife Lily and their son Jonathan. But the curses of the living are clouded and have little power. See how Jarvis, gently waking, turns to Lily and fondles her white brown-tipped breasts, smooths her smiling lips with his coarse and capable finger. Their love is blessed, not cursed. So far.

Hilary the schoolgirl, Madeleine's daughter, Jarvis's first-born, wakes at the stroke of six, feels alone and frightened, climbs into her mother's bed, and lies there sleepless, cold and lardy, against her mother's hard and feverish side (there where once her father lay and slept). She remains uneasy and uncomforted, as well she might, like any usurper to an abdicated throne.

Seven o'clock. Good morning!

Margot the doctor's wife awakes, assuming this to be a day like any other. Why should she not? The bed is warm, deep and familiar; the doctor and his wife have slept in it for some fifteen years, and made love in it some fifteen hundred times, reserving this pleasure—by and large—for each other alone. Pleasant images frequent the dreams of the doctor's wife. Why not? Since the advent of the doctor's Emergency Service, nights in this suburban corner house, where leafy ways meet, have been peaceful and unplagued by nightmares, disturbed by nothing worse than the padding of the doctor's cat off on his inconsequential journeys into the black night. The doctor's cat is a battered, randy tom, once black, now rusty, wormy within and flea-ridden without. The doctor doses his cat with free-sample antibiotics and steroids, but to no avail. Margot regards him with admiration and abhorrence mixed. He is the doctor's cat, not hers.

Good morning!

Margot, wife and mother, wakes from sleep refreshed, as befits her virtuous self. She is a little woman, smooth and plump, nicely bosomed, like some pet wood pigeon. Margot's face is round and bland; her brown and curly hair is sensibly short. Margot's sharp straight little nose still peels from August's holiday in the sun. Margot stirs. She yawns. Her teeth are white, small and even; her tonsils are healthy. Margot remains in good health not so much because of her husband's care but in spite of the lack of it.

Those who care for all the world, as the doctor does, sometimes seem to have trouble caring for just one person. Or so Margot's friend Enid once remarked, observing the neglected whitlow on Margot's thumb. Enid finds fault with any husband other than her own. Once she started on him, where would she stop?

Enid makes trouble. Enid should keep her mouth shut. Enid's words hurt more than any whitlow. She should reserve her opinion for interdepartmental memos. Enid is a civil servant.

Margot's brown button eyes fly open. She sighs. Listen now as Margot eavesdrops on herself, upon the babel of consciousness within, those multitudinous inner voices which ceaselessly define the self by shift and change, as the shore defines the sea and the sea defines the shore. Listen:

Oh, I am the doctor's wife, waking. I am Margot—housewife, mother, waking to the world I have made, a warm and homely place in which others grow, if not myself. How nice! But something lingers after sleep, some sense of sorrow, apprehension. What is it? Am I in mourning for myself, lost somewhere long ago, drowned in the sea of other people's demands, a family's expectations? [No, as the eyelids flutter, apprehension vanishes, sorrow dissolves, reality sweeps in.] I am Margot, wife and mother, folding in night thoughts before the day as a sailor folds in a sail before a rising wind. Beside me, sleeping too late, Philip. Downstairs rising too early, the children, breakfasting no doubt on cereal and too much milk. Philip's milk. Philip comes first. Husbands do.

Up gets Margot, the doctor's wife, slipping her feet into sensible Marks & Spencer slippers, wrapping her body in a blue seersucker dressing gown which goes through the washing machine without damage and needs no ironing, and is so familiar to her family, they would be at a loss to describe it. Up gets Margot, with her thick little body, wifely; her past unacknowledged, her future unquestioned, making herself useful, as women do. Up gets Margot to a day like no other.

2

Bright and early!

Up gets Lily Katkin, the butcher's daughter, Jarvis the architect's second wife, to a day like no other before or since. Up gets Lily bright and early, to prepare breakfast for Jarvis her husband and Jonathan her son. Good Lily!

Lily squeezes fresh chilled oranges into the blender, adds honey, and blends for fifteen seconds. She has iced glasses waiting. She has put them in the refrigerator the night before, as is her custom. Lily's husband and Lily's son wait obediently at the breakfast counter, their faces and hands washed, their hair combed, marveling at such wifely and maternal excellence. The coffee is filtering, newly made from freshly ground, lately roasted beans (low-calorie milk powder will be added to the cups, alas, and not cream, but never mind). Eggs from the health-food shop have been boiled for three and three-quarter minutes; the starch-reduced bread has been evenly toasted, shaken free of crumbs and placed in the little white china toast rack. The tablecloth is white and clean; the china blue and white; knives and forks, carefully washed by hand and not in the machine, retain their strength and color.

Jarvis Katkin sits, waits, watches, marvels. Lily is Jarvis's lucky ticket in the lottery of life. (So Lily's mother Ida wrote from New Zealand on the occasion of their marriage.) Jarvis has large pale-blue eyes, heavily lidded, slightly bloodshot, and thick, pale, dusty eyebrows. Jarvis's skin is loose from dieting, folding on either side of a bold, coarse-grained, handsome nose. Jarvis is not at his best this morning. Last night's drink and this morning's sex still fuddle his perceptions of the world, and he breathes heavily as he waits for his egg in the pause between orange juice and coffee. The orange juice, so fresh and cold, trickled in a chilly stream down his throat to his stomach, and now lies there, acid and uneasy. Jarvis does not like orange juice but scarcely cares to say so. He hiccups gently. Lily frowns (a pretty sight). Lily does not want anything to be out of control, least of all, Jarvis's digestion. She would have his insides on the outside if she could, the better to observe them, understand them, and control them. Lily cannot abide a mystery.

Lily has soft smooth hands which move confidently amongst the material objects of this world. Lily's nails are almond-shaped and unbroken, and the translucent pink varnish remains unchipped as now she delicately fishes in the clear washing-up water for Jonathan's mislaid silver christening spoon. Jonathan needs it for his egg. Lily cleans the spoon with silver polish every single day. Lily's mother sent it from New Zealand. The spoon is becoming very thin, almost sharp. If Lily carries on like this, Jonathan will cut his little mouth on its edges.

Lily's arms are covered not with common hair but with a soft and silky down. Lily's legs are long and full, tapering from rounded buttocks; Lily's toenails are always manicured; Lily's waist is small and her breasts are high and rounded, so that although she goes braless, she is assumed by those who do not much like her (and there are many such) to be boldly and old-

fashionedly uplifted. Lily's face has the crude regular
beauty of some painted peasant angel, colors washed
out by the passing seasons, leaving, as it were, the faint
echo of better days behind. It is the look of experience.
Lily's skin is pale; her smile is slow and sweet; her long
thick hair is a careful and expensive mixture of silver,
gold and grey, in careful disarray. Lily is twenty-eight.
She was born with the moon rising in Leo, and the sun
in Aquarius. Lily moves carefully, but with a certain
stiffness and lack of grace. Lily is the butcher's daughter. In the kitchen, in the house, she lacks abandon. It
may be very different in bed, of course.

Does this jowly man, this husband, this Jarvis, whose
waist when he married Madeleine was thirty-eight
inches and now is thirty inches, this Jarvis with his
stubby fingers and powdery nails (he draws with char-
coal, she cannot stop him: art triumphs here, as art
must), his reddish, loose and freckly skin, his full lax
mouth breathing indigestion—does this Jarvis, erect,
rouse this pale, stiff, lovely Lily to passion, flush her
cool skin with intemperate desires?

Ah yes, he does.

And Jonathan, fruit of their passion, twenty-six months
old? Jonathan is a stocky, yellow-haired child with
bright cheeks and his father's pale full eyes. Jonathan
has a stoical and uncomplaining nature, and a surpris-
ingly friendly manner. Jonathan's mother Lily seldom
picks him up, unless obliged to in the interests of hy-
giene, security or good manners. Lily is not much given
to embracing, crooning, cuddling or other pointless ac-
tivities. Already Jonathan is adept at climbing into his
high-chair by himself, scaling its frail and slippery
height with ease, waiting patiently for his regulation
Muesli, his bread and butter, his properly boiled egg,
his sharp silver spoon and his mother's distant smiles
of approval. He will never leave her, never have
enough of her.

Jonathan's father is more demonstrative. He kisses and cuddles his son when his wife is out of the room, and when she's there he will frequently catch Jonathan up and toss him in the air. Jonathan laughs when this happens, though more from shock than pleasure.

"Daddy," he croons now, waiting for his egg. "Mummy." He bashes his dish of Muesli with his spoon. Flakes of raw porridge oats and withered currants fly about the room.

"Don't," says Lily mildly in her refined, careful, loving voice. Oh, I am the butcher's daughter, but who would know it now? "Don't, Jonathan."

Jonathan doesn't.

Jarvis, with memories of the infant Hilary, child of his first marriage, smearing the tables with sugary porridge and the walls with excreta, marvels at his second wife the more. Jarvis's lucky ticket in the lottery of life. At the second draw, not the first!

But how early the Katkins rise and take breakfast. It's still only eight-fifteen.

3

Up gets Madeleine, Jarvis's first wife. Lily's enemy, Hilary's mother, not so bright and not so early.

Up gets Madeleine, putting chilly chapped feet onto brown broken linoleum. Up gets Madeleine, pulling on her old woolen dressing gown which smells (like the room) of damp and cigarette smoke mixed. Up gets Madeleine, prompted by a sense of duty, not of inclination, to at best organize and at worse acknowledge her daughter Hilary's departure for the local comprehensive school.

Monday morning—not a good one.

Hilary's tights are torn; Hilary's blouse has lost its button and Hilary's skirt has shrunk in the wash, so the waistband won't close and safety pins have to be found. Hilary does not care about any of these details, so Madeleine has to cling the more carefully to her own maternal concern lest it evaporate altogether in the general depression of the morning.

Hilary is fourteen and weighs 154 pounds; she has size-8 feet and a 38-C bust, so the missing button is important. She eats Sugar Puffs as she gathers her homework together, every now and then sprinkling more spoonfuls of sugar on the already sweetened cereal. Madeleine hasn't the energy, indeed the desire, to stop her daughter's destroying her looks. Why should she? Hilary is walking witness to Madeleine's wrongs, Madeleine's ruin. See, says Madeleine in her heart, regarding Hilary, see what has become of me? See what Jarvis has done?

And Hilary stuffs and puffs, shoveling in fuel—for what? Resentment, boredom, anxiety, despair? Or gathering her reserves against the onslaught of the next weekend?

During the week Hilary lives with her mother. On weekends she lives with her father Jarvis and her stepmother Lily, sleeping not in the spare room (which is kept for guests) but in a camp bed in Jonathan's room. Lily means to slim Hilary down. It is her earnest desire. On Saturdays and Sundays, Lily gives Hilary a

breakfast of lemon tea with artificial sweetener, two
boiled eggs and one slice of starch-reduced toast spread
with low-calorie margarine. But such a breakfast, followed by equally austere lunches and dinners, cannot,
alas, undo the damage done by Madeleine on Monday,
Tuesday, Wednesday, Thursday and Friday.

During recent months Hilary's bosom has expanded
alarmingly. Puffed wheat has become her favorite food;
yes, she is altogether puffed out. Hilary has Jarvis's
large pale eyes, her mother's sallow complexion, a
puffy face, a double chin, a stodgy body, beautiful
thick golden hair tumbling onto graceless shoulders,
and a sharp, sad mind.

Madeleine is forty-four and gaunt. Madeleine is like
her daughter; she eats and eats. Sugar Puffs by the
jumbo-size packet and tinned milk (cheaper than
fresh) by the dozen cans—but Madeleine just gets
thinner and thinner. Unlike her daughter, Madeleine is
vain. Her ragged jeans, her old brown matted sweater,
torn beneath the arm, proclaim her with a fine exacti-
tude to the world. This is me, Madeleine, what I am,
what I have become, what I have been driven to by
Jarvis. Wicked Jarvis. Madeleine goes to jumble sales,
elbowing and stamping in order to achieve a yet more
ragged pair of jeans, a yet more matted jersey by way
of illustration. She will examine herself carefully in the
mirror before leaving the flat, adjusting the armpit hole
just nicely so that it hides the wisp of underarm hair,
but not for long. Madeleine has a yellowing complexion and thick, rusty, vigorous hair which tears teeth
from combs. Madeleine's cheeks are hollow, her huge
brown eyes stare reproachfully from deep sockets.
Madeleine's voice is husky. Madeleine looks mean and
hungry, which is what she feels.

Madeleine and Hilary make their home in two basement rooms in a terrace house. It is all Madeleine can
afford—or rather, all that Jarvis will afford. The front

room has a barred window which looks out onto a white-painted basement area. This room is the kitchen; that is, there is a sink beneath the window, with a damply rotten brown wooden draining board and an electric hot plate with two burners which stands on top of a hospital locker. Thanks to Hilary, who has saved and scraped and stolen the loose change which lies about her father's house in order to buy her mother this splendid present, Madeleine also has the use of a rotisserie-and-grill. This appliance has not been fixed to the wall because the plaster will clearly not stand its weight, and so it stands, perforce, on the small prewar refrigerator bought second-hand in the market (on Hilary's insistence). Madeleine does not much care for cooking, which in any case is an expensive and time-wasting occupation. Why have toast when bread and butter will do? But Hilary likes a kitchen to look like a kitchen.

Poor Jarvis.

A brown guinea pig in a cage on the table, starting and snuffling, eats every morning what Sugar Puffs Madeleine and Hilary leave. Hilary picks up old cabbage leaves and vegetation from the street market on her way home from school to provide his evening meal, so the pig can be said not just to cost little, but to save waste on a national level.

Madeleine's back room looks out onto a damp and sunless London garden, to which only the top-floor tenants have access. In this room are Madeleine's double bed and Hilary's camp bed, and their wardrobe and piles and piles of washing. Madeleine and Hilary are the recipients of countless articles of cast-off clothing, which they neither care to wear, let alone wash, or can bear to throw away, so they lie about in heaps.

Madeleine pays £5.23 a week rent (a sum fixed by the rent officer), and receives from Jarvis maintenance of

£20 a week for herself and Hilary. Once this sum seemed lavish; now inflation makes it a dubious means of support, although it still looms large enough in Lily's mind. (Twenty pounds? Lily's father the butcher brought home fifteen at the height of his career as the best butcher in the Bay of Islands, New Zealand.) Madeleine should go out to work; she will not always be able to put off doing so. But why should she earn? To salve Jarvis's conscience? To enable Lily to buy even more expensive little pairs of white French socks for baby Jonathan's tender, much resented feet? No. And how can she earn? Hilary comes home from school and needs a mother. Hilary's school holidays last for four months of every year. Fathers such as Jarvis don't stop work on a child's account; mothers such as Madeleine are expected to.

Listen now, carefully, to their conversation. Madeleine and Hilary talk in riddles, as families do, even families as small and circumscribed as this one, using the everyday objects of their lives as symbols of their discontent:

1. HILARY: Mum, I can't find my shoes again.
2. MADELEINE *(looking):* They'll be where you took them off. *(Finding)* Here they are.
3. HILARY: Not those old brown things. My new red ones.
4. MADELEINE: You can't possibly wear these to school. They're ridiculous. They'll cripple your feet.
5. HILARY: No they won't. Everyone else wears platforms.
6. MADELEINE: In that case, everyone else will be going round in plaster casts, and serve them right.
7. HILARY: You only don't like them because Lily bought them for me.

8. MADELEINE: I don't like them because they're ugly and ridiculous.
9. HILARY: I can't find the other ones, and I'm late. Please, Mum. They're my feet.

Which, being translated, is:

1. HILARY: Why is this place always such a mess?
2. MADELEINE: Why are you such a baby?
3. HILARY: You know nothing about me.
4. MADELEINE: I know everything about you.
5. HILARY: I want to be like other people.
6. MADELEINE: Other people aren't worth being like.
7. HILARY: I know all about you, don't think I don't.
8. MADELEINE: You force me to tell the truth. Our whole situation is ugly and ridiculous and I despair of it.
9. HILARY: Then let me find my own way out of it, please.

So Hilary defeats her mother, as the children of guilty mothers do, and goes off to school wearing the red shoes with platform heels; she trips over them in the Humanities lesson, twists her ankle, pulls a video-tape machine from a shelf to the floor in so doing, and does £115 worth of damage. The headmistress subsequently attempts to ban all platform heels from the school, and fails.

Once Hilary has left, Madeleine goes back to bed and half sleeps until half past ten, when she gets up, makes herself some instant coffee, sweeps the floors vaguely, and washes up badly; and peers up through the area bars into the dusty brightness of the streets, wondering what there is in the outside world that others find so animating, and that keeps them so ceaselessly busy.

Madeleine, sweeping and dusting, thinks, feels, hurts, tries. Listen. Madeleine's inner voices cajole, comfort, complain, encourage, in equal measure.

Oh, I am Madeleine, the first wife. I am the victim. I
have right on my side. It makes me strong. I feed on
misery. But I no longer have the strength to be unhappy, not all the time. It has been going on too
long. Days drift into weeks, and weeks into months.
Three years since Jarvis married Lily, two since she
had her brat. Even so, every morning for an hour or
so, I have this sick and angry misery. It tenses my
muscles; this, or something, gives me fibrositis. Bile
rises in my mouth and burns my throat. I keep myself still and silent by an act of will, when the only
thing to give me peace would be to search out Jarvis,
waylay him, attack him, mutilate him; shriek and
scream and by the very dreadfulness of my behavior,
flying in the face of my own nature, which he knows
so well, so well, demonstrate how much, how very
much, he has hurt me, damaged me, destroyed me. I
want Jarvis to acknowledge the wrong he has done
me. I want him to love me again. I want to burn
down Jarvis's home, my home, and Lily and Jonathan with it. Jonathan, the son I should have had
and never will have. And that would be an end to
them and it and me and everything, and thank God
for his eternal mercy.

Courage, Madeleine!

If I wait, if I lie quite still, warding off, fending, pretending that these attacks—of what? hate?
madness?—come from outside me, have been sent
by the devil or his equivalent, and do not arise (as I
know they must) from within me, being as they are
the sum of every fear and sorrow, rage and despair I
have ever felt, ever known; if I forbid myself to
move, to act, to pick up the telephone, then the rage
passes. I breathe more easily. The pain in my shoulder disperses. Then the rest of the day is mine. The
devil is off tormenting someone else; he won't be
back until tomorrow, with a fresh set of mirrors, to
tease, exalt and magnify my wrongs. Alas, the devil,

once departed, leaves me not so much unhappy as
dazed and worn out and fit for nothing. My vision
still looks inward, not outward. I can wash and dry
the dishes, but not get them back onto the shelves. I
can sweep the dirt from the floor into a heap, but
not get the dust into the pan. The gardens are full of
late roses, Hilary tells me, and beautiful. I cannot
see them.

The doorbell rings.

Good morning!

Madeleine cranes up through the basement bars to see
who's at the door, sees familiar broken shoes, stocky,
wide-apart legs, a thin uneven hem, a basket of flowers, shaking as does the red hand which holds it.
Madeleine draws back into the gloom, hiding. It's the
gipsy.

Good morning!

Madeleine's flat is stuck with withered spigs of heather,
held in twists of tin foil, bought weekly from the
gipsy's basket. Ten pence the sprig. Dried heather
flowers drift into cups of tea, settle in hair, cluster like
dead insects in the corners of the room. No one wants
to keep them. No one likes to throw them away, in
case they're throwing away luck.

What luck?

Good morning! The bell goes again, harsh and
reproachful. "I know you're in there, hiding." Madeleine gives up, emerges into the light, goes upstairs, answers the bell. The gipsy's plump round face is purple
with cold, exhaustion and ill-health. Her teeth are
black and broken. A coat strains across her overfed
body. Sweet tea and sugar buns. She has tears in her
eyes, and not, as Madeleine prays, from conjunctivitis

or as a result of the cold wind, but because she has indeed been crying. Her husband has a bad heart; the hospital has sent her son-in-law home to die; her nephew has lost a leg from TB of the bone. The fares from Epping, where she lives, to Muswell Hill, where the habit of years, rather than common sense, still leads her, now exceed her takings.

"Help me out, dear. Daffs at fifty, heather at ten. Lucky heather from bonny Scotland."

Madeleine takes two sprigs of heather and parts with twenty pence out of the milk money.

"Never mind," says Madeleine from her heart. "Never mind. Good times will come again. Or at any rate, we had them once."

And so they will, and so she did. Once Madeleine woke up singing. When she was pregnant with Hilary she even sang in her sleep. Jarvis heard her. Once Jarvis loved Madeleine, drew back chairs for her, brought her tea when she was tired, held her hand in the cinema, scowled at her admirers, brought her yellow daffodils fifty at a time.

Bad times come, but can't undo the past. Mostly they come when we are ill, and old, and dying. Few of us die with dignity or without pain. But how we once lived, when we were young! How we laughed!

"I'll tell your fortune," says the gipsy, drawing Madeleine's strong, worn hand into her own red, dirty one, but Madeleine pulls it back.

"I'll do it cheap," says the gipsy. "You're a kind lady. You've got a lucky face."

"No," says Madeleine. She is frightened. She looked into her own future, at the gipsy's touch, and saw noth-

ing but blackness. Well, she is depressed. That is what
depression is, Madeleine thinks. The looking forward
to blackness. Surely.

Good morning!

The gipsy goes. Madeleine goes down to her room to
stand beside the sink, motionless, unable to make order
out of the chaos of chipped and dirty china.

I am Madeleine, first wife of Jarvis, Hilary's mother.
I am Madeleine, thorn in Lily's white soft flesh.

Lily, the second wife, Margot's employer.

4

The doctor wakes late. Margot is up; he can
hear the sound of breakfast. The doctor closes his eyes
again. These are the moments of the day he most
values, when he is most himself and least the doctor. It
is in these minutes, the doctor knows, these minutes
between waking and sleeping, that the events of the
past, of infancy and childhood, churned to the surface
by the fragmented memory of dreams, lose their hap-
hazard nature and make some kind of pattern, effect-
ing, with luck, some small improvement in our nature,
loosening the grip of resentment, altering expectation,
refocusing obsession. Thus, building on the impacted
rubble of the past, we construct the delicate filaments
of the present. Or so the doctor thinks.

The doctor's breathing becomes ragged, anxious. Listen:

Oh, I am the doctor. There is no one to help me. All night the insomniacs have held me in their thoughts. Now, as the minutes advance, it is the waking sick who direct their thoughts towards me. I can feel them. See, Doctor, my fingernail is septic; my throat is sore; I am feverish; my eye is blacked, and you, Doctor, must witness my wrongs. I have cancer, V.D., psittacosis, anything, everything. It is Monday, day after Sunday, family day. I am the doctor, little father to all the world, busiest of all on Mondays, the day after Sunday.

Up gets the doctor, Philip Bailey, Margot's husband. He puts on a suit. He has to; he is the doctor. Once he was twenty-eight inches about the waist; now, with the passage of time and the arrival of the metric system, he is ninety-eight centimeters.

The doctor is forty-five years old and has the stocky build and freckled face of some cheerful summer child. In the last couple of years his skin, once so soft and pliable, has seemed to toughen and harden; lines are etching deep into his flesh and will go deeper still. As Enid's husband Sam, the estate agent, unkindly observed at a party, Philip is like a stale French cheese, growing old before it has matured, hardening inside, cracking round the edges.

All the same, on a good day Philip looks fifteen years younger than he is. It would be unreasonable to suppose that he stopped growing older the day he married Margot, but she likes to suppose it. Margot is a good wife; she allows her husband to sap her energy and youth, and tax her good nature, and feels no resentment—or thinks she does not.

Philip stretches and bends his fingers, limbering them up
for the day. Margot does not like her husband's hands.
They express something that his face and body do not,
some stony, hidden aspiration away from her, Margot,
his wife. The doctor's hands are stiff, knuckly and red;
their palms are bloodless and lightly lined. But his patients seem to trust them, which is just as well. With
these hands the doctor manipulates their joints, presses
into their vital organs, searches into their orifices, their
dark and secret parts, judging them ill or well, good or
bad, worthy of life or deserving death. With these
hands, pulling down magic from the air, the doctor
writes his runes, his indecipherable prescriptions for
health. Dislike his hands at your peril. You will not get
better if you do.

Breakfast! Bon appetit! If you can.

The manner of the breakfast declares the aspiration of
the family. Some breakfast standing, some sitting, some
united in silence, some fragmented in noisiness, some
as in a television commercial, seeming to have all the
time and money and good will in the world, and some
in gloomy isolation. It is the meal at which we betray
ourselves, being still more our sleeping than our waking selves.

Picture now the doctor's household this Monday morning, breakfasting according to ritual in the large back
kitchen. Philip, the father, bathed, shaved, dressed, apparently benign, eats bacon and eggs delicately
prepared by Margot, reads the *Guardian* she has
placed beside his plate, and ignores the other members
of his family as best he can. At eight forty-five his re-
ceptionist Lilac will arrive, open his mail, and prepare
his appointment cards. At nine the doctor will rise, put
down his paper, peck his wife, nod to his children, and
go through to the surgery to attend to the needs of the
world.

Lettice and Laurence sit opposite each other. Lettice is thirteen, neat, pretty and precise, with her mother's build and round, regular face, but without her mother's overwhelming amiability. If the mother were unexpectedly to bare a breast, it would surely be in the interests of some cosmic medical examination. If the daughter did so, who would doubt her erotic intent? Laurence is a dark and looming boy of fifteen, with a bloodless, troubled complexion and a bony body, as if his father's hands had at last found expression in a whole person. There is little other resemblance between them.

Listen now to their outer voices, their conversation, their riddles, comprehended only by themselves, the secret society that composes the family:

1.   LETTICE: Dad, can I have the middle of the paper?
2.   DAD: What for?
3.   LETTICE: To read.
4.   DAD: You are a nuisance.
5.   LAURENCE: Mum, I haven't got a fork.
6.   MARGOT: Sorry, dear. I'll get one . . . But why do you need a fork if you're only eating cereal?
7.   LAURENCE: Sorry. So I am.
8.   LETTICE: Why don't we ever have unsweetened cereal?
9.   MARGOT: Because no one eats it.
10. LETTICE: I do. The sweetened is fattening, anyway, and not worth the extra money. It said so in *Which*. I think we should have unsweetened and add our own sugar.
11. LAURENCE: Lettice, you are not the center of the universe.
12. LETTICE: I know that. The sun is.
13. LAURENCE: You are wrong. The sun is a star of average size which is itself revolving, with thousands of millions of other stars, in one galaxy among millions in a universe that might well be boundless. If you traveled at the speed of light—186,300 miles a second, that is—it

would take six thousand million years—about twenty thousand times the total period that life has existed on earth, to travel only to the limits of what we can observe from earth with our very limited technology.

14. LETTICE: So what?
15. LAURENCE: So nothing matters.

And Laurence helps himself to the last of the honey-coated wheat puffs, the creamy top of the milk, and adds the last scrape of the marmalade in the jar for good measure.

These domestic riddles can be thus translated:

1. LETTICE: Dad, take notice of me and my changing needs.
2. DAD *(cautious)*: What kind of need?
3. LETTICE: Don't worry. Merely intellectual. All the same, I am growing up.
4. DAD: Oh dear. More change.
5. LAURENCE: Father is taking notice of Lettice again. Mother, will you please take some notice of me? My needs are not being properly met.
6. MARGOT: Perhaps I have been rather remiss. On the other hand, I don't actually want to have to get to my feet on your behalf. Do you insist, my dear? We have a good relationship, you and I.
7. LAURENCE: Quite. It's the thought that counts. Thank you.
8. LETTICE: Mother, Father cares for me, but I'm not so sure about you.
9. MARGOT: I have so very many people to look after.
10. LETTICE: I knew it. You want me to be plain and ugly and fat; what's more, I'm a better house-keeper than you, so there.
11. LAURENCE: Don't be rude to my mother, just be-

cause she's yours as well. There are more important people in the world than you.

12. LETTICE: Father is important. You're not.

13. LAURENCE: Father is not as important as you think. Enough of all this emotional nonsense, anyway. Facts are interesting, important, reassuring, and what's more, I know more of them than Father, for all his air of maturity.

14. LETTICE: Who cares about facts? They're meaningless.

15. LAURENCE: All right, then. We'll all go on as we have before, sparring for position over the breakfast table. God give me strength.

The day has begun.

5

Breakfast time! Bon appetit! If you can manage it.

Jarvis and Lily can. They breakfast in companionable silence. At ten Jarvis will go to his office. He wears a Chairman Mao blue jacket, bought for him by Lily from an expensive shop. Jarvis would prefer to wear a shirt, tie and jacket, but Lily plans otherwise, and she is, he acknowledges, quite right to do so. Those now leapfrogging over his talented head towards senior partnerships wear jeans, beards, and show their navels on hot days.

At ten to ten Jarvis puts down the *Times* and smiles at his wife. Jonathan, wiped and cleaned, has already

been set in his playpen to play with his educational
toys, which, obligingly enough, he seems prepared to
do, posting bright plastic shapes into a plastic letterbox
with supercilious ease. He is an advanced child, and
seems to know it. He begins to sing tunelessly to himself, moved by a spirit of self-congratulation. Lily, observing him, cannot understand how it is that she,
being so feminine, has produced so male a child. Is his
dexterity, his musical sense perhaps symptomatic of
homosexuality? She feels restless, agitated.

Jarvis and Lily speak. There are few riddles in this
household, which is barely three years old and contains
one non-speaking member, but let us examine such as
there are, and note how quickly pleasantries before
morning coffee can degenerate into animosity:

1. LILY: Margot Bailey is late. She's always late. I
　 shall have to speak to her.
2. JARVIS: She's not the maid. She's our doctor's wife.
3. LILY: She's an employee during office hours. It's
　 what was agreed.
4. JARVIS: Yes, but we have to be tactful.
5. LILY: She knows I've got people coming tonight;
　 I need her to take Jonathan to play group. She's
　 late on purpose.
6. JARVIS: Margot is supposed to be looking after my
　 office, not your child.
7. LILY: Our child. And if, as you claim, your busi-
　 ness is twenty percent down this year, then
　 presumably the doctor's wife has twenty per-
　 cent more time on her hands. I want to take
　 Hilary to the hairdresser to get her hair cut.
　 I can't possibly take Jonathan. He swarms over
　 everything.
8. JARVIS: Does it need cutting? It always seems the
　 only good thing about her. Still, I suppose you
　 know best. Is it all right with Madeleine?
9. LILY: Nothing is ever right with Madeleine. But
　 I can't even get a comb through Hilary's hair,

and I am paying, and it's a very good hairdresser. Today's the only day I could get an
appointment.

10. LILY: Expensive?
11. LILY: I hope you don't grudge your own daughter
a haircut.
12. JARVIS: Couldn't you do it?
13. LILY: If you worry so much about money, why
not spend less on whiskey.

Which being translated is:

1. LILY: Am I to be left all alone with this child? I
cannot take the responsibility.
2. JARVIS: Other wives can cope, why not you?
3. LILY: Because I enjoy a superior social status in
the world, and deserve to do so.
4. JARVIS: In this household, I am the one with tact.
5. LILY: Everyone's against me.
6. JARVIS: My needs are more vital than yours.
7. LILY: You're twenty percent less important than
when I married you. However, I love you and
am even looking after your daughter by your
first marriage.
8. JARVIS: I do not intend to deny Madeleine altogether.
9. LILY: Your first marriage spoils my life. I have to
make the best of what's left.
10. JARVIS: You're extravagant with my money.
11. LILY: You're mean.
12. JARVIS: You're not earning your keep.
13. LILY: You're a drunk.

At which Jarvis kisses his wife hastily before worse
befalls, does a quick farewell soft-shoe shuffle for
Jonathan, who half sneers, half smiles in response, and
departs for the office.

And the day begins.

6

Listen now to Lily's inner voice, welling up into the moral silence of her busy after-breakfast home, Jonathan playing good as gold, sunlight streaming, radio singing:

Oh, I am no longer the butcher's daughter; I am the architect's wife, waiting for the arrival of Margot, the part-time secretary, stacking well-rinsed plates in serried rows in the dishwasher (soundproofed), reserving the wooden-handled knives and forks for a warm soapy hand-rinse in the plastic bowl. It was my mother, Ida, on her wild Australasian shore, who taught me how to care so well for possessions, both material and human, there being so little of either about. How pleasant everything is since I became the architect's wife. All things around me ordained, considered, under control. The house is well converted, the plasterwork is sound, the polished floor blocks on the ground floor are both practical and attractive; the carpets upstairs are both luxurious and hard-wearing. Is this not what Jarvis has worked for, what I myself have made possible for him? How happy we are—like children. Surely nothing can go wrong?

Lily and Jarvis! What games they play, in bed and out of it. Their pleasure out of doors is to rummage through the builders' rubble heaps which line the streets, acquire the treasure within, and jeer at the philistines who flung them out. Their house at No. 12 Adelaide Row is a treasure home of trophies—here a carved Jacobean chest, once horribly painted green; there a pretty rose-wood bureau, once broken and abandoned, now beautifully restored; a Coalbrookdale footscraper, once flaky with rust, now sand-blasted and splendid. Even the water-color landscapes which line the hall were found in a folder in the middle of a bundle of old comics (in themselves items of value and interest) and have been valued at £500; and the stripped doors in the stripped doorframes, such an elegant contrast to the coffee color of the walls, once lay in a demolition yard waiting for the bonfire.

Nothing wrong with such restitutions. On the contrary, we must rescue the nation's past if we wish to rescue our own. Jarvis says so. Jarvis knows. In this wisdom Jarvis has educated Lily.

Lily and Jarvis.

When Madeleine and Jarvis lived at 12 Adelaide Row it had no such social, aesthetic or emotional distinction, It was an ordinary house, practical and ugly. In Madeleine's day Jarvis's talents never bloomed. How could they? Madeleine made no concessions to the beauties of the material world. Tat and junk, she'd say, trendy rubbish, vicious Victoriana, and millions starving in Ethiopia or burning in Vietnam, wherever that season's human ulcer happened to manifest itself. Can't you, Jarvis, turn your mind to anything more serious than a rotten old sampler badly embroidered by some miserable child in 1825? If you want to throw your money away, give it to Shelter and help house the homeless.

Because you are unhappy, Madeleine, shall there be no small delights for Jarvis?

No, there shan't.

And Jarvis earned £5,000 a year as an architect at a time when the sum meant something, but even this, Madeleine could not approve. Shouldn't you be a Council architect, she'd ask? Shouldn't you be turning your undoubted talent to some useful end, instead of designing ridiculous modern villas on unsanitary sunny slopes for ex-whores, property developers and other social criminals?

And so of course Jarvis should, and he knew it, which made matters worse. Madeleine was always right.

Nonetheless, as Lily later pointed out, Madeleine used the money Jarvis earned at his immoral tasks. Madeleine went on countless coach holidays with little Hilary, leaving Jarvis behind at the office, earning; and believing (as they both did; well, at any rate, she did) in the immorality of sexual possessiveness, Madeleine passed many a stop-over night (or so it was imagined by Jarvis, and later Lily) in bed with the current courier, exercising her sexual rights in bleak bedrooms overlooking the teeming roads of Europe and the East. Madeleine even went as far as Turkey once, and heaven knows what oriental sexual athleticism that didn't lead to! And what happened to little Hilary, alone (or so one hopes) in the next bedroom? How did little Hilary regard her mother's quest for fun and self-expression, returning from abroad even yet sulkier, blanker and snottier than when she left? Hilary's mind not so much broadened as stunned.

Poor Jarvis, poor father.

Oh, I am Lily the architect's wife. I want Jarvis to be happy, to be himself, to be with me. I even want Hilary, Jarvis's child. I want Hilary to be happy too, to make up for all the things she's lost, all the things Madeleine has taken from her. I want to show everyone what a truly successful person I am: wife, daughter, mother, stepmother. Sister? No, don't think of that.

Lily waits for Margot to arrive. Waiting, she telephones the hairdresser and makes an appointment for that very morning, to have her own and Hilary's done. It had not, until now, been her firm intention to do so, more a speculation for Jarvis's benefit. Margot's lateness and the irritation it causes drive Lily to action. Once done, she regrets it—how is she going to fit everything in? Too late now.

The milk, forgotten, would have boiled over it it hadn't been prudently placed to heat slowly on the simmer plate. Lily always puts the milk on the simmer plate. Good Lily!

And here we are at last. The Victorian doorbell rings and here is Margot the doctor's wife. She is late, she is breathless, but she is here. She has no key. Lily is very retentive of front-door keys. Margot's coffee is ready.

See how hospitable, how tolerant, how understanding of the needs of others am I? Lily the architect's wife! The servant is late and I'm giving her coffee!

Alas, the milk has turned in the pan. The coffee is undrinkable. Lily and Margot unite in deploring a world now so crassly run that the very milk is delivered to the door half sour, or what passes for sour in these days of homogenization, sterilization and so on. A new cup of coffee is made, with different milk.

"I was wondering," asks Lily at last, "if you could possibly take Jonathan to play group today?"

These two women do not compose a family; they are not a secret society; there is little need for riddles. Lily (in her white cheesecloth Laura Ashley dress, unspotted by breakfast) can ask Margot (in her navy skirt and pink fluffy Marks & Spencer jumper) a straight question and get a straight reply.

"Of course," says Margot. "Since it's Monday. Invoice day. I'll get those done with no trouble."

There are, this month, some twenty percent fewer invoices than there were in the same month a year ago. Lily is quite right to assume that Jarvis and his partners in architecture are in difficulties. There has been a twenty percent redundancy in their staff, a twenty percent inflation during the year, and a twenty percent drop in business. Lily lies awake at night, just occasionally worrying about it all, but Jarvis does not. Jarvis has an inheritance, private means. How erotic Lily used to feel when first she met him, this simple fact: Jarvis's inheritance. Later she came to see it as something which stood between Jarvis and the proper acceptance of reality—by which she meant, of course, herself. Once or twice she has even complained of having been seduced by his past. No one in New Zealand had inheritances. It seemed to be symptomatic of the English.

"I'm going to take Hilary to have her hair cut," Lily announces. "It's such a mess."

"Is she off school?" inquires Margot. Margot feels tenderly protective towards Hilary, this ugly duckling in a household of swans.

"I'll take her out of school," says Lily. "No hassle. She only has swimming this morning, and I'm sure she's forgotten her things anyway. I'll tell anyone who asks that she's going to the dentist. But they won't ask. They won't know, and even if they did they won't care. Hilary is totally anonymous in that place. Two thousand five hundred children in a school—what madness! Comprehensive! My husband was quite prepared to send Hilary to a private school, but of course Madeleine has her principles, for which poor little Hilary has to pay the price."

Lily likes to emphasize, when she can, the fact of Jarvis's basic generosity towards his first family. Jarvis rashly leaves letters from his ex-wife's solicitors for Margot to open and deal with; Lily wishes he wouldn't.

"I may be delayed," Lily murmurs. "You know what hairdressers are like. Do you have to leave sharp at twelve-thirty? I was wondering whether you could possibly collect Jonathan at twelve forty-five?"

Margot, the implication is, has arrived late, and so in all fairness, should surely stay late.

"The children come home for lunch," says Margot. "I must have it ready."

"Don't they have school dinner?"

"They don't care for them."

Silence. What, children thus unregulated and untrammeled? Jonathan, better brought up, always eats what is set before him.

"Personally, I never eat lunch," says Lily blandly. "So bad for the figure."

I live a good and useful life, murmurs stocky Margot in her heart. I would be ashamed to go hungry in order to be beautiful. Is there something wrong with me? No. I am a good and serviceable person, wife and mother. My reward is in my children's love of me, and mine in them, and in my soft, familiar, permanent bed. I am a nice person. Your husband—yes, your husband—told me so many years ago. He has forgotten—at least I hope he has—but I have not, and true, he was drunk at the time, and married to Madeleine, which may have distorted his judgment, but Jarvis told me then that he preferred nice girls to beautiful girls! And what's more, that my nipples were pale and blunt and pink and that's what he liked, he couldn't bear the harsh, brown, aggressive kind, and that, I'm sorry to say, is what yours are, slim hungry wife of my employer; I can see them through your dress.

Margot knows she is being unfair. Who of us can help the texture of our nipples? A momentary surge of irritation, no doubt, of guilt, about Jarvis, for which she will now pay penance. "I'll take Jonathan home to lunch with me," she says, "and drop him back this afternoon."

Guilt about Jarvis? Guilt, surely, is too strong a word. What, for something that happened sixteen years ago, when the world was young and still full of causes and few effects? Surely not. Margot did no wrong, or none that she could recognize. She was not married at the time. True, Jarvis was, but could Margot fairly be expected to take responsibility for, let alone stand in the way of, the imperatives of male desire? And it can't have been a good marriage anyway, or why would Jarvis have wanted to sweep her out of a party, up the linoleumed stairs and into the spare room? A one-night stand, no more, no less. True, Margot was disappointed (whoever isn't?) when the next day came, and the next, and there was no telephone call from Jarvis, no declaration of true love—no such magic, apparently, discovered in her body as would transfigure his life. But it was a disappointment muted not by experience (and experience indicates that in nine out of ten of these passing sexual encounters, no particular magic is discovered, no great alliances made, but on the tenth—ah! Happiness, fulfillment, love enough to make up for the pain of the nine? Well, more or less!) or any such calculating promiscuity in the interests of eventual respectability, but by a general apprehension of herself, a thoroughly muted expectation of life and the part she was to play in it.

Margot, born to be useful: daughter, wife, mother. This excursion into the erotic, this placing of her on him, for that was where he placed her, the better to admire her sweet pink nipples, scarcely seemed a proper part of her nature. The activity, she felt, contained its own punishment: if virtue carries its own reward, so does sin carry with it a cosmic slapping of the hand—a down, you naughty girl, you presume. When lust fades, the sense of looking silly remains—and some slight knowledge of a door having opened and closed, on the fringes of memory.

Poor Margot, only too happy, after a silent day or two, to forget.

Later, when Jarvis and Lily became Philip's patients, and baby Jonathan too, and Jarvis was overworked and underslept, and the strain of Jonathan's early feeding problems was telling on him, not to mention on Lily, it was Philip who suggested that Margot could go and work as Jarvis's part-time secretary—thus killing three birds with one stone: his wife's restlessness (well, the children were now increasingly busy with their own lives); his patient's declared need for tranquilizers; and his own monetary difficulties—the latter admittedly too great and hefty a bird to be brought down by such a tiny shaft, but winging the creature nonetheless. A step in the right direction.

Philip always had the feeling, lurking unspoken somewhere in the back of his mind, that Margot was ungrateful when it came to money and did not quite recognize the difficulty with which it was earned, nor her good fortune in being allowed to spend what was by rights his and his alone.

Margot, meeting Jarvis for the second time, going to a house which she only dimly remembered and now found altogether changed fourteen years after that passionate, private (or so she believes) encounter, recognized Jarvis at once. He did not recognize her. How could he? It had been a dimly lit party, in the days when most people smoked, and the smell of hot punch had filled the air, and one girl had been much like another, tight-waisted and teetering around on stiletto heels. But one man, then as now, not much like another at all. Poor Margot. Lucky Jarvis.

Margot accepted the offer of a job with alacrity. Why should she not? The advantages were, on the surface, so many. Namely:

a) *Ease of access*
   The Katkins lived within walking distance. Six and a half minutes (fast) or nine minutes (slow). She would not have to stand about in all weathers at bus stops, as did Enid.
b) *Good pay and conditions*
   The pay was generous and the work easy. Twelve pounds a week for ten hours' light secretarial duties in pleasant surroundings, architect-designed.
c) *Independence*
   Margot at last would be able to buy clothes without first having to persuade Philip that she needed them. (And Philip believed, profoundly, that the purpose of clothes was to keep the cold out.) She would no longer have to account for every penny which left her purse. Not that she had ever really objected to so doing—and indeed had become adept at covering the cost of unallowed frivolities, such as bars of chocolate or cartons of hot tomato soup from vending machines, under the cover of increased expenditure on washing powder, dishcloths and mango chutney (Philip's favorite). It wasn't, as Margot observed to Enid, that Philip was mean; look how he never grudged a penny on household

necessities. It was just that she, Margot, was extravagant, and he, as the breadwinner, had every right to say just how much butter and how much jam would be spread on each particular slice. What's more, she would say to Enid, she found the sense of her husband's control comforting, and even his censure satisfactory. What she did not say, however, and what made her vaguely uneasy, was her awareness that this particular comfort and satisfaction contained a languorous, almost erotic, quality, as if the financial strictures within which her husband held her had their counterpart in the bonds and whips of her (rare) sexual fantasies. Well, all that would have to stop. Employment, as Enid would say, was the answer to housewifely broodings and fantasies. Satan finds work for idle hands to do, and dreams for idle minds, while fingers play.

d) *Work interest*

Proximity to a new baby: Jonathan, sprung from Jarvis's lean loins and Lily's shapely ones. Margot, a lover of infants, finding her own children now too old for handling but still too young to provide her with grandchildren, had begun to crave babies as some people, finding themselves inland, will crave the sea; or in the middle of a plain, feel they cannot live without a glimpse of the hills. Margot would have had a dozen babies if she'd had her way, but fortunately she didn't. Philip felt that to have two children was both sensible and social, as indeed it was. (One must consider the quality, rather more than the quantity, of the human race.) As a doctor's wife, Margot was one of the first women in London to have a contraceptive coil fitted. After the initial heavy bleeding and stomach pains she settled down to it well. Again, the sense of her husband's coital interest, the gratification of his non-procreative wishes, the very carrying around inside her, foetuslike, of something she felt so strongly to be his, not hers, caused in her the

same languor, the same erotic debility, as did his
weekly checking of the household accounts: the
shrinking of the weak from the moral blows of the
strong. The presence of the coil, moreover, added a
sense of dishonesty, even of sin, to their marital
embraces and enhanced them, she rather thought,
the more. She would not, now, be without her coil.
Though sometimes she feared vaguely that it might
be going rusty within, or flaking away in the face of
her internal secretion.

Well, her employer's wife's baby would do instead
of her own. Would stop her, as she put it to Enid,
going all broody. She'd have all the pleasure, the
pride, the cooing and cuddling, and none of the
nappies.

e) *Job satisfaction*
The undercurrent of excitement she feels in Jarvis's
presence; of deceit in Lily's; the sense of secret
knowledge, of power withheld: all these entranced
her. She did not mention this to Enid. How could
she? She barely knew herself, as she barely remembered that other lost side of her which was neither
passive nor debilitated, but which long ago lured
first Philip into seducing her, and then did the same
to Jarvis.

At any rate, taking all these sensible considerations as
best she could in mind, Margot accepted Jarvis's offer
of a job, and the only query she made was as to
whether she would be expected to do any child-minding. Not that she minded if she did.

"Of course not," says Jarvis. "Lily wants to look after
the baby herself."

So Lily said. But Lily lied. Though how was Lily to
know? That was when Jonathan was just a helpless,
grateful bundle, easily passed from enfolding arms to

enfolding arms—a time when mothers will say anything and hope for everything.

Margot now says, "I'll take Jonathan home to lunch with me and drop him back this afternoon."

"That would be darling of you," says pale Lily. "I'll take Hilary out to lunch somewhere grand. Her mother only takes her to Wimpy Bars. No wonder she's so spotty. Don't worry about bringing him back. I'll send Hilary round before three." And Lily wraps a navy belt about her waist, puts on some ancient fisherman's hat, for the day is sunny and the skin of her nose delicate, and thus girded, pecks Jonathan goodbye and is off.

Jonathan leans against the front door, watching the retreating back of his pretty mother, torn between tears and the pleasures of exercising his latest skill, his newly acquired courage. Margot picks him up before the tears win. He is a heavy, comfortable child who allows himself to trust the arms which enfold him, and will relax into them. So, she remembers now, though hastily putting the memory from her, was his father, Jarvis. Laurence as a baby was much the same. Whereas Lettice, a sinewy, nervous baby and a sinewy, nervous little girl, felt lighter in the arms than her actual weight might suggest—as if, untrusting, she was as self-supporting as she could contrive and maintained by the vigor of her own nervous energy.

Margot and Jonathan set out for the play group.

7

The world! Be bold, but not too bold. Have courage, but not too much. Cross the road when you see Alsatians coming, don't walk under ladders, keep a civil tongue in your head when dealing with policemen, youths, civil servants, shopkeepers, and you may return home unscathed. And keep your home, whatever you do. You need somewhere to get back to. Poor Madeleine lost hers.

Laurence, in the graffitied playground of Woodside Comprehensive, is too bold. He intercedes in a fight between two small boys and is for his pains karate-chopped with a flying pair of Dr. Martin's boots (a brand much favored by mountaineers and schoolboys), which bruises his right hand badly. He would like to go home, but cannot. His father is a doctor and does not like his children to complain.

Lettice, in the Art room of the same school, paints a waterfall and is pleased with herself. As an after-thought she adds a skeleton tumbling to a second death. She likes painting skeletons. All her friends have their periods. She has not. She would like to ask the doctor if everything's all right inside her, but since the doctor is her father, she feels she can't. All her mother ever says is, "Wait, what's your hurry? You'll be burdened soon enough," which is no help.

Hilary, summoned over the loudspeaker to the Head's office, afflicted by the terror which dogs her footsteps, falls over her crimson platform shoes and brings down the video-tape equipment. Not bold enough, not by any manner of means. The teachers scowl, the children laugh; it is the pattern of her school life.

Philip sees his last patient of the morning: dotty old Mrs. Maguire, who calls every Monday to ask him to give her back her freedom. Philip does not know what she means. If she called towards the end of the week, he might have time to find out; in fact, he has asked her to do so, but she will not. Every Monday morning at eleven thirty-five, the busiest day of the week, five minutes after the surgery door is locked, there she is rapping on the door once again with her impatient, insistent knock. Once she is admitted, the question is always the same. "Will you give me my freedom?" And though Philip hopefully varies the manner of his answering, from yes through maybe to no, she is never satisfied; but only cries a little from rheumy eyes (and tears glistening on wrinkled cheeks are far more sad, the doctor thinks, than those that fall on young, still hopeful flesh) and then departs, leaving the doctor, as no doubt is Mrs. Maguire's intention, sadder but no wiser.

Madeleine, calling at the school some half-hour later at the Head's office with Hilary's swimming things, left behind (as Lily had predicted) in the morning's rush and quarrel, finds that her daughter is gone and is allegedly at the dentist's, taken away by a pale, beautiful lady with wild silver hair under a fisherman's hat, dressed in white cheesecloth with brown nipples showing, navy-blue belted.

Lily the butcher's daughter, from her wild antipodean shore, once turned brown by the cruel sun, now parched and bleached the color of bone. Lily the thief, the stepmother, taker and giver supreme, robbing wife of husband, daughter of mother, giving herself in return, as if this made up for everything.

Madeleine leaves the school and makes for the house where once she lived and where now her supplanter dwells. Madeleine means to make trouble. Madeleine has not been to 12 Adelaide Row for three whole years. It has been too bitter a place to contemplate, until today. See how Madeleine stretches forward with courage, common sense, acceptance? The step from depression into anger is always good!

"Would you like your hair cut?" inquires Lily of Hilary in the yellow-and-gold world of the hairdresser, "or just washed? They're very good stylists here. I'm sure short hair would suit you. It curls so prettily." "Cut," says Hilary with desperate courage.

Too bold!

Hilary's hair is washed; the shampooer, a tiny, pale, exhausted child made bitter by a daily life of insults and the detergent dermatitis on her hands, presses the back of Hilary's neck into the rim of the basin and does not care. Hilary says nothing. Discomfort, when inflicted by others, is best ignored. In Hilary's experience, protest achieves little: all it does is change practical discomfort into emotional distress, or emotional discomfort into practical difficulty.

Margot's friend Enid, happily at work, opens a supplementary pay slip, which lands in her In tray. It contains a cheque for £543.72, a back-dated raise. Enid is a senior civil servant in the Department of Education and Technology, although in the interests of domestic peace she tells her husband that she is a secretary there. Enid has £12,583 in a building society, about which her husband knows nothing.

Enid's husband, Sam the estate agent, sits dismally in his office. Business is at a standstill; how will he pay the bills and keep Enid in the style to which she is accustomed? The telephone rings all the time; any number of customers want to sell their houses. But to whom? To all those others pretending to want to buy, but without the means to do so until their own houses have been sold? For a month now not a single property has actually changed hands, although Sam has been kept busy to the point of exhaustion.

Sam's secretary Philippa, long-legged, bends and shows her knickers. She knows that she shows them and does not care. Enid, and Sam is glad to think of it, is the kind of middle-aged industrious secretary men keep to actually get the work done, not the kind of secretary that Philippa clearly is, which may give the organization a good virile name but seldom actually gets a letter into a letterbox. Perhaps one day Philippa will forget her knickers, and then Sam, having privy knowledge of her, will be better able to withstand her lack of interest in him. The slut.

Hilary's hair is cut, snip, snip, snip, by a bored young man, in the house style. On the floor lie the damp tresses that Madeleine took such trouble to encourage, attempting to disguise her daughter from a hostile world. Hilary's puffy face emerges with dreadful clarity. Even the young man pauses, but style is all. Either people can carry it off or they can't. If they can't, they shouldn't come here.

"What about cutting yours, Lady Katkin," he asks, "or is it just color today?"

"Just color," says Lily, eying Hilary's hair with increasing nervousness. She is always taken aback by the products of her own malice. "We'll leave the length for today." Lily always gives her name at the desk as Lady Katkin. Thus she is assured of quick service and good manners. Everyone else does it, anyway, she is quite sure.

I am Lily the architect's wife. I am a princess by right.
Didn't my father always tell me so?

At his play group, Jonathan, too bold, falls off the climbing frame, but is soon comforted and climbs again, too bold, and falls again. Many children break their limbs on climbing frames, but Jonathan falls easily and is lucky. He is young to be at play group, but Lily pleaded his sociable nature, and the organization was persuaded. He does not climb the frame again; he makes a puddle on the floor instead. Lily has persuaded herself that Jonathan is dry and no longer needs nappies, but Jonathan and the play group organizers know better. Now they put nappies on him. When Lily collects him she will take them off and find them dry. I really don't understand them, she will complain to Jarvis. "Nappies. They want Jonathan to conform to their image of a two-year-old, that's all. Poor lamb! What an indignity!"

Jarvis finishes reading the *Times* and turns to the *Telegraph*. He should, he knows, use his increasing amount of free time to study or to learn a language, or even to sculpt, as once it was his talent, his privilege, his pleasure to do, but of course he does none of these things. He reads the newspapers instead. Lunch-time approaches, and with it the encouragement of the daily bottle of wine which Lily does not know that he drinks. It is Jarvis's secret knowledge that wine is not fattening; on the contrary, by stirring up the metabolism, it somehow consumes its own calories. Jarvis has lost forty-two pounds in weight in the last two years and has begun to fear for the roots of his being. If the surface is so depleted, can the core be left untouched? Jarvis might die, and what would happen to Lily then?

And why does she want so little of him, anyway? Sometimes Jarvis suspects Lily's motives towards him. His stepfather, the stockbroker, frequently accused his mother of trying to poison him for his inheritance—or was it the insurance? It was said as a joke when the stockbroker put spoon to mouth and it contained his least favorite celery soup; nevertheless, the spirit of the remark made sense enough to the assembled children.

Margot types a letter on Jarvis's behalf, in Jarvis's home, at Jarvis's desk. He picked up the desk at an auction for only £2.10, in the days when the ten meant fifty pence; it is massive, oak Germanic and elaborately carved, so that Margot's knees are imprinted with the shapes of leaves and birds and foxes, and would now fetch some £400, Jarvis has been reliably informed by an antiques dealer, who nevertheless will only give him £75 for same. Margot is an excellent typist, being sensitive to the needs of others. When she has finished, she will pick up Jonathan from play group. Most of the letters are on the same theme:

> *Dear Jerry, How are things? I am sorry to bother you at a time like this, but if you could see your way to even part payment . . .*

Too bold!

Jarvis, who in the past was frequently employed by his friends, no longer seems to have many friends left.

And the doorbell rings.

8

Madeleine stands on the doorstep of the house which was once her home.

Oh, I am Madeleine, the first wife, the real wife, standing once again at my own front door. Look! Double glazing and window boxes: pretentious. The plaster in fresh two-toned beige: revolting. A giant gold K upon the stripped pine door. K for Katkin. Jokey. But the age of jokes has passed—do neither Mr. K nor the new Mrs. K realize that? The gap is narrowing between them and me, between the blessed and the damned. Long live the revolution. Long live me.

Once this was a proper home, a place where Jarvis, Madeleine and Hilary Katkin lived; it was then a place of safety, the suitable background to their lives, workaday and practical. Now look at it! It is a monument of sickly self-esteem. And see, they're growing ivy over the dustbin alcove. Why bother? What a waste of time and life. My dustbins were of battered, honest, rusty tin, much impacted with old food along the bottom seams; hers are plastic, clean and lined with polythene. She'd move house if she saw a maggot. I rather liked to see them squirming there, monument to our essential corruption.

And where is she, sickly Lily the bitch? What has she done with my daughter? I am Madeleine, the first wife, come to give the second wife what-for.

Margot opens the door. Madeleine steps inside, brushing past her. Madeleine smells oddly sweet, as if to compensate for the sourness of her mind.

Oh, I am sour; I am Madeleine, first wife to Jarvis. This is my house, if there were any justice in the world, which there is not, only solicitors, and his are better than mine. What has the second wife done to my ordinary front hall with ordinary linoleum on the floor and stairs? Lined it with mirrors and hung it with plants, built out the back, lost the broom cupboard, gained a patio? Does Jarvis the man walk into this decorator's absurdity every evening? Does he remain a man, or does he pace like a poodle? How far, how disastrously, we have progressed from the hunter's cave, and to what? To nonsense?

"What a dreadful place," says Madeleine to the stolid little body who opens the door. "Now I know why I haven't bothered to see it before. No wonder Hilary gets sick every Friday. It's the thought of Saturday and Sunday."

Madeleine! thinks Margot. Madeleine the ogre, the vampire, looking not so much dangerous as dirty and depressed. Madeleine, whom Margot once wronged, or would have in a world where women felt a sense of sisterhood and not of competition. Madeleine brought down, reduced, humbled by life and Lily.

"It's quite pretty," says Margot mildly. "You should have seen it before."

"I did," says Madeleine sourly. (Yes, of course. Madeleine once lived here. And here, under this very roof, Jarvis betrayed her.) "Of course, when I was with Jarvis he wouldn't spend a penny on a new electric fire. Mean! Well, you'll know what he's like. You're the secretary. Where's Hilary? I know Lily's taken Hilary.

I've been to the school. What does she mean to do?
Take out her white teeth and put in gold?"

"They've gone to the hairdresser," says Margot unwisely, "not the dentist."

Madeleine's anger is mitigated by the gratification of
finding Lily in the wrong, but she is nonetheless angry.
"She took my daughter out of school to take her to the
hairdresser? She told my daughter's teachers lies?"
Madeleine sits down. Her toenails are dirty; her sandal
strap is repaired with a nappy pin. Madeleine's next
sentences ought to be: "I'll go to my solicitor. I'll claim
custody, care and control. Hilary shall never come to
this house again." But Madeleine values her peaceful
weekends, her Saturday and her Sunday minus Hilary,
marked by nothing more demanding than the change of
program on the radio, so her indignation loses its force.
"I don't want my daughter's hair done by some poofy
hairdresser" is all she says. "I want her to have her
hair washed and combed like any other girl of her age.
You don't think Lily's going to have it cut? She
wouldn't dare. I'd strangle her if she did."

"It's a very good hairdresser," says Margot. What else
can she say?

"I doubt very much that it's a good one," says Madeleine, "though I dare say it's expensive."

Margot smiles unwillingly. Is there a complicity between the two women? Yes. They are united in something not very nice: a dislike of Lily for being what
they would hate to be, yet want to be. Besides, Jarvis
wronged Margot and wronged Madeleine. They are sisters in rejection, if nothing else.

"At least," says Madeleine, "Hilary's not been used to
baby-sit for the snotty brat." Madeleine slipped a disk
the week Jonathan was born, and lay on her back, in

hospital and out of it, for some three months after the birth. The pain was intense, overwhelming even grief and jealousy. These days she contents herself with referring to Jonathan as the snotty brat. Jonathan should think himself lucky it's no worse.

"No," says Margot, oh, wicked Margot, "I'm doing that today."

Madeleine smiles. "Fancy finding a human being in this shithouse," she says. "But you're the doctor's wife, aren't you? Hilary told me about you."

There Margot sits, in another woman's house, on that woman's enemy's side. Oh, Margot feels pleasure in it. A manic malice, momentary but there, felt like a contraction in her private parts. Was it malice or desire which led her up the stairs with Jarvis, Madeleine's husband? Love of the male, or spite against the female? "Jonathan isn't a snotty brat," says Margot, in the interests of truth and kindness, recalled to sanity by her fondness for Jonathan. "He's a very nice child."

"Then I can't think who he takes after. Can you?"

"Hilary is very fond of him. So am I."

"Yes, but you're very nice," says Madeleine. "The mother we should all have had." Then, the words issuing out of some blackness in her head, "If anything happens to me, I don't want them to have Hilary. I'd like you to take her."

Margot is startled. Madeleine sits on the edge of the white wooly sofa, her jeans limp with age yet stiffened by grease, dirty toe tapping. But Madeleine's face, downcast, is beautiful; her voice seems to come out of the future, or the past, to have been heard by Margot over and over again, and her very words have the ring of familiarity.

"What should happen to you?" says Margot eventually.

"I don't know," says Madeleine. "I look forward into the future, and it's black. It's my only real worry: what would happen to Hilary if I died? All kinds of things happen to people. You put all your eggs into one basket and the handle breaks. Look at me—yolk and mess everywhere. Now look!"

Now look indeed. What a handsome girl she'd been, up from the sticks, bright as a button. A father lost to another woman, true; a mother half blind, suffering from epilepsy (a war wound really; struck on the head by an aircraft propeller when a young WRAC, though she must have been half daft to begin with to have been standing in its way, as Madeleine kept remarking, entertaining her student friends with funny tales from family history—well, how else to deal with it?). But never mind, for a time, at any rate, for lovely, lively Madeleine, youth, energy and hope seemed to be winning over the disappointment of childhood, and idealism over anger, and her own griefs sublimating nicely, even creatively, into understanding and compassion. But then what happened? What does happen? The scar tissue of the past, as youth fades, hardening, coruscating, making itself more and more felt—or perhaps the prognosis was just too optimistic in the first place? Madeleine linked to Jarvis—a man amiable enough, surely, without malice (much) and an inheritance to boot—abandoning her studies, her life, herself, in the interests of art (oh, Art, Art, what deeds are not committed in thy name?), Madeleine linked to Jarvis suffered some kind of dismal change. Principle degenerated into self-righteousness, the sense of shared sorrow into self-pity.

As to love, after thirteen years of marriage Madeleine has all but forgotten what the word means. Jarvis, of course, has not. Sex is good enough for Madeleine, not for Jarvis. Jarvis falls in love with Lily. Who's to blame him? His solicitors hurried the divorce through three months before the Married Woman's Property Act came into effect. (Madeleine's solicitors, of course, had not even heard of it.)

Who will take responsibility for Madeleine's situation? No one. Madeleine must shoulder it herself. Madeleine means to do so. Something in Madeleine, something somewhere, perhaps her sleeping, not her waking, self, doesn't give up; intends eventually to return—perhaps after the menopause, when she can be her wombless, uncyclical self again—to the glory and cheerfulness of her youth.

Madeleine should get a move on, if that's the case. "Be careful," she says to Margot now, "it could happen to you."

Margot smiles, embarrassed. She feels threatened. Philip fall in love, run off, leave, abandon her? Is this what Madeleine is wishing on her, in return for that passing complicity? One should leave misfortune alone, stand well clear. Bad luck is as catching as the measles.

"You may think I'm a neurotic bore," says Madeleine, "but it seems to me the least I can do for my sex is to set myself up as an object lesson. The world being what it is—not to mention me—I'm not the kind of person of whom people say, 'What a lot of friends she has, how truly gay and popular'—using gay in either sense, though I've tried that too—and the upshot is, I'm all Hilary has. That's where it all leads one. Mother and daughter. How it starts, how it ends."

"She has her father," says Margot.

"Jarvis? He's no kind of father to her. And what kind of man is he? A nothing. Jarvis had a little talent once, but he was too trivial to sustain it. He drank it all away. And then of course Lily got hold of him. All he's got left is his business, and that's failing, and of course his cock, but who could sustain an interest in that? I couldn't, I'm sure."

Jarvis's cock. Margot shivers not just at the crudity of the word, but at the shame of the memory.

The sense of complicity has gone. Margot is alienated, as perhaps Madeleine intended. But the complicity was there for long enough. Some connection has been made, some fragile cogs have interlinked. Malice is a powerful force. Margot's malice, unacknowledged, welling up, spilling over, is perhaps more powerful than most. The flicker of an unkind smile, returned; the sly look, amusingly exchanged, and more travels between two people than you might suppose—the very devil floating, you might say, on the beam of interpersonal communication.

9

Be bold!

Madeleine, returning home, finds a letter from a computer-dating firm, giving the name and telephone number of a Mr. Arthur Quincey of Cambridge as a possible marital contact. (See how Madeleine, clinging to the past, still scrabbles for a future?) Mr. Quincy is described in the letter as being forty-three years old, tall, slim, dark, Anglo-Saxon, well-educated, owning own house and having no objection to slim dark lady under forty with own child. Madeleine rings the Cambridge number; a landlady fetches Mr. Quincey; Made-

leine finds she has agreed to be in Cambridge—yes,
Cambridge—at seven-thirty that evening in order to be
taken to the pictures. Mr. Quincey's voice has a quiet,
wheedling insistence; she recognizes it as the voice of
the male in the grip of sexual desperation, whose determination it is to bring fantasy down to the realms of
reality. It is hard to resist.

"It's like being a girl again," she complains to Renee,
who lives above Madeleine, on the ground floor. Renee
has left her husband and had her children taken from
her. It is a house full of women without men, and of
children without fathers. As you begin, so you end.
"To-ing and fro-ing to the snap of male fingers. Only,
in the old days one did it in hope; now it's in terror."

"Terror of what?" Renee is a delicate, wide-eyed
young woman, fresh, long-legged and clear-complex-
ioned, like some outdoor girl on an old-fashioned
chocolate box. Renee has two equally pretty little
daughters, sometimes with her. Renee claims to be bitter; Renee was abandoned by her father, and then by
her husband. Renee has, she says, renounced men,
Renee has her girl friends instead, from whom, physically and emotionally, she extracts comfort, company
and solace. From time to time Renee kindly offers the
same to Madeleine, in the shape of a warm and companionable bed, but Madeleine is too conscious of her
own raggedy body and troubled mind to be able to
offer herself on such simple terms. Although, as Renee
complains, she seems perfectly well able to offer herself to any passing man.

"Terror of loneliness," says Madeleine. "And of being
rejected, and of loss of status, and the general humiliation of being a woman without a man. Isn't that terror
enough?"

"You're so old-fashioned," says Renee. "You think life
for a woman has to revolve round a man."

"I can't help it," says Madeleine, the old Madeleine, to this silky young woman. "I feel it does, though I know it doesn't. Without a man to revolve around, I scarcely seem to exist. Yet when I had one, I was brave enough."

So she was. Bold, too bold! Neglecting the washing-up on the grounds that it was trivial; housework humiliating; cooking a waste of human energy and world resources. Taught within a year of marriage that sexual fidelity was meaningless, Madeleine learned the lesson well. Once having discovered Jarvis, disappeared at his own twenty-ninth birthday party to the comparative privacy of the spare room, interrupted him in mid-intercourse with a dumpy nurse on the spare bed amongst the guests' coats, and having retreated unseen, too distressed to speak or make her presence known, too shocked for action, she recovered quickly and set about using the incident to her own advantage.

"Jealousy," Madeleine would say, returning home to Jarvis from God knows where but suspiciously late, smelling of drink and sex, "is such a low, disgusting emotion! Don't you think so? Surely we're above that, you and me? We agreed before we were married that we would never be sexually possessive." And though no such agreement had ever been made, though Jarvis had no idea that Madeleine had discovered him and the transient Margot (for Margot it was, though Madeleine never knew her name, never saw her face) together on the bed that rainy birthday night amongst the damp coats, something in Jarvis, amounting perhaps to sheer forgetfulness, but no doubt bolstered up by some weakness, some guilt, some meanness learned from his stepfather, prevented him from finding the energy to contradict her. It was easier, for a time, to admire her.

Madeleine was brave, oh yes, she was, with the courage of anger. What an angry little girl she'd been, smearing the walls with far worse than puffed wheat, swearing at her mother, arms clutched round her father's pillar legs (in the process of being dislodged, she'd once had her thumb broken, so possessive, so determined, so desperate was her grasp).

"Someone's chalked a sentence on a wall in Shepherd's Bush," says Renee now. "It says, 'A woman without a man is like a fish without a bicycle.'" But Renee offers Madeleine the loan of her new white silk shirt for the evening, though it is much against her principles. Pandering to heterosexual vanities! Madeleine accepts with pleasure. Quincey is a nice name, she thinks. Madeleine Quincey.

The afternoon proceeds.

Hilary, horrified by her appearance, leaves the hairdresser in tears. Lily is irritated by this display of ingratitude; what is more, she is landed with Hilary for the rest of the day, for Hilary refuses to return to school. Not only will it be quite obvious to everyone that she has been to the hairdresser, and not to the dentist, but how can she face her classmates looking such a freak?

Margot collects Jonathan from play group, takes him home with her and serves veal-and-ham pie and salad for lunch. She bandages Laurence's bruised hand, assuming, rightly, that Philip will not have the time to do so. Lettice declines to have Jonathan sit upon her knee. Lettice always appears fearful of the demands of babies and small children.

Laurence tells Lettice that in the last six hundred thousand years some seventy-four billion people have been born and died. "So what," says Lettice. The children return to school. Philip returns to his rounds: three flu's, one pneumonia, one tonsillitis, one manic depression and one terminal cancer.

Miss Maguire, muttering up and down the High Street, calls a black man a stinking nigger. He offers her his card and suggests she see a doctor. He is a psychiatrist. Miss Maguire says she's under the doctor. The psychiatrist, relieved of responsibility, pats her kindly and walks off.

Lily goes to Selfridge's Food Store and there buys a crown roast, some *mange-tout*, some Jersey potatoes, some lumpfish roe, double cream, French loaves, cheese and six lemons. A shorn, sulky, tearful Hilary helps Lily carry the provisions home. Let us not suppose that the excursion to the hairdresser was organized totally with the image of Hilary as beast of burden in mind. Not totally.

When Lily returns home, she finds a message on the answering machine. The Bridges cannot come to dinner, after all. Harvey Bridge has flu, or so Moira alleges, in a voice brimming over, Lily thinks, with insincerity. It may be the quality of the tape, of course, but Lily doubts it.

Lily throws the Brie across the room in petulance, and Hilary stops to wipe up the spatters before finally going round to Margot's to pick up Jonathan. She wears a head scarf. It is by now three-fifteen.

Madeleine uses Renee's phone to telephone Lily, and reverses the charges, as is her custom. Madeleine speaks coldly but politely, finding it difficult to abuse or insult Lily to her face, though once it was very different! These days Madeleine suffers from the general paralysis of the defeated. She ignores the matter of the hairdresser and requests merely that Lily keep Hilary for the night, since she, Madeleine, is going out. And will Lily ask Hilary to ring her at Renee's between four and four-thirty. Lily acquiesces to both requests charmingly, with the sweet chilliness she reserves for her enemies. Madeleine has a vision of some biting summer drink, served in a thin glass with a frosted rim. Typical, thinks Lily, putting the phone down: mad Madeleine using Lily as a dumping ground for Hilary, and not in the least grateful.

Hilary returns home with Jonathan, saying that Margot is annoyed at having had to keep him so long. It is not strictly true, but Hilary will have her revenge. What's more, Hilary says, Madeleine was round at Adelaide Row, looking for Hilary and furious because she wasn't at school. Lily is horrified. Is the persecution going to begin again? Is she never to be free of Jarvis's past?

Lily forgets to ask Hilary to ring her mother. Instead, anxious to undo any damage Madeleine may have done to Jarvis's image, not to mention her own, she telephones Margot and asks if she and her husband would care to come to dinner that evening? A spur-of-the-moment affair, she claims. A panicky action, born of general upset, Lily realizes as soon as she has done it.

And done it is. Margot accepts the invitation, and then dances round the kitchen like an excited child, relieved of the necessity of cooking this, the 5,323rd dinner of her married life.

Lily actually cries.

10

Everything has meaning. Nothing is wasted. Only the young believe that they can stand alone in the world, for good or bad, their own master, independent of the past—will cross the very globe, from south to north, like Lily, in the blithe belief that she will thus put her past behind her.

As we grow older we sense more and more that human beings make connections in much the same manner as the basic materials of matter: that we cluster, in fact, as do those complex molecular structures which we see as models in physical laboratories. The linkages are unexpected; they can be of objects, plants, places, events, anything. It is perhaps why we should take good care to polish furniture, water plants, telephone friends with whom we apparently have nothing in common, pay attention to coincidence, and in general help the linkages along instead of opposing them—as sometimes, in our panic at our very un-aloneness, we are moved to do.

Consider now these linkages; these interconnections:

Miss Maguire, now fifty-seven, was at the age of 20 the general maid at 12 Adelaide Row, where Lily now lives. Her employers were a Mr. and Mrs. Karl Kominski.

Mr. Karl Kominski's sister Renate, in 1942 a refugee from Hamburg living in the Bay of Islands, New Zealand, bought a half-pound of pressed ham from Lily's father, Matthew. This was on the day before Matthew was called up and had to leave his pretty young English wife Ida behind to run the business, which she declined to do.

Margot's friend Enid, now living at 24 Kafka Rise (which incidentally lies parallel to a Thomas Mann Crescent, at right angles to a Goethe Avenue, and is bisected by Balzac Street), has a plant which originated, as a cutting, from a plant which once flourished in Hamburg in the thirties, and belonged to old Mrs. Kominski, Renate and Karl's mother.

Enid's husband Sam is an estate agent. In the golden days when money meant something and a house was a place you lived in and not the focal point of the occupier's monetary, social and emotional fears, Sam's first sale was of 12 Adelaide Row to Madeleine and Jarvis Katkin. That was in July, 1960, six months before Madeleine discovered Jarvis copulating amongst the furs with a passing party guest.

Both Madeleine and Jarvis were overjoyed at the condition of the house, which had not been repaired, let alone painted, inside or out, since 1939. But whereas Jarvis saw the house as a challenge to his architectural skill and his ability to make something new and glorious out of the wreckage of the past, Madeleine's pleasure found its source in the dilapidation itself. She did not wish anything changed. Even in those days her suspicion of prosperity and comfort ran deep, though she chose to blame her circumstances rather than herself for the bleak discomfort in which she had always lived. Madeleine declined Jarvis's offer of joint ownership. No, she wished to be free, to have no ties. No dogs, no cats, no budgies, no carpets, no potted plants, no copper-bottomed saucepans—no Jarvis, one would almost have thought. The sink, later the launderette when one finally opened in the new shopping precinct round the corner, was quite adequate to wash the clothes in.

Jarvis's early offer of a German-designed washing machine, Italian made, with the first trademark of the British Design Council hanging from the handle, was rejected with such scorn and derision, was such a defeat in that enduring domestic battle waged to and fro over everchanging demarcation lines, that Jarvis never fully regained his strength. He fought, after that, in a desultory fashion if he fought at all, and the house remained much as it was. It might be said that the house was in the end triumphant, entering the marriage as more of a third party than Lily ever was: it was the

house that tore Madeleine and Jarvis asunder. Or that
was how Jarvis saw it.

This was the house that Sam sold. Sam's wife Enid
went to school with Margot.

Margot has pink nipples; Madeleine, later Lily, brown.
Jarvis's preference for pink nipples was of the mildest
order; yet it was this appreciation of Margot's breasts,
so seldom observed, so rarely complimented, that
turned what in those days was called a snog into actual
lamentable making love—as in those days the act was
so innocently known. Poor Margot, to be so forgotten.

Poor Jarvis, in those early married days with Madeleine! It is sad to have overwhelming bourgeois ambitions and yet know in your heart that they are trivial.
Madeleine was right; that was the dreadful truth of the
matter. She was right about everything. Morally,
Madeleine was more refined, more sensitive than Jarvis, and he knew it. Heading through the fifties and
sixties towards a goal of aesthetic truth and material
nobility, shutting his eyes the while to the mayhem and
madness of the outside world, seeing only pureness of
line, curve and design, Jarvis has now run up against a
bizarre dead end. Decoration is back: frills and squig-
gles and nonsense and vulgar disposability. The squat-
ters are in next door. They light fires with pieces of
fifties' furniture which would make at least a fiver
down the Portobello Road, except that they haven't the
energy or interest to take them there. Madeleine, torn
and worn and honest, is at least in keeping with the
spirit of the times. They have finally caught up with
her, and passed Jarvis by.

Yet Jarvis, for all this, is happy these days. He has
Lily, who does not need design. Lily, Jarvis sometimes
fears, is conventional, trivial, selfish, unmaternal and
manipulative. He is better than her, as Madeleine was

better than him. He can be himself. They suit each other. Oh, they love each other. They do.

The week after Jarvis married Lily he found a model steam engine in the long grass of the garden of No. 11. A hired gardener employed by Lily had started making sense out of the jungle tangle Madeleine favored, and there it was. The engine was made out of a shell case brought home from France as a souvenir by, as it happened, Philip's father. That was in 1917.

Philip's father Alan had for a time courted a certain Phillipa Cutts, who lived in Adelaide Row. One summer evening in 1919, after lying in the long grass of the garden with Phillipa (as if he were a romantic lad of seventeen and not a shell-shocked veteran of twenty-seven), he had left the engine behind in the grass. He had brought it along to show her as an item of interest, a token of experience, but finding himself the interest, himself the experience, had never got round to reclaiming it. Why should he bother? Are not most of our treasures, in any case, offerings to romance, and well lost in its cause? Now the model engine stands, restored, polished and admired, as the centerpiece of the teak room divider on the ground floor where Margot, Alan's daughter-in-law, types Jarvis Katkin's invoices.

Alan lives in an old people's home in Crouch End. It is his habit to disconcert the morning nurses by feigning death, lying grey, stary-eyed and open-mouthed when they come to wake him. It is not so much that he wants to upset them by this habit, or so he tells Philip on his weekly visit, as that he's getting into practice. He never quite understood why he had been spared, he used to complain—one man out of the fifty lying lack-limbed and flyblown in the mud around him, dead as doornails—but being spared, he thought he might as well make himself useful. And so he was. So is Philip, after him.

The nursing home is on Heine Avenue, near where Enid lives. Back in the thirties, the chairman of the local Ways and Means Committee, had been much shocked by Hitler's burning of the books and had done his bit to compensate, to keep Europe's culture alive, when the question of the renaming of streets in the district had arisen.

All things have meaning. Almost nothing is wasted. Old friends, encountered by chance; old enemies, reunited to hate again; old emotions, made sense of and transmuted into energy; old loves reappearing; all the material flotsam washed up by the storms of our experience—all these have implication, and all lead us to the comforting notion that almost nothing in this world goes unnoticed: more, that almost nothing is unplanned.

Dumpy, flushed Margot linked to lovely, bleached Lily by chains more profound than those of employment and Margot's child-minding nature? Surely not! Lily would never consent to it.

But see the pair of them now, Margot and Philip, on their way to the dinner party. Margot scurries behind Philip, as is her habit.

"I don't like it one little bit," he flings to her over his shoulder. She is pleased. Remonstrance is better than silence, a milder form of reproof. "Don't like what?" she asks, though she knows very well. It is a windy night; the sky is alternately lowering and bright; clouds chase across the moon. "Getting socially involved with patients," he says, as expected. His suit is too tight; he has put on weight. Shepherd's pie is his favorite dish, and Margot's specialty. She is a good plain cook—plain to the point of obstinacy, he sometimes thinks. "We're only going because her other guests dropped out," says Margot, as if this made all the difference. The wind pushes her along, the moth into the flame. "We're going because his first wife turned up and you were there to witness it," says Philip. "You know what some people are like. She wants us all together in one big double bed." "Do you think so?" she inquires, surprised. But he does not reply. If he hadn't thought so, he wouldn't have said it.

Margot feels foolish. Her little feet are tight in their best shoes. Walking fast in high heels, she thinks, gets more difficult with the years, or else Philip is increasingly difficult to keep up with. Perhaps Madeleine is right; perhaps she is living in an entirely false security, and her trust in Philip is misplaced. Perhaps Philip envies Jarvis; perhaps he too would like a newer, fresher wife; perhaps he is not as indissolubly linked to her as she believes; perhaps one day he could speak of her as Jarvis speaks of Madeleine, as a stranger and enemy. The thought catches her breath, and there is a pain in her chest as if some cold hand gripped her heart. Her eyes smart. "Do you love me?" she begs him ridiculously, as she hasn't begged for at least ten years. But either he doesn't hear or doesn't want to reply. She trots a little faster. "You don't ever feel you want to start again with someone else?"

"Good God," he says, "I wouldn't have the strength," but his voice is blown away by a gust of damp wind, and his long stride takes him ahead of her again.

And Margot recalls, quite clearly, the smell of the wet furs sixteen years ago, before she was ever married to Philip—well, not ever, only some four months before; when she married Philip she was three and a half months pregnant—and puts it from her mind. The past, thinks Margot rashly and wrongly, is past.

11

Ah, bon appetit!

Lily is an altogether admirable hostess. What a happy note she strikes between ostentation and prudence, between self-advertisement and the pleasure of her guests. Dinner will be served in the dining room, French doors open onto the long garden; it is summer. The weather, contrary to the long-range forecasts, is good. The garden itself has a pale and washed-out look, partly due to the lack of rain and partly to Lily's liking for plants with pale foliage and paler flowers. A spectacular passion-flower vine covers the high trellis, which shuts out the neighbor's gardens but does not keep out the sun. The big lime tree, which once housed a wood-pigeon's nest, and every second year shed a sticky substance mortal to all growing things, and from the boughs of which the infant Hilary used to swing, has long been cut down. Pale rock plants grow obediently in the crevices between the York Stone slabs with which Lily and Jarvis personally sealed down the recalcitrant roots of the tree, for the stump refused to die for several years. (Sam the estate agent eventually suggested drilling a hole in the stump and inserting a common kitchen clove, which rite Jarvis duly performed. Whether the final death of the tree was due to the York Stone or to the clove was never known, but one or the other worked.) A pond, molded in plastic to a shape somewhere between a kidney and a heart, but its edges now tastefully mossed, is currently a home for some seven hundred tadpoles (Hilary counted, one in-

finitely boring Sunday afternoon), seven goldfish and
twelve frogs. A fountain plays, thanks to a pumping
mechanism bought cheap from Gamages in the week
before that useful emporium closed; the pump is splen-
didly reliable, except in the spring, when clogged with
tadpoles.

Bon appetit!

The guests will dine on cold consommé topped with
lumpfish roe and whipped cream, served with hot little
crescent rolls (for the greedy), followed by the
Selfridge's crown roast, served with *mange-tout,*
pommes duchesse (for the weak) and green salad;
then lemon mousse and the Selfridge's cheese served
with low-calorie crackers (which Lily will eat). Jarvis
bought the wine at Augustus Barnett; it is a light
Beaujolais and innocuous enough. Lily asserts that she
prefers Beaujolais to claret, but never gives a reason.
She would really rather not think about it. (Lily's first
sexual experience—a near-rape, alas—was with a
business executive who had taken her out to an expensive dinner, ordering filet steak and a good claret,
which latter seemed in retrospect to taste of menstrual
blood and graveyards mixed.)

Lily bleeds; yes she does. Red drops of death and
birth, like anyone else. She is bleeding tonight, though
through such a barrier of aspirin, expanding plugs of
cotton wool and proofed pants that she is able to forget
all about it. Lily's dress tonight is silver-grey, slippery,
high in the waist, low in the bust; her breasts are
clearly defined, her ankles neat in newly fashionable,
high-heeled, dainty shoes. In the kitchen, between
courses, she goes shoeless for speed and efficiency.

The refectory table on which they will dine is in faded
English walnut. It cost £65 in the days—the happy
days—when such a price seemed exorbitant. Jarvis
bought it, as it happens, in the week during which both

Madeleine and Lily lived in the house. The table mats are a pale brilliant green and come from Heal's. The cutlery is of silver and was left to Jarvis by his mother, Poppy. Lily, dear Lily, has had the dents made by Madeleine beaten out. Madeleine used the spoons, Jarvis's heritage, to open stubborn tins; she used the points of knives to change electric plugs; she used the forks to stir up the earth in the cat tray. Lily arrived in the house only just in time. As it is, Jarvis estimates that an eighth of his mother's knives, a quarter of her spoons and a sixth of her forks have found their way, via Madeleine's malice, into the dustbin. It is a matter of some grief to him.

Lily has had a waste-disposal unit installed, so any cutlery in danger sets up an instant uproar. His mother's silver remains as it should—clean, dry, polished and safe in a green felt box; on the table only on special occasions, and then briefly, very briefly, in the washing-up bowl.

On the table Lily has placed two white china candlesticks, containing pale green candles; these she will ask Jarvis to light as soon as the guests are seated. The matches stand ready. There is a posy of pale wild flowers in the center bowl (of fair-ground glass; only twenty-five pence in a junk shop which knew no better). The chairs are matching and are in mid-Victorian maple. The walls around are papered in a floral pattern: tiny white daisies and pale pink roses intertwine on a pale yellow ground. The dining-room curtains are pale yellow velvet and a mistake, but one too expensive to rectify.

The guests this evening are also a mistake, Lily fears: boring and blatant at the same time, like the curtains. The meal, costed by Lily at £24.25—she calculates such costs to a penny, including an estimate of the electricity for cooking and of two runnings of the washing-up machine after the meal—will, thanks to the loss of the Bridges, bring very little return in either entertainment, improved contacts for Jarvis or return invitations which she will enjoy. Why she ever asked Dr. Bailey and his wife she cannot now imagine. Nor can Jarvis.

Margot arrives dressed in a dinner gown bought (in Lily's estimate) in 1969, and timeless even then. It is of a shiny black material, high-necked and long-sleeved. Wearing it, Margot looks more like a plump skin-diver than a doctor's wife. The image flashed through Philip's mind as his wife dressed, but he was too loyal to utter it. If Philip has infidelities, they are in Margot's mind, not his.

Philip wears the brown suit he always wears when he goes out. He bought it at Marks & Spencer eight years ago; it is of a hard-wearing Swedish cloth, in an enduring style, and is tight round his waist. Much of his dislike of going out lies in his dislike of putting on the suit, and knowing that every time he does so it will be a little tighter, and his end a little nearer.

Jarvis, as befits the husband of a young bride and father of a two-year-old, wears jeans and Mao-blue shirt. If Lily has her way, Jarvis will hold back the passing of the years forever. Sometimes he would like to sigh and heave and sink back gratefully into a middle-aged torpor, like a hippopotamus into mud, but Lily will not have it. She keeps him slim, healthy and sober. She even cooks in margarine, not the best butter. Lily will keep Jarvis alive forever, if she can.

In the pale, plumply upholstered living room, which runs through from the front to the back of the house, Jarvis provides Margot with sherry, Philip with a glass of red wine, and himself with whiskey. He makes Lily a long Campari and soda. The glass stands waiting, frosted and sugared at the rim. Margot marvels, as Lily had supposed she would.

Conversation at first is difficult; outside their own territory the Baileys seem to be a silent pair. Philip is in the habit of thinking before he speaks, lest his patients misunderstand his meaning, as they will if they can. His family wait kindly upon his words, but in households such as these, he has no sooner opened his mouth than the conversation has leaped three subjects on. His very slowness gives him an air of wisdom, as if though clearly considering what has been said, he does not see fit to comment upon it. He makes poor Lily nervous. That, and the fact that he knows about the sometime erosions of her private parts, the result of too violent intercourse; knows her ridiculous fears of V.D.; weighed her weekly during her pregnancy with Jonathan, during which she underate absurdly, weighing as much at thirty-six weeks as she had at four; once even pushed his sheafed finger up her anus, inspecting piles. He knows too much and speaks too little. As for Margot, she clearly waits to take her conversational lead from her husband, and he is offering no leads at all. Lily thanks God she is not as other wives.

Lily's color is brighter than usual as she steers what passes for a conversation gracefully and quickly over subjects which scarcely count as politics, since they are surely open to little dispute, but which she assumes will interest the doctor and his wife.

"I'm sorry," says Lily in her cool, sweet tones, "but I think, personally, we all have a perfect right to educate our children how and where we want and to pay as much as we want for the medical attention we choose. What business has the State to tell us what to do and how we're going to live?"

No one replies. Only Jarvis, passing, grabs at her buttocks and vulgarly squeezes. Lily grows quite pink. "Personally I want the best for Jonathan, and I hope you do too, Jarvis. It's like worker's control, socialism run riot. I mean, the average person's I.Q. is a hundred, isn't it. And someone with an I.Q. of a hundred can barely read or write. How can people like that run the factories, poor things? But I mustn't bore you with politics; Jarvis is making dreadful faces at me. Why, darling? Am I being too political? Am I behaving like Madeleine? Mind you, Madeleine was red in tooth and claw, and I'm sure no one can say that of me." She laughs apologetically, and then remembers too late that the Bailey children go to the same Comprehensive as Hilary. "Oh, well," she says, "oh, well. I have my own views. I'm sorry if they don't suit. Poor Jarvis, how he suffers from his wives. What did you think of Madeleine, Margot?"

"She seemed much like anyone else," says Margot.

"Was she drunk?"

"I don't think so." Margot is quite startled.

"She usually is by lunchtime. It was always her great problem. It was very silly of her to come round here; she knows we can get the restraining order reinforced anytime we like. If she really wanted to know where Hilary was, she could have phoned. But then she'd have lost the opportunity of making a scene in front of you. Poor thing, I really feel sorry for her. I just wish she wasn't so rotten to poor Hilary; she stuffs the poor girl like a pig for the slaughter. And of course I'm good for playing nursemaid tonight, since she's off gadding somewhere. She really has a good time, that woman, on Jarvis's money, but she loves to pretend she doesn't. Are you *sure* she wasn't drunk, Margot?"

"I suppose she might have been," says Margot, betrayer. And Jarvis, to change the subject, pinches his wife. Color again. "Please don't do that," says Lily, "it makes me feel ridiculous."

"You never mind in private," says Jarvis, and Lily relaxes, bridles and giggles. Jarvis can always bring her pleasure by alluding publicly and naughtily to their private happiness.

"I expect Jamie and Judy are late because they're quarreling," says Lily, to her punctual guests, of her unpunctual ones. "Judy says they always quarrel when they're coming to us."

The doorbell rings. Jamie and Judy stand quarreling upon the step, like field mice arguing over a grain of wheat.

Jamie is fifty and feels thirty; Judy is thirty and feels twenty. That's only ten years' difference. Jamie is short, well-dieted and trim, grey hair tight and curly, face benign and wrinkled; he too is dressed in conventional Mao-blue. Judy is a top-heavy little thing; Afro hair shelters a small grey face and a spindly little body. Her thighs are taut and narrow, as if made for being forced apart, and her mons pubis is apparent beneath a startling dress of very thin red-and-yellow African cotton.

Jamie's voice is powerful, booming; hers, answering, is soft but nasal. Judy was a working girl from Liverpool, and sees no reason to forget it. Judy married a London businessman on her twentieth birthday and came south to live on a housing estate, all glass and greenery. Living next door, the other side of a couple of sheets of glass and a bush or so, whom did she find but her heart's desire: Jamie, actor and would-be writer and connoisseur. Also, of course and alas, Albertine, his wife, who claimed to be an actress but was really only a store demonstrator, unemployment in the acting profession then running at a slightly-higher-than-usual eighty-five percent. There, next door, Judy lived for eight years, during which time she had two children, made love with her husband some two thousand times, and with Jamie some five hundred times. On the five-hundred-first occasion Jamie's wife and Judy's husband, returning together from the local dramatic society's rehearsal of *Cosy Nook,* interrupted Jamie and Judy's ardors and responded not with grief, remorse and self-recrimination, but by falling in love with each other and absconding together, taking all the children—*all*—to create a cozier and more reliable nook elsewhere, and who could blame them?

Judy and Jamie, left with what they so much desired—that is, their freedom and each other—were married. Well, the other two were. Judy freaked out her hair, and Jamie took to wearing jeans; she writes theatre reviews, he runs a little theatre. They live in a penthouse, caring for a rich man's dogs while he explores the South Pole, hopefully lost forever among the ice floes. They seldom venture out so far into the suburb, but Lily is known as a good cook and Jarvis and Jamie are old friends left over from other days. Jamie went to school with Jarvis. Listen to Jamie and Judy now, as Lily opens the front door to them:

JUDY: Lily, I'm sorry we're late. Jamie has no sense of direction. That's his trouble. When I pointed out we were driving round in a circle and it was symptomatic of his whole life, he hit me. Look! Is it bleeding? His nails are very sharp.

JAMIE: I apologize for Judy. She's been drinking. It's the depressed-housewife syndrome.

JUDY: If only it were a house. You've no idea how poky a penthouse can be. Especially when it's not even yours, and you never know where you're going to be living from one week to the next.

LILY: Do both come in. No, Judy, you're not bleeding, not that I can see.

JAMIE: Of course she's not bleeding. I had to slap her. If I hadn't stopped her nagging, there would have been an accident. Judy has simply not caught

up with one-ways. She lives in the past. Women do,
over a certain age.

JUDY: Shall we just stop all this? It's very boring for
everyone.

JAMIE: I didn't start it. It's not surprising we never
get asked anywhere. Lily darling, you look angelic.
The pallor amazes. Jarvis is the luckiest man alive.
You and Judy scarcely seem to belong to the same
species. Look at you both!

Poor little grey, badly behaved Judy. Poor smarting
Jamie. There are few riddles left in such exchanges.
Resentment, fear, rejection; the desire to hurt, the
craving to be hurt; the tangle of love me in spite of
me, see how you've wounded me, offered up and
opened up for all the world to see. A cry for help,
seldom answered. Lily, good kind Lily, makes the
attempt to do so. Her own armor is not so well
made as she would like it to be. Chinks keep opening
up in her carapace of conventionality, letting in shafts
of understanding and compassion.

LILY: Judy and Jamie, do stop it, whatever it is. You
do love each other. You always have. You'll never
part, so you might as well be happy together. Do
forget it, whatever it was. Kiss and make up.

Bon appetit!

Judy catches Jamie's hand. But Jamie's hand remains
cold and hostile. Tears start in Judy's eyes. Jamie's
hand relaxes just in time. For the rest of the evening
they sit together when they can, touching flesh to flesh,
as they did when their love was still illicit and so much
more satisfactory.

"Where are the Bridges?" asks Judy now, looking
round hopefully. Harvey Bridge, the (quite) famous
architect; Moira Bridge, the lady television director. "I
thought they were coming."

"They've got the flu," says Lily. "But do meet the Baileys. Philip is our noble G.P., and Margot helps Jarvis out. Between them they know more about us than anyone else in the world. I'm surprised they came."

The shadow of the missing guests, of possible excitements and elusive good times, hovers over the rest of the evening—though Jamie does, between the jellied consommé and the crown roast, ask Philip for a diagnosis of a recurring pain under his right ribs, and Judy complains about service in the Casualty Department of the local hospital as if it were all Philip's fault.

Margot sits and smiles and speaks when she is spoken to. She may appear bland, benign and dull, but she is serviceable as a guest, and sops up aggression and tempers the general nervousness in much the same way as Lily's yellow curtains are also serviceable, absorbing noise and shutting out light.

After the crown roast, presented on a splendid blue-and-white-venison dish (picked up for five shillings on a market stall by Madeleine in the old days, when such things were plentiful and cheap; neither liking nor wanting it, she gave it to Jarvis on his thirty-second birthday) and served on crazed blue-and-white plates, each one older than the century by far; and after the Brie, and after wine and more wine, Lily leads the way to the drawing room.

What is it that Margot is whispering in Lily's ear? Lily is confused. The little girl's room? She can't be asking for the bathroom, surely; Margot works here. But no, Margot wants to pop up to Hilary's room to say good night. A little girl? Is Hilary really a little girl? Hilary looms enormous in Lily's mind—a giantess rather than a child.

"Pop up, by all means," says Lily in her husky voice. The word, repeated, sounds foolish, as Lily had supposed it would. "She's dying to show someone her new haircut. Such a relief after all that bushy doormat! One can actually see her face."

"If that's a desirable end," says Jarvis, in the disparaging tone fathers often adopt towards their daughters, as if the better to ward off incestuous notions, but in Jarvis's case it is more sincere than most. He has had more than enough to drink. So has Jamie. Philip has not. He fidgets and looks at his watch surreptitiously. Lamb gives him indigestion. The vinaigrette in the salad made him cough and splutter.

Margot goes up the pale carpeted stairs to Hilary. Does she remember going up them once, long ago, with Jarvis? No.

Hilary sleeps on a camp bed in Jonathan's room. The spare room, after all, is kept for guests, and if Jonathan is wakeful, it is simple and easy for Hilary, sleeping next to him, to soothe, change and comfort him, and means that Lily doesn't have to disturb Jarvis's essential, money-making sleep by waking herself.

Hilary is awake when Margot opens the door; she is leafing through Jonathan's ABC books by the ineffectual light of a pink bulb in a little pottery night light. Jonathan sleeps with his head cradled in his arms and his bottom in the air. Margot and Hilary whisper.

"Have they left any pudding?" demands Hilary.

"Lemon mousse? Yes. Why, will you have it for breakfast?"

"Yes."

"How's your hair?" inquires Margot.

"Don't look at it. It's horrible," says Hilary. "I can't go out of the house for at least six weeks."

"You'll feel better about it in the morning," says Margot.

"I'll have to, won't I? Mum will hate it. Her hating it is going to be worse than me hating it. I'll have both to put up with; it's always the way. You'd think mothers would be a help, but they're not."

"She might think it suited you short. She might be quite pleased."

"How can she be? It was Lily's idea, Mum rang Lily this afternoon and asked me to phone back before five. Lily didn't give me the message until half past, so when I rang she wasn't there. Lily forgot. Well, she was busy. She had to stuff wodges of mince and herbs into the middle of that bit of meat. Did Mum say where she was going? She never goes out." Hilary sounds anxious.

"No, she didn't," says Margot.

"Renee says she took the car," Hilary goes on. "I hate her driving that thing. It isn't safe. And where did she go? Why didn't she tell me? I don't like sudden things."

Jonathan stirs and whimpers in his sleep. Sleeping, he makes the same noises as does Hilary's guinea pig awake.

"Doesn't Jonathan look nice when he's asleep?" says Hilary fondly. "Mum doesn't like Jonathan. Not that she's ever seen him. She says he sounds spoiled to her. So one way and another I don't say much about here, when I'm there, if you see what I mean. You do look nice, Mrs. Bailey."

"I thought I looked rather ordinary."

"That's what's nice. I have a great craving for ordinary things in my life."

"You'd better go to sleep now," says Margot.

"Thank you for coming," says Hilary as Margot goes. "I am glad someone did." But whether or not Margot hears her, Hilary does not know.

And where is Hilary's mother, the while? Out having a good time.

Madeleine arrives in Cambridge at seven forty-five, her little mini having lost its fan belt on the way. The mini is fifteen years old and always losing something: exhaust system, door, oil, power, clutch, petrol cap. But it is loved by Madeleine. It cost £50 eight years ago, patiently saved. The car is Madeleine's freedom, Madeleine's pride. Lily doesn't drive. Mind you, Lily doesn't have to. There seems always to be someone waiting to take lovely Lily from place to place.

By the time Madeleine has found the cinema and parked the car, it is past eight o'clock. Madeleine's computer date, rather to Madeleine's disappointment, for the journey seemed pleasure and event enough, is still waiting for her in the foyer of the cinema, his pale eyes darting from side to side, distressed. Mr. Quincey is a short, pale, plump man in his middle forties. He has a nervous manner and smells strongly of acetone. Some liver disorder? Madeleine wonders. His tones are precise and careful; he comes from the Midlands. His hands are white and pudgy. He pulls at his fingers incessantly. And what does he think of me? Madeleine wonders. How will he describe me to his friends? Does he have friends? No, he blinks and twitches too much. Madeleine is sorry for him. One of the world's rejects, she thinks. As I am. Is this a good reason for us to get together? No.

After the film—a lengthy tale of handsome spies and beautiful unerotic girls—sparsely attended, Mr. Quincey takes Madeleine to a Chinese meal. He talks of loneliness over the sweet-and-sour. "I feel the same," she says, munching her egg roll, and so she does. Madeleine goes back with him to his bed-sitting room. The house smells of cabbage and his room smells of tooth powder. He is careful as he lets her in, in case the landlady sees.

Madeleine lies upon the bed without ado, and lets him make love to her. Mr. Quincey thinks he offers sex, but in fact it is love; he has books of poetry upon his shelves; he talks; he would rather talk than have sex, but feels he needs the latter as an excuse for the former. He works as a computer programmer; he was brought up in foster homes; he has been in a mental home twice; his erection is difficult to achieve, but good enough. Madeleine feigns excitement, pleasure. She does not know why she bothers, nor why she came so far to this purpose, to perform what in the end is an act of kindness. Well, it is easy enough to be kind to strangers.

She says little about herself. He does not seem to notice. Madeleine says she is going away soon, leaving the country; she cannot see him again, much as she would like to. His is relieved; it is the best possible ending to the evening. She presumed it would be.

"I've had a wonderful time. An evening to remember. Some enchanted evening . . ." he murmurs. "You begin to feel left out of things sometimes. Those girls in that film, those men—are there really people like that?" He seems to think that Madeleine, from London, is some kind of link with the outside world. He asks questions as a little boy asks questions of his mother.

Madeleine starts the journey back to London at twelve twenty-five. Her car smells of acetone, tooth powder, sex and old Chanel No. 5, from a bottle given to her in 1959 by a friend returning from a trip to France. Those were the days, the good old days, of friends, holidays, youth, possibilities. The night is clear. The motorway is deserted. The moon shines. The car rattles. It is a homely, familiar sound. Is the back left wheel wobbling? No. Too bad if it is.

12

Good night!

Hilary shuts her eyes and prepares for sleep. Hilary thinks, defining her being, naming herself to herself, preparing for her drift from consciousness, the better to awake:

I am Hilary. I am the daughter of two houses, at home in neither. I am the girl who should have been born a boy, forcing my parents apart by the disappointment. Well, something made this separation, something came between them, entered in, pierced and tore apart. Me? In all probability. My fault, but not my doing.

I am frightened of the dark. Jonathan stirs and dreams. Of what? In my mother's house I can sleep with my mother; she allows me in sometimes.

And my father sleeps beside Lily, and is a stranger to me. He embarrasses me. I know I disappoint him.

Once when I was little I used to hold his hand, but something happened to change all that.

I am Hilary, a fourteen-year-old girl with spots and short hair, a fat face and piano legs.

Hilary sings drowsily:

> *"To his nest the eagle flies,*
> *O'er the hill the sunlight dies ..."*

What comes next? She can't remember or she never knew. Mother, calls out Hilary in her heart, in the few last moments before she sleeps. Mother, do you hear me? I need your help. I am growing stunted, I know I am. If you don't do something soon, I'll fall apart like some dried-up walnut, and you'll find me withered in my shell inside. It is the sharp peremptory call of the child, bent on survival, demanding, not pleading. Mother, do you hear?

Hilary sleeps.

Mother hears something. Mother does. Blackness wells up in Madeleine's breast. Jarvis! All Madeleine can do for Hilary, all she knows how to do, is despise Jarvis and hate Lily—and what kind of help is that to Hilary?

Madeleine, driving, swears under her breath. Jarvis's fault. Everything. Lily is hateful but Jarvis is to blame. Jarvis has used Madeleine, abused Madeleine, thrown Madeleine out. Jarvis has destroyed Madeleine's life, and her child's life, and for what? For sex? For the pitiful act she has just performed with a pudgy half-person, smelling of tooth powder, on grey sheets? For sex with Lily, whose highest aspiration is to have her drawing room photographed by *House and Garden?* Is sex-with-Lily worth the ruin of so many lives? Jarvis thinks so. Madeleine doesn't.

Sex-with-Iris, Madeleine's mother: pretty, brain-damaged Iris Bates, hopeless with money, helpless without
it; half mad all the time, but who was to know it. Sex-
with-Iris ruined lives, ruined Madeleine's, drove Iris's
husband into the arms of a mistress, left Madeleine fatherless, presently motherless. Husbandless, all but
childless. For what is there left of Madeleine without
her titles? Daughter, wife, mother? Better to believe all
that, at any rate, than that Madeleine's father walked
out because his wife was losing her sight and foaming
at the mouth in public.

Oh, I am Madeleine, I am the first wife, I am the
rightful one. My house, my home, my life, gone with
my marriage. Myself left walking about the world,
stripped of my identity. I am Madeleine; I am
Hilary's mother. I cannot give her what she needs.
But what am I to do? I cannot take pleasure in her,
as Iris took no pleasure in me. There is a mist over
my eyes: the weariness of hating too much, too
silently. Hilary will wither in spite of my love, because of it, like a dried-up walnut in its shell; she
can take no nourishment from me. I consume myself; there is nothing left over.

Another minute, another mile. Sixty miles per hour.
Is it safe? No. How beautiful the night. How trivial
my complaints beneath the immensity of the sky.

I must change, thinks Madeleine. I must be Madeleine
again, myself. Neither daughter nor wife, but myself. I
see a kind of glimmer ahead, a hope of change. Could
I change? Am I still young enough? Or is anger now
etched so deep into me that to change would be to
break? That is my fear: break my habit, break me.

Courage. Change.

Madeleine, her father's daughter, her husband's wife,
her daughter's mother. Madeleine, herself, feels hap-

pier; she begins to sing a snatch of a lullaby out of some forgotten time, some happy moment, some barely recollected memory. Thus Iris once sang to little Madeleine; mother Iris all dressed up in silk and satins, mad-eyed, beautiful—longing as usual to go out, get out of the house, away from her husband's gloomy glance—but Iris delayed for a moment by the happiness, the pride reflected back in little Madeleine's brown eyes, and glad for once to linger by her bed on September 7, 1934:

> *"To his nest the eagle flies,*
> *O'er the hill the sunlight dies.*
> *Hush, my darling, have no fear,*
> *For thy mother watches near . . ."*

Madeleine sings. So Iris sang. Seventy miles an hour.

13

In the earlier decades of the century, they say, the dinner guest could expect from his evening nothing more disturbing than good food and good company.

These days the dinner guest must sing for his supper, must be prepared to accept and provide personal revelations, to acknowledge distress, his own as well as other people's, and to wake up next morning not only liverish but throbbing with personal pain. It is no doubt an improvement.

Listen to the conversation now at No. 12 Adelaide Row. The dining room, in disarray, has been abandoned. The guests sit in the drawing room. Jarvis, Jamie, Judy and Lily drank brandy. Margot drinks Cointreau; Philip drinks nothing, to Jarvis's irritation. (Those who drink heavily suspect the motives of the abstemious.) It isn't, Jarvis thinks, as if he were on call, or likely to be asked to perform an operation. He has a night service to do the first and a hospital to do the second. So why doesn't he drink?

Judy helps herself to more brandy. She is at the stage of her marriage where she drinks to keep her husband company. Presently she will stop so doing, preferring the risk of disaffection to that of hangovers, social shame and a veined complexion. But tonight she has drunk just enough to have the courage of her resentments. She eyes her husband more like an angry child than a grown woman. He speaks unwisely. He knows he is unwise. He does not care.

JAMIE: What a lucky man you are, Jarvis. To have a wife who looks like an angel and cooks like a demon.

JUDY: If you wanted cooking, Jamie, you should have stayed with Albertine.

Albertine, Jamie's ex-wife, who once played the wife in *Cosy Nook* and now plays wife to Judy's ex-husband.

JAMIE: I'm afraid my present wife is looking for trouble.

JUDY: Don't get at me in public, Jamie. I don't like it.

JAMIE: Lily, do me a favor and pour me some coffee.

LILY: But you already have some.

JAMIE: Yes, but just top it up. It's so delightful when you bend over.

JUDY: I know I'm flat-chested. I'm so sorry. Of course, there's no pleasing Jamie. Albertine had a front like a shelf and wore corsets, and he couldn't seem to fancy that, either. What it is to be a woman! You say anything about a man's cock in public and they

feel entitled to murder you, but they feel at perfect
liberty to complain about your tits.

Oh, I am Margot the doctor's wife. I cannot get used
to these new people, their new manners. Boobs is
bad enough, descriptive of clumsiness and distress.
Tits? A throwaway word for throwaway things. My
own honest breasts are scarcely looked at, scarcely
considered, except when of use to others, feeding the
babies or as a source of pleasure to my husband. My
breasts are for other people, not for me. They are
my offering to my family. Tit-wise! Oh, I am the
doctor's wife. I am staid. I am dull. But I am better
than these others. My children are happy and ordinary. By our children, you shall know us. All the
same, I want to go home. I want to be safe. I am
frightened. Philip, look after me. It is a quarter to
one. How long since we've been out this late?

But Lily is talking, and now Philip is alert and
watching her, woken from his trance. Lily is excited,
liberated. Her little white teeth gleam; her head is
thrown back, silvery hair thick and wild, neck white,
marked by little bruises Jarvis made.

LILY: I am tired of being nice about Madeleine. Madeleine is a neurotic bitch. Madeleine has her claws in
Jarvis and she won't let go. She takes our money. I
want new curtains, and why can't I have them? Because of Madeleine. Madeleine sits about on her arse
waiting to be fed and clothed, and the law says Jarvis has to do it. The world's full of women like that,
and the law's always on their side. He never wanted
to marry her in the first place; but he won't fight
her, he's soft. Jarvis looks after Madeleine's interests—what about mine? What about Jonathan's?
Three years since the divorce and she still keeps acting as if he were out on some kind of loan to me. If
her fuses blow, who does she ring up? Jarvis. She
burns electricity night and day, just for spite, so Jar-

vis will have to pay. And Jarvis won't cut down his
wine bills, nothing like that, so really it all comes out
of my housekeeping. Why should I have to pay for
Jarvis's past mistakes? And tit-wise, Judy, Madeleine is flat as a board, and twice as boring and six
times as miserable, and she had the nerve to come
whining round here this morning because I'd taken
her precious Hilary to have her beastly hair cut.
And as for Hilary, great fat creature, she has no
sense of gratitude at all. You know my only hope?
That Madeleine will find some other poor bastard
and torment him, instead of me. But who'd look at
her? Dreadful scrawny creature.

Lily pauses for breath. Philip speaks.

PHILIP: It might work out cheaper to hire a gigolo; had
you thought of that?

Margot blinks. Philip, her Philip, said that? And Lily
turns to smile at Margot's Philip, happy and relieved to
be understood, to be forgiven so much sudden, bitter
self-revelation. Jarvis is on his feet, burly and blurred.

JARVIS: A toast! I offer a toast. Death and damnation
to all ex-wives. Down with the leeches, the succubi,
the old women of the world who suck men's blood,
destroy their life force, make them old before their
time ... (and he sings) "Beauty is only skin-deep,
but ugliness goes to the bone, the bone ..."

The moon shines. It is ten to one. The hills lie silent
under a clear sky; the road is a magic ribbon.

Oh, I am Madeleine, returning home. My pants are
wet. Am I defiled? Perhaps Renee, whose white shirt
I'm wearing, is right. Perhaps sex with her, gentle,
companionable, kind, the conjunction of like to like,
would be preferable to this feeling of having used
and being used. But is Renee kind, or does she hate

the world and all its men with such ferocity, such
bitterness, that it produces this love for women as its
kind of side effect? I don't hate men. I don't. I hate
Jarvis, but then, he's damaged me and my child. I
didn't hate my father. I loved him. I hate Lily because she is evil. My gorge rises. There is a black
mist in front of my eyes. The smell of tooth powder
lingers, makes me sick. Jarvis's fault, all Jarvis's
fault. Jarvis, I hate you. Can't you feel it?

Does Jarvis feel it? Is that why he stands now, wishing
death upon inconvenient women? Listen to Jarvis, poor
Jarvis:

Oh, I am Jarvis, child of love and shame. I am
Jarvis, husband of Lily, child of Poppy. Poor Poppy,
pretty mother, all short skirts and long legs, slippery
almond eyes, kohled, and crimson-mouthed.

Who's for adventure? Who's for a fling? Oh, deary darling!

Poppy, decadent and doomed, hitchhiked north one
giddy Mayfair night in 1929, and lay with a lorry
driver, rough trade, all muscle, sweat and grime, in the
long summer grass in a lay-by south of Grantham, and
found herself overwhelmed by . . . what? Love? Or was
it only the pleasure of being defiled? Orgasm, hitherto
unknown? But off, in any case, goes Poppy to live, yes,
to live, with Harry the lorry driver in Wolverhampton,
not even married to him, leaving friends shocked, envi-
ous and excited, drooping round galleries, discreetly
sniffing heroin, dancing cheek to cheek, while Poppy,
pregnant, swelling, makes her wild, nightly journeys up
and down the old A1. There's an adventure! Except
that Harry, noticing her tightening waistband, turns her
out of the cab one rainy night just north of Doncaster.
Harry won't marry Poppy, wouldn't think of it. Harry
wants a decent girl, someone who is not defiled by him.
Who wouldn't?

And there Poppy is, presently, alone with Jarvis, her
baby, her passion, her pride, the old world lost to her,
the new one disowning her, and just as well, for the
stench of reality, of poverty, is up her flaring nostrils at
last.

Back comes Poppy to London, Jarvis tucked under her
arm, illegitimate. No social security then; no dole for
unmarried mothers (whores); no pill; no family plan-
ning clinics—just don't forget: you fornicate at your
peril. Poppy is lucky. She marries Hector, spindly
stockbroker, her own sort, who accepts Jarvis as his
own. But Jarvis is not and never will be. Jarvis has
broad shoulders; good God, Jarvis has a chin. Hector
and Poppy together make pale plump children with
pop eyes and receding chins. Poppy loves them duti-
fully, but loves her Jarvis with a mixture of passion
and despair.

Hector loves little Jarvis not at all. Neither do his
brothers and sisters. Jarvis looks strange, acts oddly,
paints, draws (what an ungentlemanly activity) in the
formality of this Home Counties house on the edge of
the golf course.

And Poppy looks wistfully out over the green of the
unnatural landscape, sipping (later knocking back) the
gin, mouth sweetly smiling, knees kept tight together
except in the course of distasteful wifely duty, lament-
ing the courage she should have had and never did,
and the sweet smell of the long grass this side of Grantham.

Oh, I am Jarvis, Lily's husband, the lorry driver's
son. I am Jarvis, Poppy's baby in that time of her
life when she was truly alive. Years pass; nothing is
resolved, little is understood. Only now I have Lily,
and I am big bad Jarvis, my father's son; I am
Harry to her Poppy. I will never abandon her or
send her away. I will keep her, love her, recompense

her. What I am doing is entirely necessary, entirely good, everyone's salvation. Why can't Madeleine recognize this, understand it, accept it and be happy?

Madeleine is like Jarvis's half-sister Ruth. "Art?" cried Ruth. "Beauty? Rot!" and off she gallops on a horse's back, pop-eyed and chinless, legs like a piano's, thwacking the horse's flanks, supremely confident, infinitely superior, her father's daughter—and Ruth was the kindest, nicest one of all.

Madeleine and Hilary have to be sacrificed; Jarvis has no choice. But why won't they lie down decently and gladly, as other sacrificial victims do? The slab is cool, clean, waiting. Not unpleasant. Their reluctance, their strugglings are indecent. All this was decreed so long ago, the near side of Grantham, the far side of Doncaster. Lovely Poppy, defiled, defiant, delighting, baby Jarvis nibbling at her white, unmarried breast.

Madeleine, I hate you. Lily, I love you. Lily, you are Poppy to my Harry. Nightly I defile, delight, relive. Madeleine, die.

Ten to one. All decent folk are asleep: life-wishing, death-wishing in their dreams.

Nine minutes to one. The back left tire of Madeleine's car, worn thin, finally worn through, deflates. The car veers off through the dividing rail, hits a post, carries on, crumbling as it goes, hits another. A twisting piece of metal from the bonnet sheers off Madeleine's right leg above the knee, and the steering wheel impacts itself into her chest; large or small, her tits, her boobs, her breasts will not help her now. The car comes to a stop. In the total silence that ensues, in the few seconds left of life, Madeleine can hear her heart still beating. It is open to the air. Madeleine is not in pain, not as she remembers pain: splitting and tearing to press out baby Hilary, as the sun split and tore to give birth to the world.

Hilary, thinks Madeleine. Hilary my child. What will become of Hilary? What have I been thinking of, these years, these times? Thinking myself Jarvis's wife, when all I was was Hilary's mother? What have I done to Hilary?

Lily shall not have Hilary. Must not. Who, then?

Madeleine's heart stops. In the distance, now, the sound of sirens, but Madeleine's world is silence. Madeleine is dead.

No, thinks Madeleine, with some spurt of power coming from God knows where, some dart of spite and compassion mixed, hate and love struggling for supremacy, as if the struggle rather than the emotions, which heaven knows are common enough, provided more than enough energy to transcend a perfectly commonplace death. No.

Who?

I am Margot, doctor's wife, in inner turmoil, smiling sweetly, sipping Cointreau.

The doctor sits up straighter, accepts brandy. Philip accepting brandy at twelve fifty-four A.M., knowing that it gives him acid indigestion, that it makes him disagreeable to his patients, not to mention his family? Philip watches Lily, Lily smiling not sweetly, smiling with pleasure at her own depravity. And Philip smiles, Margot knows, at the vision of Lily abandoned not to spite but to sexual excess. Betraying Philip. Evil Lily.

Margot feels cold; she feels horrified. The wind blows through the open window. She puts her hand to her head. She shrieks. She falls upon the floor. "My leg," she cries. Margot writhes. The others stare. This, the best-behaved of the lady guests?

Margot's breath comes in gasps; she pulls herself up and leans against the sofa. One hand slaps at her right leg with a curious waving, banging movement, as if the leg has no business being there; the other hand hits and hits her chest. Philip stares at his wife, bemused. Apart from anything else, the movements seem out of conjunction, like the limb movements of Siamese twins.

"Shall I call a doctor?" says Jarvis hopelessly, helplessly. Philip turns irritated eyes away from his wife towards his host. "Don't be more of a fool than you can help," he observes, and pulls his wife to her feet so that she can no longer hit and slap in such a disturbing fashion. "Margot," he says sharply, "stop all this."

Margot does. She moans and sways instead.

Judy and Jamie, the while, though fascinated by the lady guest's hysteria, still have eyes only for each other. Though not very nice eyes, for Jamie breathes down the back of Lily's neck and mutters, "You shouldn't have flirted with the lady's husband. See what happens?"

And Judy says, "Jamie, stop feeling up Lily. You don't annoy me in the least. You merely betray your age." And approaching from behind, she tips a little of her brandy down between Jamie's collar and his shirt.

Lily wishes she didn't give dinner parties.

"I'll never forgive you for this," says Jamie to Judy, and one can almost believe him.

Lily half shivers, half shudders, both from Jamie's hot breath and Judy's malice, and because a sudden gust of cold wind from the open window slams the kitchen door and seems to wake Jonathan upstairs. At any rate, he sets up a piercing yell of fright and rage. What an evening! Whose fault? Jarvis's, without a doubt, Lily thinks.

"Why in God's name did you open the window?" It's all she can think of for the moment, while she listens to see if Hilary will quieten Jonathan. Philip has lain Margot down on the sofa, and is busy loosening her . . . what? Her stays, Lily fears. Supposing Margot is sick? What will happen to the watered-silk covers?

"I didn't open the window," retorts Jarvis over the babel. "Why do you automatically blame me for everything?"

But before Lily can compose her reply, there's a thump-thump down the stairs and Hilary stands in the living-room doorway, apparently unconscious of the fact that her white nightie is undone and her puffed-up bosom plainly visible, and that Jonathan is still yelling upstairs. "There's something the matter with Jonathan," says Hilary. "I can't quiet him."

"Perhaps you pinched him," says Jarvis, watching the movement of his wife's buttocks as she pushes past Hilary and runs to her child. A real emergency would sober him; these current events merely make him feel dizzy.

"Of course I didn't pinch him," says Hilary with the straight-forwardness of one fresh from sleep. "I love him."

And the window bangs and rattles until Jarvis shuts it. Lily must have opened it—but why blame him?

"This house is falling to bits," says Jarvis. "One day we'll have to move. Go back to bed, Hilary. You're indecent."

Hilary blushes, clutches her open nightie together, and goes, not without a curious look at Margot, who is now sitting up-right on the sofa, pink in the face and with the buttons of her dress undone and her brassiere clearly unfastened, but otherwise composed.

"I'm quite all right," says Margot. "I'm sorry, everyone. I'm really quite all right."

I am Margot the doctor's wife, fresh from public humiliation. What will they think of me? How will I face them again? Little Margot, all of five, wetting her pants at a party. Medium Margot, all of eleven, interrupting her parent's love-making in the bath. Big Margot, all of sixteen, bloodstains on the back of her dress, unnoticed, all day. Of such stuff are nightmares made; of deeds that cannot be undone; sights that cannot be unseen; neither time nor laughter can erase. Margot on the floor, writhing from a pain that went as quickly as it came, leaving not a trace behind, except the look in Lily's eye, and Jarvis's, and Jamie's, and Judy's, and Hilary's, even, and the tired pressure of Philip's hand. When he is angry his face goes grey, heavy, like a stone. So it is now.

Philip smiles and talks, but his face is stone. "I think I'd better take you home," he says.

"I don't want to break up the party," says Margot.

Jonathan's shrieks subside as Lily reaches his door; he is asleep again by the time she is by his bed. The only sign of his distress is a damp forehead and a tear left on his cheek.

Oh, I am Lily the second wife, mother of the first real child. Why am I frightened? I have done nothing wrong. Only what I had to, and all in the name of love. See how quietly he sleeps—my son, my dearest inconvenience. Why did he wake? Does Hilary love him? Or does she only pretend—was it hatred of him, her jealousy, that swept through the house like a whirlwind just now, flapping curtains, banging doors, frightening us all? What does Hilary plan, my stepdaughter, as she bounces my son, her rival, on her pudgy knees? She could so easily harm him; he is her rival, her replacement, usurper to her rightful throne. Push him too high on a swing, let his stroller run into the road? No, she wouldn't dare. I have shown her my strength: I have made my mark on her; I have cut her hair, her pretty hair.

By the time Hilary has climbed back into her bed and Lily can go downstairs again, Margot and Philip are preparing to leave. The evening is over. Or as Jarvis says to Lily later, "Let's never give another dinner party, ever."

Jamie and Judy depart, as quarrelsome as they came. That night Judy, on Jamie's insistence, rides Jamie like a horse, taut neck stretched, head flung back, lean thighs gripping. It is not what she wants. She wants her boring husband back again, boringly on top of her, indifferent to her pleasure, quiet on account of the children sleeping in the next room. She wants to be a housewife again, despised by the world, at peace with herself.

"I love you," says Jamie.

"I love you," says Judy.

Do they? Does she? Not to want is not not to love. There are as many different kinds of wanting, surely, as there are of loving, and there are as many kinds of loving as there are of conversation. Take the population of the world and divide by two—or, if you must, three—and that's how many kinds there are. Or so says Enid to her junior secretary (who is much impressed), but not of course to her husband Sam, who likes to be the one of the family to know about these things.

Enid sleeps uneasily that night, and waking, has to go down to the bathroom. Is she pregnant? Surely not. Enid has been taking the pill for fifteen years, though Sam never wanted her to; but that was crazy, since he didn't want children either. What were they supposed to do—live in fear? Lately the reason for taking it seems largely to have evaporated, so she stopped at mid-month, for no reason she could really think of.

Sam sleeps heavily, without dreaming. He has drunk his usual nightly four whiskeys and a bottle of good wine. Such a high consumption of alcohol—as Enid keeps observing—inhibits the normal dreaming function. "Dream deprivation," she keeps telling him, "does a man no good. You end up with d.t.'s."

But Sam takes no notice. "It's sex deprivation," he says bitterly, "that's all that's the matter with me," and promptly falls asleep beside his resigned wife, Margot's friend, who composes herself for sleep. What else can she do? In the morning, if all else fails, she gets up and pleasures herself with a cucumber while Sam is in the bathroom. She doesn't mind and he doesn't know. Well, they're all getting older.

Miss Maguire, the doctor's Monday patient, stirs in the heap of old blankets and coats, urine-stiffened and cat-hair whitened, which makes up her bed. She dreams of 12 Adelaide Row, and of the days of her youth, when she and Phillipa Cutts were in service together. Poor Phillipa died in an influenza epidemic. Who remembers her now?

On the motorway, beneath the moon, ambulance men, policemen and wreckage crews work around the remains of Madeleine's car. The motorway has to be closed; wreckage has been flung across the tarmac. The ambulance men remove the body, not forgetting the severed leg, which is wrapped in a plastic bag and placed next to its owner. When they tilt the stretcher to get it into the ambulance the sheet falls away from Madeleine's face. It is the face of a living person in a deep sleep, thinks the attendant, although the state of the body is such that life cannot possibly be present. All the same, in the ambulance, he finds himself taking the pulse of the corpse, and even being anxious as his delicate fingers fail to find a response in the wrist. What was he hoping for? Is he so convinced that life is better than death?

The A.A. man is sick. It is his first night on the job.

"This is nothing," says the policeman who had closed the staring eyes. "It's when you find an eye looking up at you from a puddle . . ."

The A.A. man is sick again. He is in his early twenties and used to be in insurance, until made redundant under the last-in-first-out policy, and thereupon succumbed to the lure of the open road.

The car is towed away. The policemen and the A.A. man depart. The moon shines calmly on, untouched, over the low sweep of the hills.

The ambulance driver means to deposit the body at the Stortford General Hospital morgue, but arriving, finds their freezer unit is giving trouble, and proceeds to Custerley Mortuary. Here he has some difficulty in persuading the authorities (namely, Arthur, the mortician, white-coated and wearing slippers but no socks, and seventy-five if he's a day) to accept a body not strictly their business, and poorly documented at that. "It's asking for trouble," says Arthur.

It is Arthur's assistant, Clarence, a philosophy student on vacation, who belongs to a freer, less fearful generation, who persuades his superior to relent. In any case, Arthur wants to get back to bed.

The body is decanted onto a trolley and wheeled in, sheetcovered. Again the sheet slips from the head. The moon shines through the windows. Madeleine's eyes, open again, catch the light and glitter. Her face, drained of blood, smoothed out, is as beautiful as it has ever been.

"Poor lady," says Clarence, and the eyes close momentarily, but presumably it is only the trolley's jolting over the uneven ground that gives this effect of the dead being alive again.

"No seat belt, I suppose," says Arthur, whose custom it is to greet cadavers with some grudging remark—not so much, one might charitably suppose, because he wishes to be disagreeable, as to make himself, as well as them, feel that to be dead is not so different from being alive.

The police, meanwhile, have been doing their best to contact Jarvis. Madeleine always carries her marriage certificate, worn thin along the folds, in her handbag, together with the one affectionate letter from Jarvis she ever received. The handbag is of battered crocodile. Hilary found it in a dustbin when out on a treasure-hunt expedition with Jarvis and Lily, and hid it beneath her coat and took it home to Madeleine. And Madeleine made use of it out of deference to Hilary, and also, of course, in memory of the crocodile, slaughtered to gratify the rich and vain.

The bell of the telephone extension by Jarvis and Lily's bed has been switched to the off position. The instrument trembles fractionally as the contact is made, but no one answers. Sergeant Corvey cannot get through.

Hilary lies sleepless in her bed. It's spooky in here, she thinks, and she turns on the ceiling light to supplement the night light. Jonathan whickers in his sleep, and reminds her of her guinea pig.

Hilary sings:

> *"To his nest the eagle flies,*
> *O'er the hill the sunlight dies.*
> *Hush, my darling, have no fear,*
> *For thy mother watches near."*

So sings Hilary softly to herself, remembering what she never knew. So sang Iris, once long ago. Hilary never met Iris; she died before Hilary was born. "One of those people," as the six-year-old Hilary observed to her mother Madeleine, thus comforting her somewhat, "whose time for being alive was before ours." As if all the world, in life and death, was fair and properly regulated. Perhaps Hilary's daughter will be able to say the same for Madeleine, and as calmly. Perhaps not.

Philip and Margot are late to bed. Lettice, in some spasm of housewifeliness, has boiled up what remains of the chicken for stock, and gone to bed and left the pan to boil dry. The stench of burned bones and pitted saucepan fill the house. When the windows have been opened and the mess cleared, it is past two o'clock. Tiredness has passed; exhaustion has set in. Philip lies in bed, waiting for his wife to join him.

Margot creams her face in the mirror. "I'm so ashamed," she says. "Writhing about on the floor like that."

"As well you might be. Well, never mind. It got us home."

"I didn't think you wanted to leave. You seemed very happy."

"Nonsense. They're perfectly dreadful people"

"What was wrong with me?" she persists, although he has explained patiently, over and over again, that her symptoms, responding as they did to a harsh word and a slap, were hysterical and not functional, and best ignored and forgotten.

"Jealousy," he remarks, driven to it by a mixture of exhaustion and irritation. "Perhaps you thought it was time you got a little attention."

Margot does not reply. She removes the cream from her face and stares into her own eyes as into a lover's.

Oh, I am the doctor's wife, mother of the doctor's children; I am used, put up with, ignored; I gather scraps from other people's tables. I am the doctor's wife, my husband's wife, an only partly welcome guest; my husband's adjunct, neither smart, nor beautiful, nor successful, but useful for filling up an empty seat between two males, useful in order to make the hostess shine. I am the doctor's wife, fresh from a public humiliation I shall never forget, creaming my face before a mirror as I have done a thousand times before, seeing the detail, not the whole, as plain girls quickly learn to do—and now I find the aging woman.

Margot stares into her eye. She sings:

> "To his nest the eagle flies,
> O'er the hill the sunlight dies . . ."

"Is that you singing?" asks the doctor. "Couldn't you come to bed? I can't get to sleep until you do."

"Was I singing?" Margot inquires, and realizes that yes, she was.

"Hush, my darling, have no fear ..." she goes on, but can't remember what comes next.

"For heaven's sake," says the doctor.

Deep-set brown eyes stare back at her from the mirror. They close, momentarily. Margot sees them do so. But how can you see eyes close if they're a reflection of your own?

"Philip ..." says Margot, frightened.

"Christ almighty," says the doctor. "Don't you understand I'm tired."

Margot gets into bed beside him. She is stiff with an unfamiliar resentment. The doctor sleeps. He smells of tooth powder, she thinks. A musty, dusty, sickly smell. He who uses toothpaste. Margot sleeps.

Again the telephone by the Katkin bed vibrates, unnoticed. Lily and Jarvis are locked in a languorous embrace, which took them from the bathroom, where Jarvis soaped Lily's white body with creamy soap, up the stairs, where discomfort finally led them to their bed, where Lily all but fell asleep, and now lies on her side with him behind her, halfway between waking and dreaming. He moves inside her, it seems, like a large fish in a tiny bowl, importunate yet affectionate, pleasurable yet puzzling. All the same, the vision of Margot writhing on the floor on her side remains with Lily, holding her in the outer world. Her climax approaches, recedes; his arrives; hers evaporates. She is quite content.

"What a waste of an evening," says Jarvis. "We could have spent all of it in bed."

Lily laughs, and stretches out her white hand to flick out the light. "The clock has stopped," she remarks. "I thought I'd wound it yesterday." And so it has, although she did. Jarvis picks up the telephone to dial for the time, and hears Sergeant Corvey's voice addressing him. He is at first too confused to comprehend what is being said; it is the voice of accusation he hears, as he was accustomed to hearing it in his childhood: loud and reproachful and coming suddenly, thunder out of a blue sky, turning his life upside down. Hector, his stepfather, had a loud voice, and was given to shouting.

"Who are you speaking to," inquires Lily in his other ear, spreading her limbs over his, naked and naughty, "at this time of night? I know. It's Madeleine. It's Madeleine, isn't it? She says her drains are blocked and she wants you over right now to fix them. Tell her she can't have you. Tell her you're mine." But Jarvis quietens her with his hand and pushes her off. What is Jarvis saying? Lily listens.

"Stortford General Hospital? . . . What are you talking about? . . . Their freezer unit? . . . I'm not an electrician, I'm an architect, and it's three in the morning . . . My wife is here beside me in bed . . . Is this some kind of practical joke? . . . Madeleine Katkin? Madeleine . . . ?"

And Lily is pushed altogether aside, and Jarvis sits on the edge of the bed, head in hands, and Lily's small white hands flutter against his turned back, brown, toughened, resolute against her, and her voice in the room where once Jarvis and Madeleine walked and talked sounds plaintive and ridiculous and out of place.

Madeleine dead?

Oh, I am Lily, once the second wife, now the only wife. What is to become of me now? This was not what I meant at all. I married Jarvis, Madeleine's husband. Am I to have the full weight of him upon

me now? Jarvis, Lily's husband; Lily, Jarvis's one
and only wife?

The moon goes down behind banks of clouds; the first
signs of morning can be seen in the sky.

In Custerley Mortuary the electric light begins to seem
watery. Madeleine lies, sheet-covered, on her trolley.
Arthur has pattered off home in his slippers. Clarence
is in charge. Clarence sings a lullaby. He can't remember where he heard it; Clarence's mother was not the
kind to sing lullabies. She worked as a waitress at
nights, leaving him when his father came home. But he
likes to think she would have, if she could.

> *"Hush, my darling, have no fear,*
> *For thy mother watches near."*

Time passes. Punctually at six o'clock Goliath strides
into the mortuary to relieve Clarence, who is more
than ready for his breakfast. Whether through tradi-
tion, superstition or common politeness, the bodies of
the dead are not left unattended. To devalue the dead,
after all, is to devalue the living. At the same time,
staffing problems, here as anywhere, are acute. Goliath
is a West Indian lad, seventeen, and studying for his
A-levels in art and history. From six in the morning
until ten he caretakes in the mortuary and does his
homework the while. At ten he goes round the corner
to school, where they are pleased to see him, late or
not. From five to eight each evening he trains for the
school team in the local swimming pool. Then he helps
his father in his garage until midnight, when it's time to
go to bed. On Saturday nights Goliath takes out his
girl; on Sundays he goes to church with his family, to
whom he is a credit (as he is to the school, the swimming team, his girl friend and the mortuary). Goliath
is condescending towards Clarence, who clearly cannot
manage his life, as his shaggy hair, red-rimmed eyes
and frayed jeans indicate.

"Singing?" remarks Goliath now, reproachfully. "To my mind we owe the departed rather more respect than that."

"It quietens them," says Clarence, meaning to tease.

"Prayer does that," says Goliath, alarmed, "not song. But if you don't mind, we will discontinue this conversation. Discussion of the supernatural is not healthy; it dissolves one's senses of the reality, and renders one more open to unhealthy extrasensory experience."

"In other words," says Clarence, "if you see a ghost, don't mention it."

"Quite," says Goliath uneasily, and doesn't add, "Why? Have you seen one?" for fear of hearing an answer he'd rather not. Instead, Goliath inquires why Madeleine's body has not been decanted from its trolley and placed in the appropriate wall unit.

"Poor lady," says Clarence unctuously. "She looks so beautiful with the moon upon her face. She will never feel it in life again."

"I am a Christian," says Goliath sternly, "and I believe in the immortality of the soul. What lies there upon the trolley is dust and ashes. The soul has flown."

"Do you really think so?" asks Clarence, peering at Madeleine's white, quiet face. "She might be temporarily gone, I grant you. Off visiting, here and there, one gets the feeling she is. Busy as a little bee she's been all night."

"What do you mean?" Goliath is uneasy now, as well he might be. He loosens his beautifully white collar with his fingers, pulls at the smooth black tie he always wears to work. As the morning light increases, so Goliath's fine black face emerges out of the background, and Clarence's pale features lose their definition. It is clearly time for Clarence to go home; Goliath's time has come. Clarence is a creature of the dusk; Goliath, of the dawn.

"The newly dead do go visiting," says Clarence firmly. "I'm quite sure of it. They go off on a tour of their family and friends; they visit their nearest and dearest first, then the rest of their acquaintance in order of precedence. It can mean a lot of waiting about, if someone dies who is not very close, or not as close as you had hoped; you sometimes have to wait days, or even weeks, before you feel their spirit come to touch yours. Then they make their peace and say goodbye, and off they go wherever it is they go. After that, you stop feeling so irritated and impatient with them for dying, and begin to feel sorry about it, and presently forget them altogether. As for the dead, they lose interest in the living in the same way as the living lose interest in the dead—and as you, Goliath, no doubt lose interest in a girl once you've had her.'

Does Clarence believe what he's saying? Clarence scarcely knows himself. The day after his mother died of thrombosis—she'd had varicose veins, from a life of so much standing about—Clarence had certainly felt the breath of her presence and sensed the process of incorporation, so that later he could stand at her graveside and feel not so much grief as exaltation. But perhaps he imagined it? Perhaps it was his way of denying loss? How is Clarence to know? In the meantime, he has clearly upset Goliath.

"I am not in the habit of having girls," says Goliath stiffly. "I am in the habit of going steady, and that's the difference between you and me."

All the same, after Clarence has left, Goliath, instead of decanting Madeleine's body, as he is employed and paid to do, leaves it where it is, and sits and eats his breakfast sandwiches, first removing the ham his mother has put between the bread, for he has some aspiration to being converted to Judaism, in the hope of being able to battle on equal terms with a single-minded Jehovah rather than having to succumb, worshipfully and meekly, to the unchancy will of the Holy Trinity, as is his present obligation. Goliath finds himself singing

*"To his nest the eagle flies,
O'er the hill the sunlight dies . . ."*

and stops himself. He does not wish to behave like Clarence. Goliath has never been personally acquainted with death or suffered any great personal loss; youth and the cultivated health of his body, the surging of the blood in his veins on Saturday night, and of his heart on a Sunday morning as he lifts up his soul to the Creator, incline him to notions of his own immortality, physical as well as spiritual. Well, he is young and strong, and that is that.

This morning Goliath cannot concentrate. He feels restless; Clarence or something has upset him. The air in the white-painted room is in some kind of turmoil. Goliath is accustomed to the company of the dead, but today he wishes to be gone; he wishes he was a schoolboy like any other, and not a paragon of both the children's and adult's world; he waits impatiently for Arthur to arrive and relieve him of this noisy silence.

What would Goliath hear if he had ears to hear? He would hear the reproaches of women. What else? He knows them well, as do all the family of man. He heard them first on the day he was born. Listen. From the delivery room, where new life bursts, amidst grunts and groans, from the old: "Oh, how you hurt me, how you tear me, you beautiful boy, my love, my pride, my ruin. Ouch You devil, monster!" He will hear them, no doubt, on the day he dies: "Why are you going into that dark vale, why are you leaving me here all alone?

What is your male death to my female misery? Devil! Monster! Deserter!" He knows them well; he knows them by heart. As he knows the cacophony of female neighbors, crowding, protesting, at the door of the wife-beater, the baby-batterer, the drunkard, the deser-ter: "Villain! Devil! Monster!"

Goliath puts down his book, goes to Madeleine, pulls back the sheet from her face. She is unsmiling, intent. She seems to listen. To what? The air is thick around her body, busy with complaint. Goliath senses it. Alive, it seems, Madeleine was nothing to the heavenly female host; dead, at least she proves a point and becomes the focus of womanly discontent.

Cover your ears, Goliath! The chorus is at it again: "Why is this woman dead? Who killed her? If she killed herself, who drove her to it? Some man! Who? You?"

Goliath pulls the sheet back over Madeleine's face, breathing deeply to steady his racing heart, goes back to his place at the table and reopens his history book. Reason prevails. The dead are silent.

Be quiet, Madeleine. Lie still. So you were wronged; so were a million, million others, dead and gone or on their way. You were wronged by women as much as men; you know you were. By your mother; by your friends; by your especial sisters, those sweet flowers, by Lily, by Poppy, by Iris, sending out their sickly per-fume over the generations. And by Margot, housewife, unflowerlike, dumpy, powerful in her fertility, lying with Jarvis beneath a pile of damp and musty coats.

Be quiet, Madeleine. Lie still. Let young Goliath turn the pages of his history book in peace. You ranked first in history once, when you were his age. You can afford to leave him all alone. You had your patch of blue sky, your glimmer of sun, the awareness of your body as it took its nourishment, reproduced itself, and was finally destroyed. That's all there is to any of it. Acknowledge your mortality.

Lie still, forget, say your goodbyes and go.

No.

14

Six o'clock in the morning. Who's awake? Lily, loved by many in spite of herself.

Renate Kominski, out of Poland, aging lady withered up by disappointment and a Southern sun, loved little Lily and almost no one else besides. Who else was there to love? Her family was lost in the holocaust—all except Karl, whom she never liked and who took up residence in an old house somewhere in London. Renate herself chose New Zealand as her future home, that being the farthest she could possibly get from Europe. A Jewish agency paid her fare and gave her enough to buy a little flat, and that was all. Well, it was enough.

Renate landed in Auckland, in 1939, full of hope, but found herself an outcast in a foreign land. She kept herself alive by weaving raffia plates and baskets, which were sold to unenthusiastic buyers in the local arts-and-crafts shop. Not only was it a meager living, but her hands were always cut and sore from the sharp edges of the raffia. She was a handsome girl, but she had trouble with the language. She was too clever for local tastes; she kept herself to herself. What young

man in the Bay of Islands could understand Renate's
mind, habits, culture? Renate did not marry. The
able-bodied men soon all went off to the war, in any
case, leaving a nation of women and children behind.
They were tough women too, who could shear a sheep
and mend a roof in the morning, and in the afternoon
throw a Pavlova cake together and serve it on a lace
doily for tea. Not like Renate. No talk of ideas, or art,
or poetry; not even any recognizable political fear, of
loss of freedom or identity—just the sheer physical fear
of the Japanese, with their fiendish torturing skills,
pressing nearer and nearer to the shores of the Land of
the Long White Cloud. New Zealand! What a paradise, a pearl, a prize . . .

> *"Guard Pacific's triple star*
> *From the shafts of strife and war . . ."*

sang the little children in a frenzy of warlike enthusi-
asm.

And no one cared to listen to Renate, husbandless,
childless, crippled by experience.

> I am Renate, woman without mother, country, hus-
> band, child. I have only myself to offer. It is not
> enough.

But Ida the butcher's wife was kind; cultured, even.
Renate bought half a pound of pressed ham from the
best butcher's shop in New Zealand—the butcher himself about to go away to the war—and stood on the
sawdust floor, weeping with longing for a garlic sau-
sage. Ida, though she had never tasted garlic, recognized nostalgia when she saw it. Did Ida herself not
suffer this same sad emotion? Did she not long for the
soft, weeping skies of England? And how she was
frightened by day by the bright and glaring skies of the
Southern Hemisphere, and by night by its great cold
arch of starry sky, with all its intimations of infinity;

and frightened most of all by her own nature, which
had made her trip out of England on her little high
shoes, in her little peekaboo red hat, and follow her
butcher to the very ends of the earth. The Land of the
Long White Cloud.

Ida tried to get away from him once. She bedded with
a poet during the butcher's short absence in the Philip-
pines, but all she got from that was Rose, Baby Rose,
with her thick curly hair, and a whole lot of trouble
when the butcher returned with an amputated big toe.
Fingerless, toeless man. Ugh! How lovely.

Lily has a mourning ring which her mother gave her
when she came to England. It contains a lock of Baby
Rose's hair. Lily keeps it, not for Baby Rose's sake,
but for her mother's.

Renate comforts Ida through her trials. Ida learns to
weave raffia plates; together they teach the butcher cultural ambition and Lily cultural discontent.

Renate one day receives several thousands of pounds
in compensation from the German Reparations
Board—for loss of mother, country, future. Renate
gives it not to Ida so that Ida can pay her fare back to
England and start her life again, but to the butcher, so
that little Lily can be properly educated and get to the
Northern Hemisphere, where by now, ambitious and
discontented, she spiritually belongs. "You're too old,
Ida," says Renate. "You're too old, like me, to start
again. Blame the war, not me. Besides, we have to
think of the children."

Renate, female in spite of her situation in the world,
abandons her own generation in favor of the next. Ida
and Renate quarrel and part.

Ida smiles at Lily now, distantly, on her return from
boarding school. Lily has stolen Ida's heritage. Well,

she was bound to. It is what daughters do, given half a chance. Daughters steal youth, beauty, hope and future—or so mothers are inclined to think.

"Mother darling," sighs Lily, boarding the plane for England, home, safety and the secretarial college, "I'll miss you so much. What will I do?" But she doesn't mean a word of it. And Ida knows it.

Goodbye, daughter.

"Father dear, oh, Father . . ." But the butcher is an old man now, waving stubby fingers in farewell, and old men are better left. If you can. Not so easy.

Goodbye, Father. Goodbye, Mother. Hello, life! Lily, once in England, sensibly finds work as a secretarial assistant on an elegant women's magazine, and from its monthly column sets about bettering her appearance, refining her manners, improving her conversation, and changing her culinary repertoire from mulligatawny soup and bacon-and-egg pie to consommé and garlic.

Goodbye, Father. Goodbye, Mother. Hello, Jarvis. Public school, stockbroker belt, but an artist nonetheless. Going to waste with Madeleine.

Oh, Jarvis.

Six o'clock in the morning. Who's awake?

The doctor, the doctor's wife, the doctor's children, and of course the doctor's cat, loved and hated by many, whose courting habits caused an uproar as dawn broke over Muswell Hill, waking the entire household with its screeching and yowlings.

Laurence, the doctor's son, climbs out of bed and gropes his way into the garden to rescue the cat, whom he assumes to be in great distress, both physical and mental. The circle of cats, disturbed by his big bare feet, stare at him with hostile eyes before dispersing, their coven's communion broken. Laurence picks up the doctor's cat, soothing and comforting, and carries the unwilling creature inside. Laurence's feet are wet from the damp grass, his pajamas damp from drizzle; he does not care. Lovingly he feeds the cat with the chicken breast left uneaten the night before by Lettice and himself. The kitchen still smells of poultry bones boiled dry.

I am the doctor's son. I am the cat's protector. No one in this household loves him properly. Chicken is too good for us, not good enough for him, that's my opinion of the world this morning.

Laurence gets back into bed, damp and chilly, he sneezes and drifts back into nightmares. The cat forgives him and comes to sleep on his bed. Thus are the virtuous rewarded.

The doctor's wife awakens with a tightness on her chest, which she puts down to last night's drink and dinner, and with an unfamiliar feeling of resentment, which she attributes to her husband's callous behavior of the night before, though in what respect it was callous she cannot now quite remember. The doctor rolls towards her, embraces her, murmurs comfort in her ear, and folds himself upon her. Margot's resentment remains with her; her body goes as usual through its familiar warm and compliant rites. But this is ridiculous, thinks Margot spitefully. It's ridiculous and boring. He's using me, pretending, giving nothing of himself. I don't really like him at all, let alone love him. And Margot's heart stays as cold as her body is warm. To be thus unusually separated mind from body, feeling from act, gives her an almost pleasant sensation of freedom and power, and since it in no way interferes with her orgasm, but even heightens her sexual response, she is not as dismayed by the alteration in her-

self as she might have been. Philip notices nothing.
How could he? Only afterwards Margot says, "You
smell of tooth powder, or that stuff my grandfather
used to drop his false teeth into every night," which
slightly takes him aback. When Margot's grandfather
died, Margot's grandmother, much taxed in the past by
a husband overfinicky about his food, took to wearing
the false teeth of the deceased in the interests (or so she
said) of economy. It used to upset Margot's mother
Winifred dreadfully, and for a time she ceased to visit
her mother at all; to see her father and her mother
speaking from one mouth was more than Winifred
could endure.

Lettice wakes to find her crotch sticky and spots of
blood upon her bottom sheet. Her instinct is to call her
mother for help: "Mother, come quickly! See, I am
hurt, wounded, ill in some dreadful way." But the truth
of the matter is soon apparent to Lettice: she is men-
struating for the first time, as to all accounts was only
to be expected. A dreadful gloom falls upon her; she
has the vision of a life to come which is womb-cen-
tered, messy, uncontrollable: a whole future of preg-
nancies and miscarriages, cysts, fibroids, erosions, V.D.,
breasts swollen with milk, riddled with cancer, the
sorry women sitting in her father's surgery. She is at
the end of her neat, self-controlled prepuberty prime. I
am finished, thinks Lettice, not without truth. No age
will suit me as well as my late childhood. Five days a
month like this for the rest of my life? One week out of
every four, or as good as? Sheets and knickers stained
and messy? My lifeblood draining away monthly?

Lettice's grandmother, Margot's mother, Winifred, re-
ferred to menstruation as "the curse," and to Lettice's
mind the description is more apt than that offered by
her brisk and sensible teachers, who present, with evi-
dent untruth, the genital and reproductive processes of
the human female as ordinary, pleasant and orderly.

Lettice, who never cries, cries, and lies as still as she can for fear of making yet more mess.

Miss Maguire wakes early; she, who rarely dreams, had a vivid and disturbing dream that Mr. Karl Kominsky and his wife have returned and taken up residence in 12 Adelaide Row, and that Phillipa Cutts rose from the dead from amongst the long grass in the back garden and helped her make pressed-meat sandwiches. Miss Maguire unfolds herself from her blankets and sets out to see if it is true. She wears the same clothes night and day.

Sam wakes earlier than usual. He has a headache; he has been mixing his drinks again. Enid, his wife, though feeling sick herself to the point of retching, runs to fetch him an Alka-Seltzer. Enid normally rises at six, Sam at eight-thirty. Every morning she brings him his breakfast in bed, sorts the clothes for the washing machine, washes up, sweeps, dusts, tidies, and leaves a note for the milkman. This morning she has time for a cup of coffee before she leaves for work, although not time to sit down while drinking it. Enid is an efficient woman. Sam complains that she moves unrestfully fast. Enid will shop for food in the lunch hour and collect Sam's suit from the dry cleaner's. She travels by public transport, much weighted by shopping bags. Sam does not think she has enough concentration to drive, and would be a danger on the road to herself and others.

Only sometimes on a winter evening, waiting in the rain as bus after bus, overloaded, pass the stop without pulling up, will Enid feel sorry for herself. Otherwise she remains cheerful, stoical, and happy to love Sam and be loved by him. She cannot talk to him about her work but she can listen to him talking about his, and she can always tell Margot, her confidante, all about everything on Wednesday evenings.

A sex shop has opened just by her bus stop. Enid toys with the idea of buying a vibrator, but the bus always comes before she plucks up courage to go in. Just as well; the use of a simple cucumber seems far less disloyal to Sam, besides being cheaper and less potentially dangerous, electrically speaking.

At 12 Adelaide Row, Hilary and Jonathan sleep. Some bond between them, some quiet companionable love, sets up a barrier against disturbance and allows the two of them an hour or so's grace before waking to their dreadful day. Thus, so far, has Hilary armed herself against her mother, and grown from Madeleine towards Jonathan, that lovely child, born of love and need, whom Madeleine so unreasonably detested in her life and in her death.

Jarvis and Lily are awake, never more so. Lily lies on her back in bed, furious and resentful. Jarvis paces the room, his face flabby with lack of sleep and last night's alcohol, and pale beneath its stubble. Jarvis's pajama trousers gape open and Jarvis's genitalia, disregarded, fall out. From time to time tears burst out of his eyes, and he groans and gasps at air.

And Lily, lying watching him, remembers vaguely but with repugnance some other such scene from out of her past: the collapse of some other male personality. When? Who? She would rather not remember, but eventually she does: Lily's father, the butcher, in tears in the cold room, stumbling amongst the hanging mutton carcasses, blinded by grief, stabbing uselessly at the smooth white flanks as they swung towards him and away from him. Is it a real memory, or an imagined one? She does not know. At any rate, it enables her to view Jarvis's present collapse with distaste rather than despair. He will recover, as did her father, to hold her hand and give her treats again. At least partially. Well, Jarvis must recover. If anyone went on like this for long, Lily thinks, he would clearly have to be put in a lunatic asylum. She takes some comfort from the thought.

It is Lily's habit to let her mind race along to the very worst that might develop out of any given situation, accept it, and deal with it as best she may. She has already worked out in detail how she would survive in the face of most losses—if she were widowed or Jarvis was bankrupted; if Jonathan was lost, kidnapped, brain-damaged or killed; if Hilary or herself were raped; if the house burned down; if the H-bomb fell— but never, oddly, has the death of Madeleine entered into her calculations. Perhaps it was an event too devoutly to be wished, although now that the actuality is here, she finds it acutely upsetting. Who is to tell Hilary, and how? And if Jarvis loves her, Lily, as he alleges and she has believed, and has put Madeleine out of his life, why is he now so totally out of control?

It will be a great saving, thinks Lily, looking, as always in moments of crisis, at the positive side. (So her mother taught her.) Twenty pounds a week, clear of tax, will be added to their income. The new roof can be started, the hall recarpeted—unless, of course, Jarvis decides to send Hilary to a private school. But that will surely no longer be thought desirable, for Hilary will have the civilizing influence of Adelaide Row as her permanent home, and won't have to put up with Madeleine any more, and Lily will have a baby-sitter every day, not just on weekends. On the other hand— no, don't think about it. Not yet.

"For God's sake," says Lily to Jarvis, "either come back to bed or get up. It doesn't make any difference to anyone you wandering about, tearing out your hair. Dead is dead."

"I know it means nothing to you," says Jarvis bitterly, "but she was the mother of my child."

"Of one of your children," says Lily, and Jarvis stops pacing to glare at the butcher's daughter, that upstart lady.

"Death is not such an awful thing," announces Lily, getting out of bed, peeling off her nightie and standing nude while she searches for her knickers—and the awful thing is, she means it. Death lurked over the sandy beaches of her childhood; she is accustomed to the end of things. Why else does she pay such reverence to what is here and now? Dead birds, dead wood, dead sailors; in the end, even a dead little sister lying on the white dry sand, washed up by the Pacific waves. In the end it was the pounding and dragging, pounding and dragging as the oceans of the world slopped this way and that beneath the circling moon, which in the end made a silence in Lily's shell-like ear, blotting out all but the most vivid sounds of distress.

After her quarrel with Lily's father, the Bay of Islands butcher, Lily's mother Ida, that delicate lady from the Home Country, took herself and Lily and the newborn Rose off to Long Bay, Coromandel, where she lived and sulked the war out, running the Kiwi Tea House for the benefit of swimmers, ornithologists and truckloads of American servicemen, then on leave in this New Zealand paradise, resting after Okinawa. The teahouse was little more than a wooden shack perched on top of a sand dune, vibrating like a drum when wind and rain bounced upon its corrugated iron roof. Ida made it nice: nice as middle-class England in the thirties, when the servants knew their place and the servants doffed their caps. Ida served tea in china pots on checked tablecloths, weighted down against the wind by cowrie shells; she served passion-fruit ice cream in scallop shells, and slices of cherry madeira cake and crab sandwiches besides, and if the sand flew into your mouth as you ate, there was nothing she could do about that, except to request you to keep your mouth shut while you ate. The bay was sheltered from the open passions of the huge Pacific; here the sea ran sluggishly, the waves were an apology for the huge rollers Lily loved. Everything here was second best, Lily used to think, like her mother, like her life: little bleached girl on a hot dry beach, thin arms lifting trays, filling teapots, taking tips from the large-teethed, yellow-skinned, open-faced Americans, with their free, loping gait. In the winter the beaches emptied, the tea-house closed, the shutters went up over the windows, and Lily's mother Ida occupied her time dreaming of England, home, green fields and tea dances, teaching little Lily the art of English housewifery, and looking after Baby Rose, that little bundle of sorrow and shame, while the set sand whipped against their oil-lit, wood-warmed cottage, and Lily wondered if she would ever see her father, or a school, or the real world again.

"What did Madeleine have to look forward to, anyway?" inquires Lily. What indeed? The fading of her youth; the growing estrangement of Hilary; the falling value of twenty pounds a week; the encroachment of rust through the fabric of her refrigerator, and wet rot spreading through the draining board? Some households, as Lily is aware, like some people, if left spiritually unattended will move steadily away from grace and towards corruption, will become a prey to the breaking in of thieves and rust and moths. As to Madeleine, as to her home—"What did she have to look forward to?" Lily repeats.

Under his wife's disparaging gaze, Jarvis straightens up and defends himself. "Life," he replies.

"She must have died about the time you were wishing her dead," says Lily unforgivably, "so I think you're being very hypocritical. I can't bear hypocrisy in a man. It's the last quality one looks for. And what's more, the clock stopped at the time she died." She says it in triumph, as if this last fact somehow proved her value and his worthlessness.

"I wondered when you were going to bring that up," says Jarvis. "I wondered when the farago of superstitious nonsense was about to begin. I know what we'll be having next. It was Madeleine's ghost swept through the house last night, opening the windows, sticking a cosmic pin into Margot Bailey's leg, another one into Jonathan, and another into Hilary, but missing you altogether. Is that what you believe? It wouldn't be like Madeleine one little bit. Why should she have anything against the doctor's wife? It was you she didn't like, and with good reason."

"Good reason?" inquires Lily dangerously, and with what remains of her common sense.

Jarvis refrains from pursuing this particular tack, which would consist of variations on the theme of Lily as home-breaker, marriage-wrecker, child-stealer. But two can play at that game, and he knows it. "If you and I are going to get through the next few days, Lily," says Jarvis instead, with that paternal pomposity to which his wife reponds so well, "we are both going to have to behave. And you can start by not implying that it was I who killed Madeleine by wishing her out of the way. I'm sure you were wishing harder than me, in any case."

Lily is quiet, for she is frightened. What is Jarvis implying? That Madeleine, at the moment of death, did indeed send her spirit through 12 Adelaide Row, Lily's home, with its pale new carpets and its pale clean walls? Stop the clock? Why should she? Madeleine hated the house in her lifetime, had been heard a hundred times to say so, had at one time quite deliberately broken its windows and torn out its flowers; she had left no part of her spirit here. Everyone agreed. Otherwise Lily would have insisted, yes of course she

would, that Jarvis and she start their married life in a
new house. She could only enter No. 12 as its mistress
by virtue of the fact that Madeleine had left so remarkably little mark upon it. If Madeleine's spirit was to
turn up anywhere, thinks Lily, on its way to wherever
it was that spirits went, surely it would be at her
present basement home? Yes, Lily can quite imagine
that. She shudders.

"What's the matter?" asks Jarvis. "Is someone walking
on your grave?" And Lily begins to giggle, and then to
laugh, and then to cry, and then to have hysterics, so
that presently Hilary and Jonathan, wakened by the
noise, come into the bedroom and stand staring at her
in horror—cool, quiet Lily, Jonathan's mother, Hilary's
stepmother, for once so flushed and noisy—and Jarvis
their father, feeling too dull and indifferent to so much
as slap his wife and bring her to her senses. She has to
do even that, or its equivalent, for herself; she bites her
hand hard.

"What's the matter?" asks Hilary.

"Your mother's dead," says Lily, just like that. Well,
once Lily's mother said to Lily, "Your sister's dead,"
and Lily felt only relief, so why should Hilary feel dif-
ferently? All Hilary says, in any case, is "I don't believe you," thus betraying stupidity, ingratitude and
callousness, and making Lily want to scream once
more. Is this what she's going to have to cope with
from now on?

Jarvis takes another swig of whiskey and puts the
bottle down on the floor. Jonathan totters over, picks
up the bottle, and copies his father. Lily gets to her
son, but not before he's taken at least a couple of swal-
lows. Lily snatches, Jonathan wails, Jarvis rants, Hilary
asks unnecessary questions about the manner of her
mother's death, and Lily is left to ring the doctor to
ask his advice about Jonathan's drunkenness.

Philip Bailey, awakened from early-morning sleep, says not to worry, let him sleep it off, and puts the phone down without, Lily realizes, so much as a thank-you for last night's dinner. She wishes she'd never asked him. She can see that she's going to have to change doctors, sooner or later. Some other finger will have to inspect her cervix.

Breakfast is clearly going to be late.

Well done, Madeleine! More effective in death than in life. At least at breakfast time.

Eight o'clock.

"I don't believe you," cries Hilary, beating at her stepmother with clenched fists as Lily tries to make Jonathan vomit by sticking her finger down his throat. All Jonathan does is bite. "You're lying. My mother isn't dead."

"You'd better get ready for school," says Lily. "You'll be late."

"School?" says Hilary blankly.

"S-c-h-o-o-l," Lily spells it out. "You have to carry on. We all have to carry on."

So Hilary puts on her red platform shoes, stumbles off into the day, and carries on.

Eight-thirty.

Breakfast at the doctor's house is similarly disturbed by Margot's ill-temper and the doctor's early awakening. Margot, hollow-eyed, strips the stained sheets off Lettice's bed with unnecessary force and a muttered "Well, its started now."

"What's started?" demands Lettice. "What?" She is pale and furious.

"Trouble," says Margot, and that's all she will say. Margot, suddenly cruel mother, offers Lettice neither comfort, advice nor help, beyond handing her a towel, a belt and a couple of pins, which Lettice knows to be hopelessly old-fashioned. What's the matter with her mother, Lettice wonders, this morning of all mornings? Can she be jealous? The notion cheers her up a little. "Will *you* tell Dad?" she murmurs to her mother later, with some faint notion of being proud of her new status as fecund woman, but Margot merely stares at her daughter and says bleakly, "Tell him what?" so that poor shattered Lettice goes off to school feeling resentful and miserable.

And when Laurence insists on telling his mother in detail about the behavior of matter in black holes, the doctor's wife remarks, "Facts never made anyone intelligent," so that he, too, leaves the house upset and hurt. And then when the doctor asks his wife why she is limping, she retorts "I'm not," although the pain in her thigh still comes and goes.

She burns the bacon and eggs, tips the lot into the bin, and starts again. "What's the matter with you today?" he asks. "Isn't that rather wasteful?"

"No more wasteful than your *Amateur Photographer* every week. It's not as if you ever even opened it."

The size of the weekly newspaper bill is a matter of some grievance to Margot. Through the letterbox every day comes the *Times,* the *Guardian* and the *Mail;* and on Sundays, the *Observer,* the *Sunday Times* and the *News of the World;* and once a week, *New Scientist, New Society, The Statesman, The Listener,* the *B.M.J.* and the *Lancet;* and once a fortnight, *Amateur Photographer.* The doctor does not like to see unopened newspapers and periodicals thrown away. Margot stacks them, badly and unwillingly, in the hall between the kitchen and the surgery. One day the doctor (he claims) will get round to reading them. In the meantime, a nest of field mice lurks unseen but sometimes heard in the 1971 back numbers.

One day.

One day, in 1948, when Philip was sixteen, prize pupil at the grammar school and form prefect, he entered a photograph in a local amateur photography competition, "Artistic Nude" section. The photograph was of his sister Jill, then twelve, who took off her clothes for her brother not only willingly but almost eagerly. Perhaps something of her smiling complaisance showed, because the photograph won first prize locally, and then nationally, and appeared in all the national newspapers. (Those were the days when photographs of naked girls needed to be backed by an excuse of some kind—artistic, medical or geographic.) Jill had to be taken away from school, out of range of the sniggers of her contemporaries and the shocked disapproval of their parents, and sent off to boarding school. Mr. and Mrs. Bailey did not in any way blame Philip—after all, they had given him the camera for Christmas—but the whole episode was distressing. Jill contracted infantile paralysis at boarding school and lost all movement from the waist down. Mrs. Bailey nursed her at home for some five years, until herself contracting cancer of the spine.

In those days the word cancer, like the word bankruptcy in the previous era, was whispered; it was a disease as socially embarrassing and as little understood as insanity. Mr. Bailey, that lover of open spaces and wild flowers, was tied to a home of shame and illness. Philip abandoned his ambition to become a newspaper photographer and became a doctor instead. His parents were much relieved by his change of plan.

It seemed to them that the cloud which had descended on the family the day Jill took off her clothes and posed for Philip had finally lifted, and the purpose of Mr. Bailey's survival of the battlefields of World War I was made clear at last. Philip was to be a doctor.

Even though he spoiled things rather by presently marrying Margot, a little pregnant nurse.

Since the doctor started in general practice he has had little time for photography, let alone remorse. His sister's death from pneumonia, by comparison to many deaths he has seen, seemed merciful; his mother's lingering end no worse than many: his father's condition, living in a nursing home in the daily expectation of death, of no great moment. He has trained himself in compassion for others, and has little left for himself. He expects Margot to be likewise, and she is.

She is the doctor's wife. She is there to help. When the telephone rings, she replies patiently and carefully. When her husband is tired and cross, she understands. When he is unreasonable, she forgives him. When he is selfish, she makes allowances. When young women undress for him, she knows his interest is in public health and not in their sexuality (as once his interest lay in lighting, grain and texture, and not in the naked body of his little sister Jill. Or so he told his parents, and they certainly believed him.) His patients' needs, in fact, are greater than hers; she knew that when she married him.

Not today. Today she brings the subject round to the unread copies of *Amateur Photographer* and the size of the newspaper bill, or (if we're translating riddles) the unacknowledged and painful traumas of his adolescence. It is a declaration of marital war to which he responds with alacrity. He has spent a disturbed night, after all, and his digestion is still laboring under the strain of last night's lamb, vinaigrette and Beaujolais.

"Since I earn the money," retorts her husband, " I can surely spend it how I please, and if I want to buy seven thousand copies of *Amateur Photographer* and never read one of them, it is nothing whatsoever to do with you."

It is a statement which normally she would accept as self-evident truth, but today she feels argumentative. "What nonsense," she observes. "You can only earn the money in the first place because I set you free to do it, washing and cleaning and cooking and looking after your children."

So saying, she drops a cup and breaks it. Is it accidental? She scarcely knows. Certainly it is Philip's favorite cup—bowl-shaped, the better for tasting the flavor of coffee, and given to him by an emergency lady patient from Paris, whose peritonitis he diagnosed when all others had failed to do so, and whose life he (allegedly) saved. She was a very French, very blond, very grateful patient indeed.

"What is the matter with you? The cost of breakage in this house must run to hundreds."

"You could always deduct it from the housekeeping," observes Margot. "It's what they used to do to servants. Charge breakage."

"A very good idea," says Philip. "You might learn to be careful."

For once, the doctor's wife is not wearing her seersucker dressing gown, but her oldest skirt and an old grey jersey she uses for spring cleaning. There is a hole in the armpit. No doubt if she included jeans in her wardrobe, she would be wearing those.

"Are you going to work like that?" he asks.

His wife seems confused, plucks at the jersey, regarding it with some astonishment, and says, "Of course I'm not."

"Why not?" he inquires. "Sackcloth and ashes might well be appropriate."

"I couldn't help being taken ill." She is hurt now, and subdued.

"If that's what you call it."

"What else?" she begs.

"Very well. What diagnosis would you prefer? Hysteria or brain tumor?"

Philip surprises himself by his own competence, unpracticed as he is, in this flare-up of hostilities between them. He is almost enjoying himself. The second lot of bacon and eggs is burning in the pan. He looks at his wife with the hatred she seems intent on inviting. Shaken, she turns to the stove. She is getting scrawny, he thinks, lanky and sinewy, like some tough old lady in the Appalachian Mountains. "All I can say," he observes to her back, "is that as a servant you're a failure, and not worth the wages you're paid. Look at the state of this place."

It is certainly not tidy, but then, when was it ever? The injustice of his own remark troubles Philip; certainly he does not normally regard his wife as a servant. On the other hand, the lanky, angry creature at the stove, her back set against him, burning his breakfast, seems to expect and deserve abuse. He has the feeling that he is required to provide it, much as it goes against the grain.

Margot turns back to him. There are tears in her little button eyes. "You've gone mad," she says. "And what about you last night, anyway, ogling Lily like that and suggesting they find a gigolo for Madeleine."

"So that's what it's all about. You're such a prude," he laments. "I was only entering into the spirit of the evening, after all. I thought that's what you wanted." His long fingers drum upon the table. His hands seem to have declared their own independent war against his wife.

"You're turning into a dirty old man," she says. "I suppose you fancy her tits. Brown-nippled bitch."

Philip is quite shaken. Perhaps his wife has a brain tumor after all? "Margot, my dear," he says, all his own animosity evaporating, his fingers quietening.

"Don't you 'my dear' me," says Margot. "I know you and your dirty tricks. Sticking your hands up women when there's no need. And weren't you sorry when you got a night service and had to stop visiting your slut. I knew where you were going, up and off in the middle of the night, don't think I didn't."

Once, long, long ago, when Philip was thirty-three and feeling older than at any other time in his life before or since, when Margot was pregnant with Lettice and his life seemed to be closing in upon him, as once his father's had, Philip had an affair with a patient. An affair? It was hardly worthy of the name: more like a scuffle, three times enacted in the back of a car, and then boredom interceded—or was it prudence?—and Philip, in the interests of honesty, harmony—or was it fear of blackmail?—confided in his wife. She understood, as a good wife should. (By that time Lettice was born and Margot was struggling to establish breast-feeding.) Where had she been herself, after all: deserting her post, off at the ante-natal clinic, concerned with the pressure of the baby (unborn) on the sciatic nerve, and (born) on her nerves, rather than with her

husband's emotional and sexual needs, and so on. He'd
been lonely, the girl had thrown herself at him, and
how could he—why should he—resist? He loved his
wife, after all. It had meant nothing. The girl, alas, was
less easy to throw off than he had assumed girls were
(Margot being his model of femininity). This one was
an artist's model who worked at the local art school,
and spending, as she did, most of her time naked and
observed, had developed a fine sense of her own im-
portance. Throughout the ensuing years Philip would,
from time to time, at two, three, four in the morning be
summoned to emergencies at strange addresses, and
when he rang the bell, why, there she'd be, naked on
the step, inviting him in. He either had to have her
certified or pay for a night service. He chose the latter,
regretfully; it saved him sleep but cost him money
and the good will of his patients. But this, he acknowledged, was the price one must expect to pay for
professional indiscretions. He was lucky it was no
worse and that Margot was such an understanding
wife.

Not this morning. This morning Margot is all the
wronged women in the world; and being so, he finds it
all the more natural to wrong her. "My patients are
waiting," the doctor observes, and so saying, he leaves
her, her Madeleine-mouth still open in abuse, and, as
one might say, egg around it.

Oh, I am the doctor, I am any man leaving home
with a jaunty step, off to work, putting the trial of
breakfast time behind me; off out into the world
where I can deal fairly and squarely and be the decent man I know I am. And pray God by suppertime she is herself again.

Oh, I am the doctor's wife, any wife, Jarvis's one
and only wife, left with the dishes as the front door
closes. My own words corroding my own sweet
mouth; his still rankling in my ears, unforgivable. I

shall feed off them all day, and they off me. It's a poisonous diet, but I'm hungry, and if there's nothing else, it will have to do.

Poison indeed! And the only antidote is love. If there's a scrap of it left, find it.

Presently Margot does so, and feels better. The cat emerges from under the table and jumps on her lap. The doctor, after all, has not left the home; he is only on the other side of the dividing wall. She can almost hear his patient voice, slow and reassuring, that he sympathizes with, understands and heals the whole world and its populace—with the single exception of herself. Well, it has to be put up with.

Margot thinks of Hilary, poor Hilary, with her shorn hair, and the thought lifts what remains of the oppression on her spirit. She clears the table, sweeps up and presently goes to the bedroom, takes off the sweater and skirt, puts on her navy and white suit, looks in the mirror somewhat nervously, and is pleased to see her own plump and easy face. It is more than time for the doctor's wife to go to work.

Ten o'clock. Bonjour! Lettice's French class commences. Last year Lettice ranked tops in French.

Arthur the mortician arrives for his day's work. Goliath gathers his belongings together and prepares to leave for school.

"What's she doing out?" inquires Arthur of Madeleine's body, sheeted and harmless on its trolley.

"Well, she's not doing any harm," says Goliath.

"Enough of your lip," says Arthur. "That's a white woman lying there, let me remind you." Goliath smiles grimly but patiently at his aged superior.

Margot arrives at the Katkin household in command of herself and cheerful, her earlier breakfast behavior all but forgotten, so little does it accord with her normal experience of herself. In much the same way will a virtuous woman expunge from her mind the memory of an untoward sexual adventure, attributing it—if she thinks of it at all—to some split-off part of her personality for which she can hardly be expected to accept responsibility.

Margot is let in through the stripped pine door, and there, staring and distraught, is Lily. Lily's face is paler than ever, and her lipstick more scarlet, more clearly edged than usual. Lily wears the same dress she was wearing the day before. Lily's finger is bleeding.

"I'm sorry I'm late," says Margot, feeling that perhaps an apology may help. "You know what family breakfasts are." It is not the kind of remark she usually makes.

"I do indeed," says Lily, and continues to stare unflinchingly at Margot.

"It was a lovely evening we had last night," says Margot. "I'm sorry I was taken ill."

"You're quite better now?" asks Lily politely.

"Perfectly," says Margot. "Is everything all right?"

"No," says Lily, "it isn't."

"I'm sorry," says Margot. "Why not?"

"My husband is drunk," observes Lily. "He is drinking whiskey with his bacon and eggs, and seems disinclined to go to the office. Madeleine is dead. She was killed in a car crash last night. It was to be expected—she drank very heavily, as you know, and she kept her

car—Jarvis's car—in dreadful condition. In fact, the
only surprising thing is that she only managed to kill
herself, and not a dozen other people as well."

"Where's Hilary?" asks Margot, a reaction well within
character. In times of stress the doctor's wife always
thinks first of the children.

"Gone to school," says Lily. "The thing to do is to
carry on as usual. Well, isn't it? Was I wrong?"

Margot says nothing. She is conscious of a spasm of
rage. She limps into the kitchen, and there sits Jarvis
slouched over the table like an old man.

"I'm sorry, Jarvis," says Margot, "I'm really sorry."

Lily snorts behind her; a mad bull's snort through delicately flaring nostrils. "Jonathan bit very deep," she
complains, waving her hand. "Do you think I ought to
have a tetanus injection? God knows what's got into
the child."

"Can't you think of anyone except yourself?" Jarvis
demands. "You are a callous, selfish, monstrous bitch."

Margot retreats to the study to nurse her sense of
shock. Hilary. What's to become of Hilary?

"Nicely spoken," Lily remarks to Jarvis, cool as a cucumber, "and in front of witnesses too. However, you
did marry me. You did prefer me to Madeleine. If you
feel like joining her, please feel free. I shan't stand in
your way."

"Lily," groans Jarvis, "for God's sake, allow me to be
just a little upset. She was my wife for thirteen years."

"Twelve years," his wife corrects, "and very miserable
years they were, too."

"Leave her alone, she's dead," says Jarvis, but Lily's refusal to allow him to mourn is having its effect. He is beginning to feel better already.

"Dead she may be, but her spirit's going to hang round for some considerable time," observes Lily, with more truth than she knows. "At least it will if you go on behaving like this. The truth of the matter is, some people are better dead, and Madeleine is one of them."

What can Jarvis say to this? He does his best. "When you first went out with me, Lily, you knew I was a married man. In fact, you only went with married men; you boasted of it. How are you going to get on with me now that I'm a widower?" And with that, he goes back to bed.

Oh, Jarvis, old-fashioned Jarvis, with your public-school tie at the bottom of your drawer, tucked away beneath the Mao-blue shirts. Jarvis, last of a long line of English gentlemen, revering women yet fearing them, flying to the bottle for comfort, consolation and to fan the tiny female spark of creativity to flame; finding there the strength to insult, combat and defy the female principle in its crude and cuntish form. Jarvis, born of woman, fashioned by man, yearning yet despising; full of talent on a good day, full of rubbish on a bad; terrified of stridency, of the raising of a female voice and yet embracing it; showing your love in bed but seldom out of it. When Madeleine saw through you, raised her voice to crush and crucify, it was time to go.

And what are you to do with Hilary, Jarvis? She is not beautiful, but she is a woman. Jarvis is confused. Poor Jarvis.

Poor Jarvis, Madeleine sometimes felt, sometimes feels; she leaves Jarvis alone, as latterly in her life she left him alone, reserving her spleen for Lily, her sweet betraying sister, and innocent Jonathan, who had no business to be born.

Madeleine's spleen burst. Even had she been wearing a seat belt, she would have died, would have been lost to Hilary, who needed a mother and never had a proper one—though she might have found one, breathing, living, happy and recovered from a lifetime's desolation, given just five minutes more down the motorway and a phone call or two from Mr. Quincey.

Poor Mr. Quincey, rising with Madeleine's sweet breath still warm upon his nostrils, strong and eternal in his memory, as his tooth powder is in hers.

Bonjour!

Margot starts work on the invoices, and so the morning proceeds.

Hilary is sent home from school; she was sick in the Art room. When asked if there was anyone at home to look after her, she says, "Yes, my mother," and is then sick again. She ate quite a lot of lemon mousse, it becomes apparent, between hearing of her mother's death and going off to school. Had Lily kept Sugar Puffs in the house, Hilary would have eaten those. As it is, the lemon mousse sits uneasily on her troubled stomach, and is finally ejected, to the great inconvenience of pupils and staff.

When Hilary gets to her basement house, she feeds the guinea pig a couple of withered carrots left at the bottom of the vegetable box, and automatically tidies away the jumble of clothes Madeleine left out in her hurry to get to Cambridge and Mr. Quincey, her Dial-a-Date. Then Hilary lies down on her mother's bed and goes to sleep. It is the heavy, dreamless sleep that comes after shock or great mental distress, as near to death as anything.

Jarvis sleeps.

Jonathan sleeps, as the doctor had predicted he would. Lily worries. Perhaps Jonathan has suffered some kind of alcohol-inflicted brain damage?

Bonjour! Bonjour! The French teacher moves on to take Laurence's class. Last year Laurence ranked twentieth in French, and only twenty-two in the class. He prefers the sciences.

The police arrange for formal identification from the deceased's husband, and for an inquest. Again, a formality. The car wasn't fit to be on a side road, let alone a motorway. Women drivers, the policeman in charge snorts. Arthur snorts too, in sympathy. There are three other traffic fatalities, all male, in the mortuary, but safely shut away.

Madeleine sleeps.

Arthur worries about her; he put her away in the cool, but now he keeps opening up the hatch to make sure she's still there and still dead. Once, in Arthur's youth, an apparently dead woman sat up on the trolley, threw back the sheet, and demanded to see her daughter. And the cremation was only hours away. Of such stuff are nightmares made. Of course, clinical tests determining death are more refined now than they were in Arthur's youth, and there is no logical possibility that Madeleine's corpse can retain any vestige of life. All the same, Arthur will feel happier when Katkin, Mrs. M, with her sweet, sad face, is properly identified, inquested, taken to the undertaker's and safely buried.

No one, in her lifetime, could have described Madeleine's face as sweet.

Bonjour!

Lily telephones Judy to tell her that she is an only wife at last. Judy bursts into tears and says she knows her ex-husband Billy wants her dead, and she has a thrush infection of the vagina from taking the pill, and she wants her children back, but Jamie won't have them. He says they have each other. At the same time, she has recently overheard Jamie making a secret assignation with his ex-wife Albertine. Everyone wants Albertine back, it appears; even the Amateur Dramatic Society she left in mid-production is willing to forgive her. No one seems willing to forgive Judy anything. Why is that? Lily gives up trying to talk to Judy about Madeleine.

Enid faints at work whilst chairing a meeting on the implementation of the Anti-Discrimination (female) Bill. The assembled trade unionist and management delegates look at each other in dismay. Is this the stuff of which the future is made?

Mr. Quincey telephones Renee from Cambridge and asks to speak to Mrs. Katkin. The warmth of their encounter is still fresh upon his flesh, and he feels he cannot rest until he has at least spoken to her, and at best slept with her again. He is disappointed to hear that she is out. Where, he wonders jealously.

Phillipa, Sam's secretary, makes this the day to come to work without her knickers. Observing, Sam thinks longingly of Enid. He is not altogether happy in the permissive age. Nakedness, he fears, is becoming clinical rather than erotic. The hairy redness of Phillipa revealed is not, in the end, exciting. It merely puts him in mind of childbirth scenes, as seen on television. Dear Enid, thinks Sam. She is such a good and uncomplaining wife; unexciting, true, but always reliable, not very bright but restful. Perhaps it is unfair of him to require so much from Enid whilst lusting so desperately after younger, sexier women? But how can he help it? It's the way he is made, after all, and in the meantime, two phone calls from reasonably serious clients indicate that the property market is looking up. The trouble with Phillipa, Sam concludes, feeling more himself again, is that she's not as young as she was. Pushing thirty, if she's a day.

Quelle horreur!

Lettice, ever obliging, helps the caretaker sprinkle sand over the yellowish slime left by Hilary on the Art room floor, and shovel the resultant sludge into a bucket. "What can she have been eating?" Lettice remarks. She has recovered from her morning's despair; she bought Tampax on the way to school, and discarded her belt and towel in the girls' loo.

"I am a doctor's daughter," Lettice says to herself, scraping away with a will, "and neither disgusted nor disturbed by the by-products of the body." Though this resilience may in fact come from her mother's side: Lettice's great-grandmother Alice, Winifred's mother, Margot's grandmother, wore a bracelet composed of her own gallstones, polished to perfection. When old Alice rattled and shook her bracelet and chomped her husband's teeth, how she defied her own mortality!

Lily is sulking. Well, why not? It's a perfectly horrible day and none of it her doing. She looks at her sleeping husband and feels a pang of horror at his sudden, apparent decrepitude. He seems inappropriate to her life and times. The bedroom is so young, so clean, so fresh, in its muted pinks and greys, the bed itself so delicately wrought in brass; her little jars of cosmetics (Lily's mother Ida contented herself with sensible tubes of sheep lanolin), so expensive and so pretty on the pine dressing table—and here in broad daylight, gross, un-shaven and snoring, lies this man, this husband, this creature, surely of the night, from whom admittedly all money flows but on whose absence during the day she totally relies. She shakes Jarvis awake and tells him it is time he went to work.

"Do stop telling me what to do," grunts Jarvis.

Lily sulks the more. How can you help anyone if they abuse you for trying?

"Where's Hilary?" inquires Jarvis, remembering his daughter.

"She went to school," says Lily.

"She what?" demands Jarvis, angry.

"She wanted to, so I let her." Bad-tempered men must expect to be lied to.

Jarvis does not altogether accept Lily's version of events, but cannot find the emotional energy to query it. "She doesn't seem to have any proper feelings," he laments.

"No" says Lily. "She finished up every scrap of lemon mousse before she went, and there was a whole lot of cigarette ash blown into it from somewhere. I'm sure if my mother died, the last thing I could do would be to eat."

"Perhaps I'd better meet her out of school," says Jarvis.

"You'd never find her," says Lily. "Two thousand children all let out at once. It's mayhem."

Downstairs, Jonathan misses his mother and begins to cry. Margot, typing letters, hears him perfectly well, but for once does not go to his rescue. Spoiled brat, she thinks. Jonathan starts upstairs.

Jarvis pulls Lily down on the bed and embraces her. Her resistances disperse.

"I shouldn't drink so much," he says. "Then I could cope better."

"It's all right," she says. "All right. Of course you're upset. I'm sorry I was so nasty before."

"I suppose it will be a relief to you," he says, "not having Madeleine on the other end of the telephone all the time."

"That's right," says Lily.

"You'll be a full-time stepmother now," he warns. "Will you mind?"

"Of course not," says Lily, but she lies in her little white teeth. Her little sister Rose's hair, blond, thick and curly, was not unlike Hilary's. Hilary's hair on the hairdresser's floor; Rose's hair on a sandy bare-wood floor, while mother Ida grumbled and whinnied and snipped and snipped—so much hair on such a tiny thing! Hair everywhere! What makes me think of that now? wonders Lily.

I am Lily the butcher's daughter, Rose's big sister, fled ten thousand miles, but still the memories come back. My husband lies on top of me, my dress pushed up, everything rucked and rumpled. Never mind, never mind; despoiling is what it's all about. My mother never understood it; the cycle of cleaning in order to dirty, dirtying in order to clean. I am an advance on my mother, and that's something, surely. Socially, sexually, I am one step forward. And that's the meaning of my life.

So thinks Lily, sly eyes shining, sly lips slippery beneath Jarvis's own. Coitus is what we owe the dead, thinks Jarvis. The only answer to death is life, and more life.

Jonathan stands in the doorway observing his parents with no little wonder. He is pale.

Hangover, thinks Lily, disengaging herself, straightening herself: all that whiskey before breakfast. Just like his father.

Downstairs the doorbell rings. Margot stops typing and answers it.

Miss Maguire has come visiting, her smell strong upon the wind, asking for Mr. Kominski.

"Mr. Kominski moved away fifteen years ago," says Margot, "when Mr. and Mrs. Katkin bought the house. Can I help?"

Ah, the doctor's wife, always helping! But you have nothing to offer this poor old lady with her swollen, ulcerated legs and her trembling hands. Your husband has, perhaps; not you.

Miss Maguire shuffles off, confused. Margot closes the door, but something seems to have slipped into the house while it was open; at any rate, Madeleine's presence seems strong in the room—or is Margot only now emerging from the shock of hearing Madeleine is dead? Here she stood yesterday, thinks Margot, poor wronged soul, and now she's dead, and what was all that struggle, all that anger for? I never said I'd take her child, thinks Margot. I never actually said I'd look after Hilary. She asked me, but I didn't reply. I am excused. It would be impossible, in any case. I have my own family to look after. Your child, Madeleine, not mine. Nothing to do with me. Nothing.

I am Margot the doctor's wife, Winifred's daughter, Alice's granddaughter. Let me hold on to that. By our titles you shall know us.

Yes, I came to this house once, years ago, so long ago it doesn't matter. You were queen here then, Madeleine, and a sorry queen you were. You should have looked after your kingdom better. But I don't remember you at all. I remember no glints from the jewels on your crown. I remember feeling sick from too much gin; I remember following Jarvis up the stairs, giggling and stumbling. He led the way; I followed. I can hardly be blamed for following; it's in a woman's nature. I owed you nothing; I never met you.

Margot feels again the tightness of her chest, and gasps for breath; I'm ill, she thinks. I must leave, I must go home. She gets up, goes to the door and calls up the stairs in a hoaky old voice scarcely her own, more like her grandmother Alice's, "Where's Hilary? What have you done with Hilary?"

But no adult hears, which is just as well. Only Jonathan, who comes tottering to the top of the stairs, unattended. He stares at Margot, unblinking and unsmiling, then wavers and almost loses his footing, and Margot/Madeleine, instead of rushing to protect him, stays exactly where she is and hopes to see him fall.

Jonathan does without the witch's help, regains his balance and saves himself. But his face puckers. He changes his mind about coming downstairs, and goes back instead to stand silently on guard outside his parent's door, where it's safer.

15

"She knew she was going to die," says Margot to Philip at lunch. She serves veal-and-ham pie and salad. Laurence and Lettice are relieved to see the familiar slices and to know that their mother is herself again. Philip reads the *Lancet* and the *B.M.J.* while he eats. He smiled at his wife when he came in, so she knows their breakfast quarrel is forgotten—or at any rate, that she is forgiven.

"People who say they're going to die frequently do," remarks Philip. "But there's nothing magic about it. They say they're going to die because they want to, and if they want to die, they usually do. One way or another."

"It was an accident," Margot protests.

"Bad tires aren't an accident," says Philip. "They're negligence. If you want to live, you don't travel the motorways in old cars."

Margot does not reply. Philip knows best.

Philip discovers and laments the existence of a new crack in the salad bowl.

Lettice dissects the pie-crust from the veal-and-ham pie (in the interests of her figure) and queries the necessity of its existence.

Laurence helps himself to her discarded crust and discourses on the existence of charm quarks in particle physics.

Philip asks for tomato ketchup, Lettice for pickled walnuts, and Laurence finds that the salt cellar is empty. Margot gets to her feet during the first ten minutes of the meal some five times. "If I dropped dead from overwork," says Margot/Madeleine to her family on the fifth occasion, "I don't suppose any of you would bother to come to the funeral."

Fortunately, neither Philip, Laurence nor Lettice hears, either because Margot/Madeleine's voice does not have much power (so far), or because they are too busy with their own lives to pay attention to Margot's.

"Look," says Lettice. "Green fly. Never mind," and with the coarseness consequent upon her new status, her arrival at the menarche, she actually devours a couple of the green translucent creatures, to her brother's horror.

"Six people a year in this country are killed by cows," he announces for no particular reason. "And four are blinded by champagne corks."

"Someone was sick in the Art room," says Lettice. "I helped clean it up."

Margot limps as she goes to fetch a fresh bottle of Heinz salad cream, and turning, says to her husband in Margot/Madeleine's voice, "I think we should have Hilary to live with us."

"You must be mad," is all Philip says, and goes back to his paper, and the pain in Margot's leg gets worse and worse, and her breath comes in gasps, and she wonders why she ever married her husband, and remembers: because she was pregnant.

In the afternoon she irons her husband's shirts.

Seven o'clock. Bonsoir! Suppertime. Shepherd's pie, and the tomato sauce has run out and all the shops are shut.

Quelle horreur!

Clarence starts the second half of his shift. The air inside the mortuary is still and close; the tile and formica surfaces seem not so much hygienic as grubby. Arthur, unusual for him, has not cleared away his tea things. Everything seems to Clarence to be in need of sweeping and wiping, as it seemed to in his mother's house after her death. Dead spiders and crumpled daddy-long-legs are swept up in corners; rust flakes fall from the rows of empty trolleys; the shrouds, which should be neatly folded, white and crisp upon the shelves, lie in grey untidy heaps upon the floor. How did they get there? Clarence picks one up and starts to fold it. But it is too large to be folded by one person; the width is beyond the reach of his arms. Clarence leaves the shrouds where they are. Someone else's job, he thinks, not mine. I am here as guardian of the dead, not as a cleaner.

Clarence opens his book on the works of Bishop Berkeley, but cannot concentrate. There is a smell of something—toothpaste? tooth powder? He sniffs around, like some shaggy, untidy dog, but cannot trace the smell to its source. Clarence does not clean his teeth. He has been heard to say to his girl friend that if God had meant us to clean our teeth, he would have made us with bristles on our fingers. His teeth are filmed over with plaque and have a yellowish greenish color, but are in perfect condition. Clarence's girl friend cleans her teeth after every meal, goes to a dental hygienist who regularly picks away at the build-up of plaque, uses both dental floss and tooth sticks daily, and has very painful, very sensitive, very rotten teeth.

The smell of tooth powder reminds Clarence of his girl friend, and he feels a stab of painful lust.

New identity forms, properly completed, must now be attached to Madeleine's body. Clarence performs this distasteful task. He prefers dealing with the bodies of men. Madeleine's eyes are closed. She appears to listen. When her eyes fall open on their easy hinges, she appears to watch. Still, thinks Clarence, listening is better than watching. Clarence's father lost a leg in the Second World War; Clarence's mother grew cross and sluttish in his absence. Clarence was born in the satisfaction of his father's inordinate (according to Clarence's mother) demands. Clarence's father groaned long and loud in the face of his misfortunes. Clarence's mother reproached Clarence's father until the day she died. Clarence, like Goliath, is accustomed to the complaints and reproaches of women.

"How can I manage on the money you give me? How can I cope with a growing boy with you out at work all day? Of course the place is untidy; I'm at my wits' end coping with the mess you make. If you'd ever played football with the lad, his hair wouldn't be the length it is. Just because your peg leg hurts and you're too mean to get a new one, stainless steel, articulated, and with toes that even wiggle? How you ill-treat me, monster! Villain! Going off to war with two legs, coming back with one, and not even hurrying home, either. Beast! What kind of husband is that? What kind of fate? Oh, my heart, my poor heart . . ."

Shut your ears, Clarence. The chorus is at it again. "Who killed this woman? This poor woman, with her crushed chest and her perfect face?" Mother, sleeping, silent while her eyes are closed. "Who killed her? Or failing that, who drove her to her death? Someone must have. Some man, some devil, some monster. Who? Was it you? Clarence? Your guilt, by virtue of your maleness, your beard, your yellow teeth (how she begged you to brush them!), your hair, grown long to annoy?" Clarence closes Madeleine away again, in her little chilled cupboard in the wall.

Lie still, Madeleine. Lie quiet. Don't think about Lily. Was it really her fault? People do the best they can and only steal what they have to. Husbands, lovers, children.

No. Not Hilary. Not my child. Never.

Lily pours herself a pink drink in a frosted glass. Madeleine can touch her not at all. Is there something already dead about Lily, so that the touch of the dead on her mind seems nothing untoward?

It was Lily's father the butcher who made a lady of Lily in the end, and not Lily's mother, the Home Country miss. It was Lily's father who rescued Lily from the white sands and randy servicemen of wartime New Zealand, who sent her to a good school and paid for a course in flower arrangement. How did he do it? With money lent him, long ago, by Karl Kominski's sister Renate. It was Lily's father who paid for the fare to England, home and safety. It was Lily's father who told her she was a princess, and made her one, so that in the end she outstripped him, passed him, all but forgot him. Lily writes to her mother, the expatriate Englishwoman, not to her father, the retired butcher, with the tops of his two forefingers missing and two phallic stumps left behind.

Bon appetit!

Margot heats up the water for the frozen peas, to serve with the shepherd's pie, Philip's, Laurence's and Lettice's favorite dish. The curtains are drawn and it's cozy and nice.

You sly bitch Margot, cries Madeleine now; you hypo-
crite, with your secret knowledge and your self-satisfied
wifedom and your smug motherhood—it was you who
started the whole thing off. I remember you now.
Beneath the coats with Jarvis. It was you. You owe me
something. Look after Hilary now.

Margot winces, suffers, sighs, and feels such a wave of
spite and anger against all the world that Hilary, poor
Hilary, is quite forgotten in the wash of it. It is left to
Renee that evening, child-loving, man-hating Renee, to
take Hilary in her arms, fold her bosom against her
own, and gently swaying, gently murmuring, offer the
child comfort and a place for her tears.

"All right," says Madeleine in their ears. Is she passing
by? "All right for the moment, but not for long." At
any rate, Hilary cheers up, and Renee wonders
whether the landlord will let her have Madeleine's two
basement rooms in addition to her own, in which case
she could then reapply for custody of her daughters.
The judge rejected her last application on the grounds
that Renee could not provide the girls with proper ac-
commodation, though Renee herself believes that the
real reason is her avowed bisexuality. My husband's
heterosexuality, she wished to say, has been more damaging to our marriage than my homosexuality, but no
one seemed interested. He has custody of the girls, and
to look after them, employs a succession of au-pair
girls, with whom he sleeps if he can. Renee's friend
Bonny drifts between Renee and her own husband, unable to make up her mind which she prefers, finding
Renee more consoling but her husband more exciting.
Bonny is just eighteen.

Renee sends Hilary back to Jarvis and Lily, and offers
to feed the guinea pig until a decision concerning its
future can be made.

Some deaths move us; others don't. One friend dies, and we remain indifferent; another dies, perhaps less intimate, and we see ourselves as dead, and weep, mourn, tear our hair or find ourselves caught up in the madness of the wake, competing with others as to who was closest or who now suffers most, until the passage of time—or, indeed, the visiting of the Dead—dissolves these unholy linkages and we can let the dead alone at last. We are all part of one another. Separation is bound to come painfully.

Renee is not much grieved by Madeleine's death, and that is that. She thinks that perhaps Madeleine had it coming. She wishes she had not lent Madeleine her new white blouse (the remains of which now mingle with Madeleine's torn flesh, discreetly covered by the white mortuary shroud). Renee feels the same kind of impatient, companionable sympathy for Madeleine dead as she did for Madeleine living. So much, thinks Renee, for vanity. Madeleine punished at last for her assorted, dismal heterosexual cravings, which in the end did her so little good. Madeleine adorned for the delectation of the predatory male, dressed up like a lamb, dead as mutton.

Bon appetit!

"Onward Christian soldiers," sings Clarence loudly and valiantly as his shift ends and the murmurings in his ears subside.

16

Good morning again. Or so they say.

Is this all, thinks Margot, waking hollow-eyed, is this all my life is to be? My children growing older, my husband growing fatter, myself more bored and boring day by day?

Disloyal, discontented Margot! She wants to pinch her husband; instead she caresses him, a timid, unexpected flutter of her hands upon his inner thighs, but he sleeps heavily and does not respond.

Up gets Margot, furious. All this bad temper, she thinks, peering at herself in the mirror, is wreaking havoc with my complexion. It seems to her that her skin is yellowish instead of its usual nutty, freckly, healthy self.

The telephone rings. She is alarmed. Bad news travels unduly early or unduly late. But it is only Enid, Margot's friend, ringing before Sam gets up. Enid thinks she's pregnant. Does Margot, the doctor's wife, think it's possible?

"I thought you were on the pill," says Margot.

"I gave it up a month back," says Enid. "It hardly seemed worthwhile. Only once or twice a month, the way things have been lately, and it's not as if I'm a young woman any more. Thirty-nine, after all."

"Young enough," says Margot, and feels such a stab of jealousy as quite confounds her. Is Enid to have husband, career and now a baby too? "What does Sam say?" she inquires.

"I haven't told *Sam*," says Enid in disparaging tones that Margot has never before heard Enid use of her husband.

"You'd better come and see Philip," Margot says. "He's quite good about that kind of thing. So long as you're not married to him, of course."

And Enid has never heard Margot speak of Philip in such tones before. "I'd rather do a test," she says. "You see them advertised. It just might be an early menopause. I'd rather it was. Can you see Sam with a *baby?*"

Good morning!

"It's no use moping round the house," says Lily briskly to Hilary. "You really should have gone to school. You can't take days off just because you feel like it."

Well, look what happens when you do! Lily snatched Hilary out of school to have her hair cut, and what ensued? Madeleine was lured back to her one-time home; an unholy bond sprang up between her and the doctor's wife, and now look. It did not go unnoticed, after all, that Hilary's lovely hair lay in piles upon the hairdresser's floor. Better she'd stayed safely at school—or as safe as her platform heels would let her be.

Lily feels it, too late.

This morning Jarvis has gone to Custerley to identify the body. Hilary wanted to go with him, but it was not allowed. She stayed in bed instead, until it was too late

to go to school. Lily actually had to go out and buy
Sugar Puffs to entice her tearful stepdaughter down to
breakfast. Lily the tea-lady's daughter, showing culinary kindness, at which she excels.

"I don't believe she's dead at all," says Hilary now,
stuffing and puffing. "There's some mistake. She doesn't
feel dead to me."

"We have to face facts," says Lily. Facts? Lily's little
sister Baby Rose, face downward in a rock pool,
drowned long, long ago—was that a fact? Ah yes, and
a fact to be faced fearlessly, even joyfully. Even her
mother's sorrow was muted by the usefulness of the
event. After Baby Rose died, Lily's mother, duly punished, could go back to Lily's father and to his fleshy
overpowering love, crude as the knives he wielded,
tough as the flesh he pierced, and delicate as his hands
as he so elegantly deftly, jointed, rolled and strung.
Ida's husband was the best butcher in New Zealand,
everyone knew. Poor Ida! She who should have married a solicitor, a scientist, an art historian, bound by
the flesh to a Bay of Islands butcher. And decades
later, here is Lily, succeeding where her mother failed.
Married to an English architect. But all Lily feels for
her mother is a kind of proud, harsh anger.

"Daddy might not know it's Mummy," says Hilary,
"it's so long since he saw her."

"Don't be ridiculous," says Lily.

"He didn't even like her," his daughter persists. "He
might make a mistake."

"Of course he liked her," says Lily, angry as she always is in her lies. "He was married to her."

She has never said this before, never quite admitted it.
The marriage between Jarvis and Madeleine was real,

real as her own, though in a different time. Or if not quite that, real as her mother and father's was real. The acceptance makes her softer. "Poor Hilary," she says, and stretches out her cool hand to touch the flushed and dumpy Hilary, but moving away, all Hilary says is "I wish I hadn't had my hair cut. Everyone pointed and stared and laughed."

"I'm sure they didn't," says Lily, but she knows quite well that of course they had.

"Anyway," says Hilary, cheering up, "there's always Jonathan, isn't there? Can I take him for a walk?"

"Better not," says Lily, fearing she knows not what.

"Why not?" Hilary persists. "He'd love to go to the swings."

"No," says Lily sharply, and that is that.

So Hilary plays patience instead, and waits for time to stretch itself between her sense of now and the occasion of her loss. She imagines it will have to stretch itself to the very ends of her life before this day can join the others and fit neatly and painlessly into the receding patterns of the past. When she is eighty or ninety perhaps, she will be able to say, "Oh yes. When I was a girl of fourteen I lost my mother. She was killed in a car accident," and feel no pain.

Madeleine is wheeled out, ready for inspection by her next of kin. Jolt and jump. Her eyes fly open. Hi there!

Jonathan develops a little fever. His nose is running, his eyes are bleary. Perhaps he would have done better over at the swings, with Hilary standing, as was her custom, between her half-brother and her mother.

Lily does a little gardening, snip, snip amongst the thorns. She wears white gloves. She does not like the notion of Jarvis having to visit Madeleine, dead or alive. She thought she'd put an end to all that, years ago.

Oh, I am Lily the tea-lady's daughter, the tired U.S. serviceman's delight. Little bleached girl amongst piles of spiky white driftwood, seen by nobody, missed by none; them so large with their bold exploring hands, and me so small, skinny-thighed, tiny-breasted. No older than Hilary in years.

Hilary has no instincts, thinks Lily, despising her—though what good Lily's early instincts did her is not, in the long run, apparent. Lily did what she wanted at the time: what she needed. At least she was too young, too small, too unformed to get pregnant. Hilary will get pregnant at the first opportunity, thinks Lily; she is the type—generally messy, overflowing and prone to emotional demonstration. I must get Hilary on the pill, thinks Lily. At least I'll have control of that aspect of her upbringing from now on.

Jarvis, where are you?

Jarvis the absentee father! Can he not protect his daughter from the ravages of his wife? Any more than the butcher could protect his daughter, stolen away from him as she was?

Jarvis looks at Madeleine's face. He had not known quite what to expect of the faces of the dead. But here is Madeleine—looking, moreover, as he would most like to remember her: on the point of saying something nice and not something nasty. A frame frozen at a singularly fortunate time. The trouble is that living with Madeleine's successor, as he does, Jarvis has trained himself in the remembrance of bad times. "I thought the dead looked more dead than that," he observes to Arthur.

"Most do," says Arthur. His legs are troubling him. He has spent a lifetime standing about on cold floors with hard surfaces, the better to be washed and purified of the putrefaction of the dead.

Jarvis reaches out his hand to touch Madeleine's cheek.

"Don't," says Arthur sharply. "Please don't touch the corpses."

But Jarvis has already done so. "She's warm," he says. And then, as if relieved, "No. My fingers have been resting on cold metal, that's all. She feels warm by comparison. Well, that must be it."

Does Jarvis want Madeleine dead or alive? Does the possibility of her resurrection gladden him, or disappoint him? Alas, it seems he would prefer her safely dead; his relief as her skin grows cold—or his fingers grow warm—demonstrates the truth of the matter. Still, it cannot be denied—nor would he wish to—that he was shocked and saddened by the manner of Madeleine's dying, and his own part in it.

Jarvis fills in the necessary forms. Arthur recommends an undertaker. The inquest will be a formality and will take place on the following day. The deceased has no near relatives. Even Hilary is not Madeleine's any more—not since the divorce courts made Jarvis her guardian. How sadly depleted Madeleine leaves this world.

And how richly Jarvis, looking forward, will leave it: by virtue of his temperament, his masculinity, his will to life and sex, his attachment to domesticity and the trivial trappings of this world—all those things which Madeleine, in her pride and in her youth, rejected.

And how unfair it all is! How little is virtue rewarded. In the white-painted room, with its cold floors and colder occupants, its green-tiled walls and the dead daddy-longlegs swept up in corners, the air is alive again with a confluence of comment, indignation and argument. It is as if Madeleine's body, so little regarded in life, has in death become the focal point of some kind of group energy, some social concentration, some common search for consensus, of the kind which sends our communities lurching in one direction or another towards their gradual betterment. Unfair!

Jarvis will have a grand and well-peopled funeral; it is his very proper ambition. He hesitates to consider the solitary glumness that will be Madeleine's. Will he be there to watch? Will anyone? Or will he allow the disposal of Madeleine's body to be attended to in the same spirit as the inquest—as a formality, symptoms of society's determination to acknowledge the quantity of its members, every one of them: to number them, list them, to record their beginnings, their middles, their ends, their births, marriages and deaths, while yet ignoring the quality of these events?

Jarvis cannot decide. He is upset. He has a cold in his nose. He goes back to London, eying all the dents and breaks in the motorway's central barrier with morbid fascination. Was it here, or here, that Madeleine met her death? He leaves the motorway to find a pub, and has two double whiskeys and a pork pie. He feels better. He is putting on weight. Unfair! Some people, like Madeleine or Lily, can eat and eat and stay slim; others, like Jarvis, eat a pork pie and develop a paunch.

Arthur plods over to the window to shut it yet again. The daddy-longlegs have whirled from the sill in a gust of turbulence and disintegrated. Someone, Arthur thinks, must keep coming in here and opening the window. He will be glad when Madeleine's body is gone. He has felt similar unease about perhaps three other bodies in all his years as mortuary attendant, but prefers not to let his feelings harden into opinions, let alone conclusions. Dead is dead, or else his work becomes impossible. Unfair!

The Dial-a-Date agency tries to locate Madeleine on Mr. Quincey's behalf, gets hold of Renee, and phones Mr. Quincey back to say that unfortunately his date is dead. Mr. Quincey cries, and is comforted. It is something, in a lonely life, to have someone to mourn. Presently he telephones Renee and tries to ascertain from her the time and place of the funeral. He would like to come, he says. But Renee is chilly and evasive. She does not know; she has not heard; she herself does not believe in funerals. Neither did Madeleine. Dead is dead; bodies should be carted off by the Council. She'd heard Madeleine say as much many times. In any case, in what possible capacity could Mr. Quincey attend Madeleine's funeral? Besides, if Madeleine hadn't gone to Cambridge, she'd still be alive and there wouldn't be any need for a funeral—a point which had already occurred to Mr. Quincey. Unfair!

When Mr. Quincey puts the phone down he is gripped by a fierce pain in his stomach, so fierce that he collapses groaning on the floor of the hall. The landlady calls the doctor, the doctor the ambulance; at the hospital they diagnose a peptic ulcer, allay his pain, and keep him in for tests. He likes the hospital; it is warm, friendly and crowded. He sleeps better that night than ever he did at home; the constant murmurings, outbreaks of coughing and varieties of breathing in the ward remind him of the companionable dormitories of his orphanage childhood. The night sister reminds him of Madeleine.

Unfair! Miss a pill and see what happens! Enid has brought a Pregnancy Home Testing Kit. It is a pretty, transparent box lidded with magnifying glass, in which is inserted a yet prettier test tube containing a mix of this chemical and that, to be combined with a drop of early-morning urine. If, once the urine is added and stirred, the contents of the tube settle down within two hours to look like the sun in eclipse, a dark circle lined with a ring of fire, why then, Enid will be pregnant.

Enid sets up the test when she gets out of bed. Even by seven o'clock there is no doubt about it. The sun is in eclipse; the corona leaps from its dark circumference with fiery beauty. Enid is pregnant.

Enid takes Sam his breakfast tray. Her parents never wished Enid to marry Sam, for reasons never quite specified, beyond the fact that her father didn't trust him. But then, he trusted no one. Enid is an only child. Her father was fifty and her mother forty-one when she was born. Enid was a quiet, good, competent little girl, much in the habit of carrying trays. Here and there, up and down, in and out of the kitchen: breakfast, tea, late-night cocoa. Thank you, darling. No poison, I suppose? Ha-ha!

"You're a good girl, Enid," says Sam, waking, not unwillingly, from dreams of Phillipa in which that knickerless girl took tea with his mother.

"Thank you, Sam," says Enid, pleased.

On the way to work Sam notices the glass box on the mantelpiece. "That's pretty," he says. "What is it?"

"A table decoration," says Enid, and Sam looks slightly puzzled, but lets it pass.

Years ago Sam and Enid decided not to have children. Sam has a generalized horror of pregnant women: of stretch marks on bellies, of figures lost beyond redemption, of curlers and nappies and toys on the floor; he finds the notion of breast-feeding grotesque. And watching, as he does, the end result of all this reproductive misery, the schoolchildren sauntering past his office—swearing, smoking, jostling; long-haired, scruffy, of assorted race and creed—Sam is the more thankful not to have exposed himself and Enid to the messiness and inconvenience of parenthood.

As for Enid, she realized long ago that she hasn't the time, the energy or the inclination to look after a baby. There isn't a spare moment in her day, as it is. Already she begrudges the minutes she has to spend in the bathroom being sick. Well, she can talk to her friend Margot, the doctor's wife, and ask her what to do.

Good evening!

Wednesday evening: Sam's night for playing poker, Enid's for visiting Margot, Lettice's for a piano lesson, Laurence's for shaking out the cat basket and spraying for fleas, Philip's for doing his tax accounts, Phillipa's for washing her hair, Hilary's for cleaning out the guinea-pig cage, Renee's for visiting her two daughters in the presence of a third party, and Jarvis's for taking Lily to the cinema. Once it had been Madeleine's night for telephoning Jarvis to complain of some domestic difficulty or unfairness to Hilary—or is none such could be found, for making anonymous and abusive phone calls to Lily. Whic was why Jarvis and Lily presently made it their weekly night out.

Good evening! Wednesday evening round again. How quickly time passes! Madeleine's lips are dead, cold and dry. The guinea pig is hungry; Renee has forgotten to feed him. His cage, however, uncleaned by Hilary, is rich and cozy with his own dung. Jarvis has taken Hilary to the pictures to cheer her up. Lily has been obliged to stay home to baby-sit for Jonathan, who is developing quite a nasty fever. Lily was prepared to leave him with a strange baby-sitter from an agency, but Jarvis wouldn't hear of it. Jonathan had clearly been sickening for something or other during the day. Lily left him with Margot while she shopped, as was her custom, but poor Jonathan cried from the moment his mother left until the moment she came home, shrieked whenever Margot approached, and even bit her hand when she attempted to lay it upon his infant brow to gauge his degree of fever. "I'm afraid we're all rather upset," as Margot observed to Lily, attempting to excuse the child to his mother. "I daresay that's all it is. Children are so sensitive to atmosphere." "Upset?" inquired Lily coolly. She'd bought a charming little brown-and-white woolly hat and matching scarf. "Why should we be upset? Do you think this suits me?"

It did, of course. Her color was good that day. Her period was over, her normal relations with Jarvis resumed—enhanced, if anything, by the shadow of death. But when Jarvis took Hilary to the pictures and it became apparent that she, Lily, would have to stay home and baby-sit, her face became quite pale and pinched again.

Wednesday evening!

Sam loses heavily at poker. In the morning he will wake bleary-eyed, hung-over and heavy with a remorse so extreme as to be almost pleasurable. "What have I done?" he will cry, as on so many Thursday mornings. "What a fool I am! Lost! Everything lost." Though whether it's tens, hundreds or thousands of pounds he's referring to, Enid has no means of knowing, and does not ask. "Everything lost!" It is a cry of cosmic, not financial, agony, she knows quite well.

Good evening!

Enid brings her own cry of distress to Margot. They sit alone in the kitchen. Philip, Lettice and Laurence absent themselves on Enid's arrival. No one dislikes Enid, but no one seeks her company. Plain, obliging, respectable women beyond their first youth may be good enough company for each other, but not for the rest of the world. Unfair!

"What shall I do?" cries Enid. "What shall I do? At my age! I can't possibly have it. Sam doesn't like babies. And what about my job? I shall have to have an abortion. Philip will just have to write me a note to the hospital. He can't refuse."

"Philip has rather complicated views on abortion," murmurs Margot. She is feeling tired and her chest hurts.

"What do you mean, complicated?" inquires Enid uneasily. "You mean he's old-fashioned and reactionary?"

"Women do get rather depressed afterwards," says Margot tentatively. "He's not in favor of abortion on demand. And of course, it can reduce one's fertility."

"I can hardly be more depressed than I am now; I don't want to be fertile. I think Philip is being very hypocritical. He talked you into an abortion once, I know very well."

Had he? Was that what happened? Margot puts on the kettle for tea. "It was the only sensible thing to do," she says presently. "It was a long time ago."

So it had been, back in the late fifties, when abortion was illegal, and even a nurse—as she had been—had trouble finding (at best) a rogue doctor or (at worst) some enthusiastic amateur willing to terminate a pregnancy. Margot's best friend Katriona had nearly died of septicemia following an abortion, and had awakened one night in a hospital with the police at her bedside and a criminal prosecution to follow.

"What possible difference can it make—being a long time ago?" asks Enid persistently. The same petulant persistence has made many a colleague concede a point to Enid at the conference table.

"Just that I can hardly remember that time of my life," says Margot.

"But you did have an abortion?"

"Yes."

"And it was Philip's baby?"

Philip's baby. Yes, certainly she can remember that it was Philip's baby. Philip was a medical student, on the same ward as herself. The maternity ward: she clearly remembers that too. Philip was too young, too boyish, to really attract her, but it was Christmas Eve and she'd had too much of the patients' sherry to drink. So had Philip. He'd come into the supply room; she'd turned into his arms; one thing had (presumably) led to another, because there they were, rolling around together on the floor behind the stacked piles of linen. In a confusion of new experience her hymen had been broken—what a strange, sudden pang—and the labor-room bell meanwhile blared unheard in their ears, while a baby all but strangled in its own umbilical cord. That had been a lesson to them—and then again when she found she was pregnant. Life in those days had seemed all lessons.

"Yes, it was Philip's baby," says Margot now to Enid.

"And he did talk you into having an abortion."

"It wasn't him so much as his parents."

Philip's parents had high ambitions for him, socially. After all that, why shouldn't they have? He was a doctor at last—what an attainment! A nurse, a nobody for a wife? Never! Surely he could marry some young deb, or failing that, at least some girl with a family, an education or an unearned income to her name. There were plenty of girls around in London who would answer to his parents' requirements, nice virtuous girls only too happy to salve their social consciences by marrying some young doctor and devoting their lives (and their education, income and background) to him and humanity. But Margot? That ordinary, bustling, plain little nurse with nothing to recommend her but a pleasant nature—and not even a virgin any more?

And Philip's mother didn't have forever to live; and Philip's father had his ambitions centered on his son; and Philip's sister Jill had her heart set on a grand white wedding for her brother's eventual bride, since she couldn't have one herself. A lace train streaming out behind a wheelchair? No, thanks. Even worse than walking up the aisle with a bride clearly pregnant, dressed in white.

Since there was to be no marriage, it was left to Philip's parents to arrange an abortion. An unsavory business, they felt, but necessary, since Philip wasn't prepared to take the only other sensible course open to him—namely, to deny paternity and abandon the girl. He was, they felt, being rather naïve. If Margot would with Philip, she would with anyone; just because she said it was his baby didn't mean it was; she was a girl of low moral fiber, and quite capable of pinning paternity on Philip in order to catch him as a husband. And so on.

Well, Margot did as Philip's parents said. She had her abortion. Margot was a nice girl. She didn't want to marry Philip if it meant ruining his career, and apparently it did. Of course, her own career was at an end in any case. Her inspired union with Philip in the supply room had become publicly known in the course of the inquiry into the unanswered labor-room bell—but *why* didn't you hear the bell, Nurse Armitage?—and although male medical students were allowed, even expected, to be sexually active, nurses were not. Nurses had to be responsible. Margot would have to be dismissed for negligence and behavior unbecoming the noble calling of nursing.

And so she was creeping back to her mother Winifred, ashamed and in disgrace. Winifred was not too upset. She never expected anything except disaster, in any case, and found it quite comforting to have her worst fears realized and her view of the universe reinforced. Besides, in her heart she had always wanted Margot to be a secretary, for then, if she played her cards right, she could marry some rich businessman or stockbroker who could afford to keep his mother-in-law in comfort. It wasn't that Winifred was mercenary, just practical. How else was a woman to live but off men? Looking back over the generations, how else indeed?

Philip felt badly about Margot losing her job. It was hardly fair. He even quarreled with his parents and Jill on her account, and that took some doing—quarreling with one distraught father, one mother with cancer, and one sister in a wheelchair. Good God, he might have said, don't you think we need a nurse in the family?

But everyone knew (as Winifred had warned Margot) that nurses were a hard and worldly lot, and rarely virginal, certainly not in mind, if occasionally in body, having seen too much with their girlish eyes and touched God knows what with their pretty fingers. No, the Baileys certainly did not want a nurse in the family.

They felt a need of raising, not lowering. As indeed did Winifred, pinning her hopes on stockbrokers.

Philip and Margot agreed not to see each other any more. The forced parting added poignancy to their relationship, added the overtones of love to what started, really, as a state of having nothing whatever to say to each other. Sex, of course, does instead of conversation. Just as conversation does, for those beyond it or before it, instead of sex.

Good evening!

"I'm sure Sam will come round to the idea of your having a baby," says Margot cozily to Enid.

"Supposing you got pregnant," says Enid dangerously. "What would Philip do?"

"I can't get pregnant," says Margot. "I wear a coil."

"Whose idea is that? His or yours?"

"His," says Margot. She coughs and coughs. She wishes Enid would go; she does not like this conversation.

The telephone rings. It is Lily. "Margot," she says, "could I speak to Philip, please? It's Jonathan. He's so terribly hot, and he just lies there panting, and Jarvis is at the pictures with Hilary . . ."

"What are they seeing?" inquires Margot.

"*Jaws,*" says Lily. "But that's not the point . . ."

Jaws? Margot feels a spasm of anger. It seems a tactless choice for a girl who has just lost her mother in a road accident. "I shouldn't worry about Jonathan," she says. "Children do run high temperatures, you know. Keep him warm and give him half an aspirin, and I'm sure he'll be better in the morning."

"You don't think he ought to see Philip?"

"I'm afraid Philip is out," says Margot.

"I hate making a fuss," says Lily, "but Jonathan looks so strange."

"Perhaps he's sickening for measles," says Margot. "I thought he might be this morning. Have you taken his temperature?"

"I haven't a thermometer. We're never ill."

"Well," says Margot, "I'll tell Philip when he comes back. You really ought to get through to the night service after six, you know."

"I don't trust them," says Lily, and puts the phone down.

"What's the matter with your voice?" asks Enid. "It's very hoarse. And why did you say Philip was out when he's not?"

"Because there's nothing the matter with her snotty little brat," says Margot. "She's just in a fury because Jarvis has gone out with Hilary, and she's after Philip, I know she is. Nasty predatory little bitch. Anything in trousers will do for her."

Enid frowns, puzzled. "But you usually say how lovely she is," she remarks.

"And fancy Jarvis taking Hilary to a film after all that," says Margot, thrusting her fingers through hair barely long enough to make the gesture worthwhile. "Mind you, he never thought of anyone except himself.

It just wouldn't occur to him she might be upset. And if it did, he'd forget it pretty quick, in case it interfered with his enjoyment!"

Jarvis's enjoyment! Margot's too. Long ago. At Madeleine's expense.

Good evening!

It was much the same for Margot when she encountered Jarvis on his twenty-ninth birthday. She found herself dancing with him but having nothing to say, a social predicament which in those days she dreaded. Easier to kiss Philip in the supply room than think of something creditable to say. Easier to follow Jarvis upstairs than say something witty, sophisticated and sparkling.

Margot had gone with her friend Katriona—who later so nearly died of septicemia, and who'd been at college with Madeleine—to the birthday party. It was some time after Margot's abortion, and she was feeling low and bored with her secretarial course, and lonely in her bed-sitting room, and yearning for Philip (or so she interpreted the pain of the stifled surging of her young life), and she was pleased to be asked, though she could not see the hostess anywhere. Mind you, it was a large house. And a whole house! Everyone else Margot knew lived in a hostel or a bed-sitting room, or at best shared a flat.

Jarvis dances with Margot; his eyes seldom leave her breasts. He has had too much punch to drink. He says nothing. If she tries to speak he puts his fingers across her lips, thus solving many of her problems. He seems to be including her—this host, this man of property, sophistication, friends and temperament—in some kind of conspiracy. She is flattered. Their bodies bump together, melt together. Bodies do. He takes her by the hand, draws her out of the room, still secret, silent, conspiratorial, and with drunken precision leads her up, step by step, stair by stair, to the spare room, where the remains of the wallpaper put up long ago by Phillipa Cutts's father—great splodgy roses on a fawn ground—now peels from the wall, and the broken bed sags under the weight of the damp coats of the guests. There he forces punch down her more than willing mouth, and by the pressure of his body against her, eases her on her back upon the bed; a V-neck sweater slips easily off one arm, and then with a little pressure, off the other; her bra is easily removed and her breasts exposed—and if she hadn't wanted that to happen, would she have worn such a sweater?—and then at last he speaks. "You have pink nipples. Thank God. I can't stand brown ones."

But if she speaks, he lays his finger on her lips, and really, she would rather his fingers were elsewhere, so she remains silent until she is totally unclothed and seated on top of him—what is happening she scarcely knows, so little does this experience accord with any information her mother, her friends, her nursing manuals have given her. So far as she ever knew, the man lay on top of the woman—in bed, according to them; in the supply room, according to her single experience. She did clearly hear Jarvis say, "Don't worry. I'll only put it in a little way." Did he? Is he? It doesn't feel like it, but how is a girl to know? She can't look; that would be indecent. She can only feel, and feelings, physical sensations, when related to such an unexplored, uncharted area as her own genital organs, might not necessarily accord with what is happening to them and in them.

Presumably he is right and she is wrong. Men know what they are doing. Any man, however drunk, knows better than any woman, however sober—or so Winifred had brought her up to believe. The more you defer to the male, the more popular you'll be and the richer you'll end up. The door opens once, twice, closes again. Margot does not hear, does not know; this is the best, the most valuable, the most transfiguring experience of her life so far; she is blind at last to sense and prudence. How wonderful!

Presently, in any case, Jarvis falls asleep, though in a companionable manner, not a rude one. Has he finished? She does not know; she cannot tell. She disengages herself quickly from her host, dresses quickly and guiltily—supposing she is surprised by the hostess, the host's wife?—goes downstairs, and quickly out of the house and home to recover.

Later that very night Philip her true love comes knocking on her door, begging to be let in. He cannot live without her. He'd been to the party, looking for her, failing to find her. "I came home early," she said. "Nothing's any fun without you." Bitch. Liar. But how nice to believe what you want to believe. Four weeks later there she is again, pregnant. Well, Jarvis said he'd only put it in a little way, so presumably he had, and in any case, wouldn't it all fall out, that way up? She'd been wet enough. And nobody knew. And though Philip wore a French letter, everyone knew they weren't reliable. In the light of events, he, at any rate, assumed it had been faulty.

That was in the days—remember?—before the pill or the coil, when men took responsibility (or didn't) for birth control, and girls relied on abstinence (or the good intentions of men) to keep themselves unpregnant, and diaphragms were available to married women only. Otherwise, the theory went, promiscuity amongst the young would know no bounds (the fear of pregnancy being the beginning of morality).

Margot forgot the Jarvis episode as best she could. What else could she do? It was too shocking to be true. Two men in one night! When up till then her average had been one man in twenty-two years—and that on only the one occasion, in the supply room of the maternity ward, and the proper way up. She had the feeling, in any case, that the other way up didn't count. She developed a quite inflated notion of Philip's fertility. He'd done it once; he'd done it twice.

This time, at Philip's insistence, Margot proceeded with the pregnancy. She was married in a church, in splendid, radiant white, four months pregnant with Laurence. Margot's mother Winifred acknowledged defeat and even paid for the wedding and the reception out of her savings, since Philip's parents declined to attend. But Jill came in her wheelchair and took the wedding photographs. She'd taken up amateur photography as a hobby. You can do so quite well from a wheelchair.

"Why don't you just have the baby," suggests Margot now to Enid. "Babies solve so many problems." And so they had, for her.

But Enid is not to be convinced. Her work at the department has repeatedly indicated that babies are the cause of many problems, both practically and statistically: unemployment, low family income, immobility of labor, inflation—you can put the lot down to babies.

When Margot gets up to show Enid out, her foot is dragging again. "Are you limping?" asks Enid.

"I don't know what the matter is," says Margot, "Philip says it's psychosomatic."

"I bet he does," says Enid unkindly. "I suppose it's something to have the use of both legs. Madeleine Katkin had one of hers cut right off in that car crash. She and Jarvis were Sam's first customers. He's quite upset about it."

"Right foot or left foot?" inquires Margot.

"Now how would I know a thing like that," says Enid crossly. She has come for advice and commiseration, and Margot seems prepared to give her very little of either. "Anyway, that was beside the point. What's a missing leg or so? Her chest was crushed right in. The steering wheel was sticking out of her back. I'd have thought you'd have known—or don't they talk about it? I suppose when the first wife dies, no one quite knows what to say to the second. You can hardly say congratulations."

"They don't say much at all," says Margot, "they just drink." Enid stares at her friend. Margot's in a strange mood, she thinks, and she's not looking well. Her eyes are hollow and staring.

"Poor thing," says Enid. "Though why she just didn't get herself a decent job I can't think. I'd never live off alimony. But then I've got too much pride and I'm not afraid of hard work."

How those who can manage to despise those who don't. Unfair!

"She had Hilary to look after."

"That's what I mean about children," says Enid gloomily. "They stop you doing what you want. Madeleine always looked such a mess, didn't she? I've noticed that about mothers—they always have such an ungroomed look. No wonder Jarvis went off with Lily. Madeleine drove him into her arms, Sam says."

Sam would. Enid leaves.

Only the fair deserve the brave. Only the fair. Well, of course, in a manner of speaking, that's what Madeleine did. She drove Jarvis away. What with her untidiness, her coach journeys, her couriers and her talk of sexual freedom—a liking for all men, it seemed, just so long as they weren't poor Jarvis, as if Jarvis had suddenly become too old for the fancying on his twenty-ninth birthday.

To be sure, Madeleine denied it all afterwards. She said she'd only made it up about the couriers; she'd said it in order to tease Jarvis because he was neglecting her, never going on holiday with her, never leaving his work for a single day on her account, let alone on poor little Hilary's. Sex on her holidays? How could she do anything like that, lugging Hilary along?

Oh, panic!

It had all been talk; anyway, she'd never stopped loving Jarvis; it was just that she couldn't stand his attitudes, his coldness to herself and to Hilary. If she'd nagged, it had only been revenge for his coldness and indifference—couldn't he understand that? She was sorry, terribly sorry. Couldn't they just start again?

But by that time it was too late to say sorry. Jarvis had become enamored of Lily, his partner's secretary, slim, sweet (sweeter, in those days) and lovable, and that was that. Jarvis told Madeleine all about it—hadn't they agreed always to be honest? (Well, she'd agreed for both of them, back in the old days of her ascendancy. He'd just nodded, for the sake of not missing *Match of the Day* on television.) Jarvis was a great soccer fan: his phony working-class yearnings, as Madeleine described them (oh, unkind, desertable Madeleine). Jarvis was quite affronted when she objected to his relationship with Lily. Madeleine had driven him to it, after all, showing her boredom in bed, flaunting her infidelities. What had she thought would happen?

Jarvis brought Lily home to meet Madeleine. Lily thought that Madeleine was singularly overpossessive, jealous, and careless of her appearance. What, it was both their refrain, had Madeleine thought would happen? Madeleine deserved to lose Jarvis. Poor, overweight, unhappy, bronchial Jarvis—and all due to Madeleine. Her fault, not theirs. What did Madeleine think of Lily? Jarvis wasn't listening, and actually, Madeleine was too stunned to speak.

Jarvis moved into the spare room. Presently he moved Lily in there, too. Well, he had to. Lily was pregnant. What else could he do? No, he wouldn't give Madeleine a divorce. That would mean selling the house and breaking up Hilary's home. Hilary was the only important person in all this mess, everyone agreed. If Madeleine didn't like it, she would have to go. No, she couldn't take Hilary; Hilary was his by law. Madeleine was a bad mother—whoring on holiday in Hilary's presence. Everyone knew. Madeleine had boyfriends by the dozen; couldn't he even enjoy his one true love in peace? What was all the fuss about, he'd like to know?

Panic!

Madeleine stole Hilary out of bed one night and ran away with her. Mutual friends, fearful of interfering between husband and wife, mindful of the sanctity of marriage, declined to take her in. She got a living-in job as a cleaner, child not objected to. Lily moved into the main bedroom. Jarvis sued Madeleine for divorce. She'd driven him to driving her out. Everyone knew.

Panic!

The pain in Margot's leg gets more intense; her breath comes in gasps. It's psychosomatic, thinks Margot. It must be. What else can it be? Philip is right. It's hysterical. That's all. Control it; don't fight it. Enter the pain; don't resist it. Now that I know how Madeleine died, of course it's worse. Leg *and* chest.

Margot takes aspirin, three, four, five tablets, but the drug has no effect. She reels, she gasps, she crawls on the floor. No one comes to help. Who's going to? No one knows that Enid has gone, and Margot's voice no longer seems her own to summon them.

Presently Margot crawls to the telephone and dials Lily's number. "You bitch," says Madeleine/Margot in her new hoarse voice, in response to Lily's best fluty hostess tones. "You filthy murdering bitch. You stole Jarvis. You shan't have Hilary too."

"Who's that?" demands Lily in panic. "Who is it? What are you talking about?"

In the past Lily has received many such phone calls from Madeleine, and discounted them, on Jarvis's instructions, as sick, mad ravings—the very reason, after all, that Jarvis had to leave mad Madeleine and cleave to Lily. But Madeleine is dead. This voice is not quite like Madeleine's, not quite. Did Madeleine have a sister, so far unheard of? Is there someone still left to pursue, reproach and threaten poor Lily for following her heart's desire? Poor Lily! Has she not given Jarvis back his youth, his health, his happiness? How can she deserve such persecution?

Margot puts down the phone. The pain has dissolved and she feels better, quite herself. Who was she telephoning? She can't remember. And hush! Philip comes in, weary and worn from taxes. Such paper work! What has it got to do with healing the sick? Listen:

1. PHILIP: Enid gone?
2. MARGOT: Yes.
3. PHILIP: How was she?
4. MARGOT: Pregnant.
5. PHILIP: Don't tell me. I'll know soon enough. Who's the father?
6. MARGOT: Sam, of course.

7. PHILIP: What, after all these years? You're joking.
8. MARGOT: I think that's very cynical of you.
9. PHILIP: All women are the same, my dear—except you, of course.
10. MARGOT: And that's very patronizing.
11. PHILIP: What's the matter with you tonight?
12. MARGOT: Nothing.
13. PHILIP: Were you on the phone just now?
14. MARGOT: No.
15. PHILIP: Oh, I thought I heard it pinging.
16. MARGOT: Don't you believe me?
17. PHILIP: Of course. You're very edgy, Margot. Perhaps you should have a tranquilizer before you go to bed.
18. MARGOT: Perhaps.

Which, being translated, is:

1. PHILIP: Is it safe?
2. MARGOT: Yes.
3. PHILIP: I'll try to be polite, though I don't feel like it.
4. MARGOT: Actually, Enid's not as boring as you thought.
5. PHILIP: Yes she is. Boring and immoral.
6. MARGOT: She's nothing of the kind.
7. PHILIP: I have some knowledge of human nature.
8. MARGOT: You're not the man I married.
9. PHILIP: I have a low opinion of women, especially you.
10. MARGOT: I know what you really mean.
11. PHILIP: Why are you reacting to things as if I were saying them for the first time?
12. MARGOT: I'm not telling you anything.
13. PHILIP: Women. Always gossiping.
14. MARGOT: I shall retaliate by lying.
15. PHILIP: But I will catch you out in a lie.
16. MARGOT: Am I in the custom of lying?
17. PHILIP: You are a difficult woman and I am a very patient man. I make no distinction between you

and my many middle-aged, neurotic female patients.
18. MARGOT: That's unfair.

Margot and Philip go to bed and lie far apart. Margot
lies awake; Philip sleeps.

Margot/Madeleine gets up and stalks the room, hollow-eyed. Devil, she thinks. This devil I'm married to.
He uses up my youth, saps my strength, exploits my
good nature; he uses me as servant, whore, a punching
bag for his ill-humor. He gives nothing in return. I am
married to the devil. See how he smiles in his sleep?
He is impervious to my distress; worse, he grows strong
on it.

The doctor's wife pinches the doctor's arm sharply and
suddenly. The doctor wakes and cries out in alarm. "I
want us to have Hilary here," says Margot/Madeleine
with the gravelly taste of blood in her mouth. "Do you
understand?"

The doctor stares at the doctor's wife. Long years of
practice—in the days before the prudent introduction
of his night service—have enabled him to wake suddenly from sleep and face emergency. "What makes
you think she'd want to come here?" he inquires.
"Why should she? Stop behaving like a mad woman.
You're perfectly sane."

To which there is no reply, so Philip falls back asleep.
Presently Margot feels better and creeps back into bed
beside him. When she closes her brown button eyes,
her face falls into its usual sweet, complacent lines; the
doctor's wife sleeps too, and does not dream. It is the
cold, hard, dreamless sleep of the dead, all the same.
As if, in mimicry of Philip's father, who never wanted
her, never acknowledged her, Margot is trying death
out for size, getting into practice, as the womb will get

into practice months before a birth, with a few trial contractions. Just in case you forget.

Margot was not exactly asked to Philip's mother's funeral, and did not attend. She went to Jill's, however, the following year. Well, Jill had been to Margot's wedding and taken some lovely photographs, which now stand on the bedside table.

Margot's younger, sweeter self smiles down on Margot's cold, grey unconsciousness. If you come to my wedding, I'll go to your funeral.

17

Ah, possessions!

"Someone's got to go through her belongings," says Lily.

Jarvis does not reply. Jarvis the architect and Lily the architect's one and only wife are watching television. Their dinner (lamb cutlets, salad and Camembert) is digesting, and their comforts are around them. Their chairs are designed for maximum viewing comfort and their distance from the screen for minimum eyestrain. They sit side by side, hand in hand, their drinks beside them. Hilary is in bed reading; Jonathan is asleep. "There is nothing wrong," Lily keeps telling herself. "Nothing to be anxious about." But she cannot concentrate. Events in Ulster seem to have even less to do with her than usual; she cannot feel enthusiastic about the plans of the young Conservatives. She wishes Jarvis would pay less attention to the screen and more to her, and she is worried about Jonathan.

Earlier in the evening she quite panicked about Jonathan. He was clearly ill and very feverish; his forehead burned to her touch. He lay in his crib, whining and grizzling, slapping at his leg with his hand. His eyes were cloudy, like the eyes of fish on a watery marble slab. She rang Philip Bailey, but could only get through to his night service, which with some reluctance agreed to send out a locum.

The locum, a sallow and disagreeable young man, unmoved by either Lily's beauty or her distress, protests at having been called out unnecessarily. The child's temperature is normal, or so the thermometer says.

"But you can *see* he's ill," says Lily.

The locum shakes his head; he can't see it at all. All he appears to think is that Lily, though beautiful, is an overprotective, hysterical nuisance of a mother. And it is certainly true that the minute the doctor walks into the room, Jonathan stops his grizzling and tossing, and the turning up of his glazed eyes, and becomes a perfectly ordinary, plump small boy, with a cold in the nose and eyes red from crying, who doesn't want to go to bed.

But after the doctor has gone the dreadful keening and tossing starts again, and only stops when Hilary in desperation takes him into the camp bed with her. Lily hates to see them thus so entwined, so comforted the one by the other; her golden boy enclosed, suffocated, trapped, by Madeleine's lumpy, puffy, sulky girl. Supposing, Lily thinks with horror, anyone thinks Hilary is *mine?*

Ah, possessions. Some reflect credit on us, others don't.

Lily turns off the television. She'll have Jarvis's attention through fair means or foul. "Someone's got to go through her belongings. Do try and face facts."

"Let the Salvation Army take them," says Jarvis. "Clear the place out. Sell what it can and throw away what it can't."

"But everything there is ours," says Lily. "After all, you supported her. Everything she ever owned comes from you."

"I don't suppose there's much there," says Jarvis. "Do you mind if I watch television?"

And he turns the set on again, so Lily has to speak over the voice of "Our Man in Israel." "What about all the things she took from here?" she demands.

Some six months after Lily moved in and Madeleine moved out, Madeleine returned one day in Lily's absence with furniture removers, breaking the law, defying the injunction not to molest, and took away the brass bed which she and Jarvis had once shared but which now was Lily's own, by custom and convention.

What a lovely bed it was, too—not one with ordinary coarse bold brass bars at head and foot, but delicately filigreed into a glittering pattern of flowers and peacocks. Madeleine, Lily knew, didn't really want the bed—she could hardly have had pleasant memories of it, and couldn't even get it into her little flat—but had simply had it removed and sold, motivated by nothing other than spite. Not by sentiment—her sexual relationship with Jarvis had been totally miserable, almost nonexistent, or so Jarvis assured Lily—merely by a dog-in-the-manger attitude. Jarvis, you see, had at one time to have a restraining order taken out against Madeleine, who in the early days would lie in wait outside the house for poor Lily (who'd be returning tired from the ante-natal clinic, as like as not) and spring out at her, abuse her and pull her hair, poor mad soul. Even Lily, her victim, could feel sorry for her, so awful and dreadful did Madeleine look.

And then Madeleine started making obscene telephone calls in the middle of the night, so that the number had to be changed; and then she started breaking the window, and pulling up the flowers (leaving poor little Hilary without a baby-sitter the while, no doubt, just as she'd left her alone on all those coach journeys whilst having it off with the courier—poor Jarvis!). And damage to persons and feelings is one thing, but damage to property is quite another, so Jarvis and Lily were obliged to go to law. The threat of prison if she persisted quietened Madeleine down considerably, and after the theft of the bed, the visitations stopped altogether.

Madeleine, taking to visitations once again. The Visitings of the Dead.

But the day Madeleine and Hilary left Jarvis in that taxi (what extravagance! Wouldn't public transport have done?), she took with her not just her and Hilary's personal belongings, but some very nice fluffy towels and some hand-embroidered table linen to which Lily had taken an instant liking in the few days she and Madeleine were under the same roof. Lily under the spare-room roof, waiting; Madeleine under the bedroom roof, hesitating.

Possessions! Who cared? Lily, certainly, and Madeleine, rather more than she thought. For Madeleine had no right to take them; they belonged to Jarvis, who'd paid for them. Jarvis paid for everything, after all; it all belonged to him.

Jarvis, Lily thought, was altogether too neglectful of his own interests. "Let's hope the tablecloths aren't too ruined," she says now in retrospect, as the tanks

rumble over Sinai. "I don't suppose there's much hope
she did them by hand—just bunged everything in together in the launderette, I expect. At least that's what
Hilary's clothes always looked as if she did. We could
get the poor child some new ones, now that we know
they won't instantly be damaged by Madeleine. You
must admit, Jarvis, there must be a lot in the flat worth
salvaging. I know it's distasteful, but I'm afraid that's
the other thing about people dying: there's just a lot of
work to be done."

When Baby Rose had died, drowned, what a clearing
up, a packing, a throwing away there'd been! "You're
such a good little worker," Ida had said, tears in her
troubled eyes. "My only little daughter."

Lily wears steel-grey tonight: a slippery, shiny, shape-
less dress. Her pretty feet are bare, her toenails scarlet.
Her big toe is not altogether straight; in fact, it all but
folds itself over the adjacent toe. She has difficulty buying shoes.

Jarvis does not reply.

"And apart from anything else, all Hilary's shoes are
there," says Lily. "We have to have those. She says the
red ones hurt her. Well, of course they do; those heels
are absurd. I don't know what Madeleine was thinking
of."

"Can't she have new ones?"

"We're not so rich we can afford to throw money
away, Jarvis. Besides, I hate buying shoes."

"If you want to go down and loot," says Jarvis, "go
ahead."

Jarvis is worn and frayed. Identifying a dead body is
not pleasant. Lily seems to have no idea of it. And he's

hungry. Cutlets, salad and Camembert may keep a man thin but they do not keep him content. All he wants to do today is eat, drink, sleep and suffer in peace. But Lily keeps to her rules. Food as consolation? Never. Look how fat it made you before!

"It is not looting," says Lily, "it is common sense. And I'm not suggesting for a moment that I do it. Why should I? It's not my fault Madeleine killed herself in that ridiculous car she couldn't afford, and ran at your expense, while I don't even have a car at all but have to go everywhere by taxi or public transport; all *I* do is slave my guts out running this house, carrying your child, looking after a stepchild with no help, let alone gratitude from you, putting up with your moods, your drinking and your abuse; and now poor little Jonathan is ill, but you don't care, you go off to the pictures with Hilary, leaving me alone to cope with the doctors, and I have to take responsibility for absolutely everything and I'm sick of it—and what's more, you don't even seem to *like* me any more." And off she goes to bed.

Jarvis drinks half a bottle of whiskey, goes to the kitchen and eats half a loaf (Jonathan's) with a lot of butter and some plum preserve (Lily's make, for displaying rather than eating), before coming to bed and telling Lily that he is paying for Madeleine's funeral. When she opens her mouth to protest he slaps her.

It is Jarvis's way to meet attack by attack. He rarely responds to the detail of accusation, only to the spirit behind it. It makes him difficult to live with, Lily thinks, as Madeleine knew. He and Lily are either totally happy together, or completely miserable. This evening they are completely miserable, and hate each other. They have both been unforgivable. They sleep on far sides of the bed, not touching.

It is the same filigreed brass bed as once Jarvis and Madeleine shared, but neither of them thinks of that now. Lily found it for sale in an antiques shop on the Portobello Road a year ago, and had to pay £90 for it. But it was worth it, she felt, so as not to let Madeleine have her own way.

Ah, possessions!

18

Property, possessions!

"I wonder," says sweet Lily to mad Margot the next morning, "if you could possibly take Hilary round to Madeleine's and bring back some of her things? In particular, some decent shoes, so she doesn't go on making the rest of us feel like dwarfs?"

Or as Philip says to his wife at lunchtime, over bacon-and-egg pie and baked beans, "What is the matter with that woman? Why should you have to go rifling through the relics of the dead? Tell her you won't do any such thing."

But Margot has already said she will.

"You get yourself too involved," says Philip, over peach slices and custard. "You're not a friend of the family, only an employee. Margot, this meal tastes remarkably like the school dinners of my past."

Is it a complaint or a compliment? Margot decides it is the latter. Philip liked his school. His winning of a national photography competition, and with a nude photograph, had made him something of a hero.

"I had to sieve the custard," she remarks. "There's something strange about the powder. It keeps going into lumps."

"Why doesn't Lily do it herself?" persists Philip.

"She's rather upset."

"That's obvious," says Philip. "Calling out a doctor in the middle of the night to a perfectly healthy child. I wonder what she's been up to."

"Up to? Why should she have been up to anything?"

"Heaven knows. It's just my experience of overanxious mothers," says the doctor, "that they've been having a bit on the side and expect lightning to strike."

"Lily and Jarvis have eyes only for each other," says Margot, in the language of the films of her youth. And all the doctor's wife can offer the doctor, in the way of temptation, is sliced tinned peaches and custard, however smooth, however lovingly sieved, preceded by egg-and-bacon pie and baked beans. No time, no life, no emotion left for anything more adventurous. Quite suddenly, quite painfully, she feels such a stab of envy that her hand slips as she makes the instant coffee, and she splashes her fingers with boiling water and has to hold them under the cold tap until the pain abates.

"Jonathan's not himself," says Margot. "Lily's worried. He cries if I go near him, and he's usually so good with me. He only seems happy with Hilary, so Lily's kept her out of school again."

"You complain if Lily sends her to school, and you complain if she doesn't," says Philip. "You don't seem to like her very much. I don't know why you envy her. You have just as good a life as she does. Don't you?"

Yes, of course Margot does. A good life.

Does the doctor's wife envy the architect's wife, as the doctor claims? Yes, she does. He's right. And why not? Well, none of our lives are so perfect that we wouldn't want to change them—or at any rate, some part of them—with some other person of our choice. Only when we are in love, and loved in return, does the pleasant singularity of being oneself fill the heart with joy—when we are the recipient of that insane love that on occasion comes from another, by-passing all defects, ignoring all faults of appearance, age, history, conduct, character and humor. Such love would alter, if it improvement found, so at such times we can be reconciled for once to our imperfect selves.

Margot envies the architect's wife, but it is the talent of the architect's wife (for she is in love with herself) to envy Margot hardly at all, except insofar as she imagines that to have a doctor for a husband would be useful when one had an ailing child. If Lily envies anyone, it is Judy, not because of Jamie, but for Judy's courage, her ability to follow her own rash inclinations to their bitter, stylish end. Judy in her penthouse is not suburban, and sometimes Lily fears she is suburban. She has journeyed the length of the globe, but can never quite reach the center of things.

Property, possessions! Quality or quantity?

The undertaker arrives to measure Madeleine. Five foot three in death, five foot four in life. Some jolting of his hand makes the corpse's eyes fly open. "Funny eyelids," says the undertaker.

"Very," says Clarence. Arthur is at the hospital, having his varicose veins injected. Clarence wishes Arthur would come back. His own feet feel cold. The shrouds, which he and Goliath folded earlier, are in heaps on the floor again. The cleaner, perhaps, being careless— except that there is no cleaner. Or did Arthur sweep them all to the floor again in anger, perhaps because they were not perfectly folded? Goliath was good at folding, being accustomed to helping his mother with the sheet off the line, and Clarence soon got the knack of it; only the shrouds were not evenly shaped, and no sooner had you got one edge to meet another than everything else was out of true. Difficulties.

The eyes close again, like the hinged eyes of the more expensive kind of Kewpie doll when laid on its back, with a strictly mechanical motion.

19

Spaces, places! Some places we approach with dread: they carry the burden of our anxieties if we have failed to shoulder them ourselves.

I am Hilary, daughter of a dead mother, scuffling through a pile of shoes at the bottom of a wardrobe. This is my home, no longer a home. It's below ground level; I never thought of that. It's as if we lived in a hole, and a hole was all we were fit for. When I looked up to heaven, all I could see was the feet of strangers passing behind bars. But here my mother lived for years, slept and woke, and ate and cried and sometimes laughed. Here, every Saturday night, we played Monopoly for my sake, to keep me happy; and every Saturday night I bent the rules (which only I remembered) so she could nearly win but let me do so in the end. We were kind to each other, my mother and I, quite apart from what she felt she owed me for having brought me into the world she made, and what I owed her for having given me life, to make of what I could. I shall remember my mother with love when I have my own children. If I ever do. If I stay with Lily, I never will; I will shrivel up completely in my shell, in the glare of something far too strong for me.

I am Hilary, daughter of a dead mother, child of a lost father. I am Hilary, Jonathan's friend. I am Hilary, Lily's obligation, Lily's servant: Lily, spinning through the universe, a brilliant star, and me, a poor dead planet, revolving hopelessly around her. I am Hilary, lost to Lily. Almost.

"Have you found them, dear?" inquires Margot, as bright and brisk as she can manage. She and Hilary are sorting through the jumble in the bottom of Madeleine's wardrobe, searching for Hilary's sensible brown shoes. So far only one has been found.

In the end, Lily sent her as one sends a servant on an errand. "Margot, be a dear. Poor Hilary! Stumbling about in those ridiculous shoes! Too dismal for her to go alone."

"Yes," said Margot. "She'll need something quieter for the funeral."

"The funeral?" said Lily, as if mystified. "Oh, she won't be going to the funeral. It wouldn't be suitable for a child. Is there going to be much of a funeral? Jarvis said something, but surely he was joking. The expense! And for what? Who would go? Madeleine has no family. Surely they'll just bury her, cremate her—whatever it is that people do to corpses. It's not as if she was religious. What a dreadful subject for so early in the morning. I've never been to a funeral. Have you?"

Lily is herself again: wild and wan in washed-out jeans, brown nipples bold through a white shirt, crimson-belted. Jarvis relented at 6:45 A.M. and they made love—ah yes, and love it was. He to her and she to him. So many kinds of sexual congress! As many as there are of conversations. Sex with love, and sex without it, sex hostile, sex friendly, sex perfunctory, sex enjoyable, boring, disgusting, sanctified, disquieting, destructive; as many kinds as there are partners; as many with the same partner as that partner has frames of mind. This morning between Jarvis and Lily there is sex with love, and in the silence of mutual forgiveness.

Breakfast is on time this morning. Kippers for a change, boiled in a plastic bag. Lily enjoys dissecting the flakes of flesh from the flimsy bones. And Jonathan seems much better, although he has a nasty little blister on his heel which Lily has just discovered. It looks to her rather like a cigarette burn. Perhaps that was what was hurting and making him grizzle and keen, and why he didn't want to be picked up? But how could he possibly have a cigarette burn? Lily doesn't smoke, and Jarvis stopped when they were first married. When he was with Madeleine he smoked at least sixty a day, and of course, Madeleine smoked like a chimney, then and afterwards. It was ridiculous the way Madeleine kept pleading poverty while wasting all her (Jarvis's) money on cigarettes. Everyone thought so.

Lily puts antiseptic cream and a plaster-dressing on Jonathan's heel. Margot, watching, is about to suggest, from the strength of her position as the doctor's wife, that the burn would be better left uncovered, or at any rate, with a simple dry dressing upon it, but she holds her tongue. Why? What new meanness is this?

"I can't think how it came to be there," Lily persists. "You don't suppose Hilary's a secret smoker, and brushed his heel with her cigarette, or something, and didn't like to tell me? I wouldn't put it past her . . . She's so guilty about everything. Poor little Jonathan."

And she hands Margot Jonathan to hold, as she has done a hundred times before, but Jonathan's face puckers, so she sets him down instead, and he totters off towards the door, in his haste, banging his head on the edge of the table, as not infrequently occurs, but this time stoically refusing to mind, just so long, it seems, as he can put as much distance between himself and Margot as possible.

"When you're there, Margot," Lily goes on, in the fluty tones she uses when she's in an organizing mood, "just have a look round. See if there's anything of value."

"What do you mean by value?" inquires Margot. "There is the guinea pig, I suppose."

Lily looks blank.

"In the sense that anything alive is of value."

"I certainly don't want the guinea pig around here," says Lily, aghast. "I hate small animals, don't you? They're dreadfully dangerous for small children. They carry any number of germs."

"What's to become of it?" asks Margot. "Hilary's very fond of it."

"Oh, Hilary . . ." sighs Lily. Margot, she notices, is limping. Perhaps she is in pain; perhaps this explains her unusual sharpness. This plump, soft, little body, the doctor's wife, with her pouter-pigeon chest and her warm brown eyes and her brave little smile, is today all sharp edges and disapproval—or so it seems to Lily.

What's more, her stockings have a run in them. Amazing, to achieve a run in stockings made of such tough and sensible stuff, runproof to the point of total if shagged opaqueness. Still, there it is. There they are: run, unrunnable stockings. The doctor's wife looks a mess, thinks Lily. Not just boring, as she usually does, but dismal. "Isn't your leg properly better yet?" she asks.

"It still aches."

"What does your husband say?"

"He doesn't."

"Oh." Lily is nonplused. If Lily has a broken fingernail, Jarvis is all anxiety and concern: Lily his most precious possession, damaged!

"He's very busy," apologizes Margot, after the fashion of wives.

"I know a marvelous osteopath . . ." Well, Lily would. What a kind and handsome man! It hurts? Poor thing, of course it does. Here, let me help. And a twist and a stretch and a snap, and there we are, some kind of violent muscular orgasm, and ah yes, that's better, pain is passed and a dull ache remains, like the memory of a sorry love affair, but how much better than the sharp nagging of desire. Ah yes, Lily knows an osteopath; Jarvis hates her going.

"By something of value," murmurs Lily, "I meant—well, antiques, good towels, tablecloths, anything one wouldn't want to go to the Salvation Army. Just have a look."

So off Margot limps to Madeleine's flat with Hilary lurching and looming beside her. Hilary is going to be

as tall as her father, Lily fears—come to think of it,
she already is in the red platform heels.

So here they are now, as evening falls, in this dismal
place: Hilary crouched in front of the wardrobe, scuffling through the rubbish left by the partly living. Her
head is bent in a way that reminds Margot of someone.
Whom? Lettice? No, lithe, neat Lettice has nothing in
common with this lumpy, overflowing creature. Something of Laurence, perhaps? Hilary's hands. Yes, Hilary's hands are like Laurence's hands. They are large
and red, and chilly-knuckled. But that can only be coincidence; Laurence inherits his hands from Philip.
Surely.

Hilary's father's hands? Jarvis's fingers? Margot gasps
at some sharp pang of memory; there is an indecent
fluttering, an awful plucking at her private parts—
gone, almost before she's conscious of it.

Fifteen years ago Jarvis had young man's fingers,
forceful, charming: drunken, certainly, but with the
nice, the altogether legitimate, inquisitiveness of the
young, and whose touch is not, as in an old man's fin-
gerings, merely to remember.

Oh, I have wasted my life, cries Margot in her heart.
I am nearly old and I have known nothing. Only two
men in all my life: Jarvis and Philip. I have wasted
my youth, the body God gave me; I have muffled it
up with respectability and the terror of experience. I
have given myself away for the sake of my children,
my husband, my home; I have been the doctor's
wife, mother to the doctor's children; I have been
daughter to Winifred. Is there nothing left of me?

She moans. Hilary turns to look at her curiously.
"Don't you like it down here?" she asks. "It *is* rather
spooky. Do you think Mother's haunting it? I am a bit
frightened. Though why one should be frightened of

one's own mother ... We had awful rows sometimes. She'd get angry with me and I'd get angry with her, and that was fine except I'd stop being angry and then I'd feel dreadful, as if there was nothing beneath me to walk on, only a kind of nothingness. I feel a bit like that now. There's black all around." She raises her voice. "Mother, Mother, do you hear me. You had no business dying. Leaving me alone like this."

"Quiet," begs Margot. "Hush."

"Leaving me to Lily," shrieks Hilary into the blackness. Then her anger ebbs and she cries instead. "It was awful at the pictures last night," she complains through her sobs. "I couldn't think of anything to say to Jarvis. I never can. It's so embarrassing."

Margot is dizzy. Her breath comes in gasps. Objects around her lose definition: piles of clothing lie like hills in a night landscape. "If you want to come and live with me," she says, "you can." And instantly feels better, except for panic that Hilary might accept, and then what would she do? What would Philip say? Lettice, Laurence?

"With you?" Hilary is bewildered. She stops crying. "Oh no," she says. "I couldn't leave Jonathan. He needs me. I'll tell you what," she adds. "You could take the guinea pig. Renee comes in and feeds him, but he needs company."

The guinea pig stares at Margot with brown button eyes which remind her of her own, and whiskers.

"Of course," says Margot. The room is cold and dank. Both of them feel it. Shoes lie littered around her feet. There are the lace-ups which Madeleine wore for every day, their laces worn and knotted. There are the sandals with the broken straps, which Margot last saw on

Madeleine's knobbly, aging but still living feet. Madeleine seems not far away.

"Let's go," says Hilary, standing up. "Please let's go. It's horrible down here all of a sudden. It's not like it used to be one bit. We were quite happy here—really we were."

"You go back to Adelaide Row," says Margot. "I'll stay here and clear up." Though it's the last thing she wants to do, for once.

Clearing up! Is it Margot's instinct, or Margot's destiny, that leads her always to be Martha to other women. Mary? Little Margot, sweeping up under Gran's heavy chair, sifting with tiny deft fingers through the litter of horse hair, apple cores, orange peels and sweet papers which lay beneath, while Alice cackled, entertained and ruminated above, jangled gall stones and chumped ill-fitting teeth: was Margot born to it, or led to it? Later, little Margot clearing up after Winifred's long scented bath ("Remember, darling, men love a girl to smell sweet"), diving with skinny arms to remove the plug, retrieve the soap, replacing the shampoo top, refolding the towels, mopping up the water. Was it love she felt, or hate?

Later Winifred would introduce Margot to her men friends as "my little orphaned sister." Well, they felt like sisters: Winifred the pretty one, Margot the plain one—though how as sisters Margot could be orphaned and Winifred not, Winifred never explained. But after all, Winifred was only sixteen when Margot was born; it had always been ridiculous for a girl of Winifred's age to have a daughter Margot's age, and the older they both became, the more ridiculous it got. So they settled for sisterhood. Or at any rate, Winifred did, and if Margot resented the demotion, the diminutive in title, she did not say so.

Margot's father was a Battle of Britain pilot, shot down in flames over Sussex Fields when Margot was just a little girl. Or so Winifred says, and there was certainly a war widow's pension to prove it, and a special scholarship for Margot, £5 a term for the clever children of fighting men killed in action. Otherwise Margot might not have believed it, so much of what Winifred said being so often untrue.

Margot always tries to tell the exact truth, to make up for her mother in the general scheme of things. As a child, she had the feeling she was born by parthenogenesis; she has no sense at all of having had a father. He is seldom talked about, and if he is, she feels it is nothing to do with her.

For all her scented baths, her lying and scheming, her powdered cheeks, brilliant lips and pointed falsies, Winifred did not marry again. She remained husbandless, with all the loneliness and humiliation that this entailed, and Margot remained fatherless, making herself useful, clearing up.

Winifred, mind you, never much cared for sex, and the cause of her enduring widowhood may have lain more in herself than in the callousness of men: though in Margot's memory she brought three suits for breach of promise (and threatened many more) and lost them, every one. Her appearance told against her. Try how she might to look like Greer Garson in *Mrs. Miniver*, she never really managed to look anything other than (at worst) her chomping, clicking, randy old mother's daughter, or (at best) Margaret Lockwood in *The Scarlet Lady*.

Now Winifred is nearly sixty and works in a bookie's office on the South Coast, powdered and rouged, making out betting slips and flirting happily with the male customers from behind security bars. Her vision of a leisured old age, supported by a rich son-in-law, has evaporated. She has a vague sense of grievance against Margot, and by and large, prefers to forget her existence. Though once a year, over the Easter holiday, Margot takes the children to stay with her, and does Winifred's spring cleaning and gives the flat a general going-over and cleaning-up, and Winifred smiles at Margot and approves her usefulness.

Clearing up! How gratefully Margot clears up after Philip, Laurence and Lettice. It is her privilege to do so. To have a man, a husband of her own, and children too? Margot never thought it could happen to her. Such riches! She lives in fear lest they evaporate like phantasmagoria, and she finds herself once again living with Mother, and with Gran, and her happiness only a dream, and all her clearing up concerned again with the debris of the past, and not making way for the future.

Oh, backache! Margot, clearing up, picking up, bending down and putting back. Philip's dirty socks and shoes; Philip's wallet, always lost; Philip's memos, here and there; Philip's tissues, nail parings, hair clippings. Well, someone has to do it. He's a busy man, about more important business than Margot will ever know. Laurence's dirty socks (earlier, nappies) and ironed shirts; Laurence's homework, gerbils, pencil sharpenings, badges, spilled cocoa, sports gear, shoes. Lettice's discarded tights (earlier, nappies) and pressed blouses; Lettice's homework, letters, diaries, ointments, drawings, shoes. Well, someone has to do it. Those who are grown must serve those who are growing. And what else has Margot got to do all day, in any case?

And what will she do when they have gone? Her job? More clearing up, though mostly on a typewriter, and not so hard on the small of the back. Tidying up Jarvis's assorted notions and muddled demands on the outside world, translating them to his financial benefit.

Clearing up. It is the task of mothers after children have departed. Now Hilary flees from gloom and inconvenience, leaving Margot behind, ankle-deep in discarded shoes and old clothes. Margot stands by the barred window until Hilary's platform heels and solid legs have passed.

And still she stands, and does not bend, her back to the open door, staring out of the window, thinking of she knows not what, out of this world, this time, and then she is conscious of a sound behind her, an intake of breath, and whirls, expecting to see Madeleine, back to do her own clearing up. But it is Renee, pale, open-mouthed, curly-haired, pretty, proud. Mary to Margot's Martha.

"I thought," says Renee, "I thought for a moment it was Madeleine. I thought there'd been a mistake, after all. That she wasn't dead."

"I don't look like Madeleine," says Margot the doctor's wife.

"You do in this light," says Renee. "It's always so dark down here."

I am Renee, mother of two stolen children. I sort through my days as best I may, vitalized by anger, enriched by hate. I have youth on my side, and beauty, and a vision of a world not yet too old and tired to change. Not quite. I have my women friends, my pride, my dignity. I walk down the street with my head held high and my jeans stretched tight; I look over my shoulder, and yes, there they are, the men, sniffing after me, slavering, coarse-jowled, flabby-lipped, bald-pated. I spit; I slam the door in their stupid faces; I laugh. One day I'll get my children back. I am Renee, mother of two, wife to no man, disgusted by men, full of love, passion, generosity, the feel of other women's breasts upon my fingertips.

I am Renee. Who is this stranger, standing silent in dead Madeleine's room? I don't like her. She's against me. I can always tell. In her navy-and-white-spotted suit from Marks & Spencer, her smug little smile, her neat little hands; she is man's slavey, she is the enemy. If I stretch out my hand to her, she will recoil. But I am her sister. I will try.

Renee stretches out her hand.

Something happens; oh, events!

Something of Madeleine bursts free from the restraining discourse that surrounds her body, now encoffined and on its way through discreet back streets to lie at the undertaker's office until the funeral.

Something happens. A cyclist swerves under the hearse's wheel; the driver slams on the brakes; the hearse skids into a bollard, turns over and lies on its side like some great black stranded creature; the glass sides shatter, the back doors fly open, Madeleine's coffin slides out onto the ground, beneath the wheels of a braking mini-van; the wood splits, and there Madeleine lies, face upturned to the open sky, eyes open yet again, glittering in street light reflected off the mini-van's wing mirror. Well, that must be it. Such dull brown eyes by now, glassed over like fish for dinner not too freshly caught.

Well, accidents do beget accidents, everyone knows. Ambulances crash on their way to the hospital. While lightning strikes, the milk boils over. So this week Madeleine was in two road accidents.

The cyclist is unhurt, but gives his bicycle away thereafter. Of such occurrences are nightmares made. The driver of the hearse suffers backache for some months after the accident—the whiplash effect compressing the vertebrae of his spine—and presently seeks relief, and finds it, from the same osteopath which Lily recommended to Margot. An ambulance takes Madeleine back to the mortuary, where Arthur, Clarence and Goliath welcome the body back with a kind of gloomy pride.

After the injection of his varicose veins, Arthur is supposed to walk at least two miles a day. He spends much time pacing the length of the mortuary, backwards and forwards, backwards and forwards, until his slippers are quite worn down at the heel. No doubt it is the vibration which causes the shrouds to fall yet again from the shelves, and set Clarence and Goliath to their folding and refolding once more.

"Out visiting," observes Clarence to the shaken Goliath on Madeleine's return. "You can tell. Close the poor lady's eyes, Goliath."

Goliath does so. They spring open again, and he turns his back on Madeleine thereafter. He'd rather not see.

At any rate, something happens. Margot sees Renee's outstretched hand with Madeleine's eyes. The doctor's wife, Hilary's mother, does not recoil; she comes closer, takes Renee's hand and places it on her bosom. "I'm clearing up," Margot/Madeleine says in her new gravelly voice, profound as a very good claret. "Such a mess." Then a feeling of sickness, of suffocation, wells up inside her; reality recedes out of color, into sinking black and white, and then to black and nothingness. Margot faints.

Something happens! Jonathan whines and plucks at his plaster. Lily removes the dressing and is horrified to see that the affected area has enlarged; it is now not a neat blister, but a big round flat red sore, peeling back at the edges, revealing more flaky layers of skin than Lily knew a child could have, covering the entire side of his heel from flat of foot to ankle. Lily hastily smothers it with more cream, covers it with the largest plaster she possesses and tries not to think about it. Of such stuff are many mother made. Do not blame them.

Something happens! Enid is at Philip's evening surgery, demanding an abortion.

> I am Enid, Sam's wife; that's all I want to be. All the rest is playing games: offices, careers, affairs of state . . .

"Babies born late are often the best," says Philip. "The most beautiful, the best loved." What does he know about it?

"I was a late child myself," says Enid. Still am, she thinks. A naughty child. Marrying without permission. Not a real marriage at all; that's why I have to work so hard at it. Enid's executive case is in the waiting room. It contains ministry files. She hopes it will be safe.

"You're a secretary, aren't you?" says Philip. "You can pick that up again easily enough when the child's old enough for school."

"Yes," says Enid.

In five years, thinks Enid, all going well, I'll be an Under-Secretary of State. Sam's bound to find out. Then what, when I am finally revealed as better than he is? He'll take up with some dolly bird, I know he will, who never argues, never questions, just lies there and admires. Panic surges in her bosom, which is too small for Sam's liking. He has a fondness for large breasts. A tit-man, is how he refers to himself. Enid suffers from feelings (she knows) of inadequacy: that is, she endures torments of jealousy, of fear of abandonment, of dread lest Sam should have the affair he threatens, and go off, even for a one-night stand, with someone better equipped sexually (in Sam's terms) than she.

Affairs of state, she wishes to say to Philip, are child's play compared to the affairs of the home, of Sam, of the intricacies of a marriage and the marriage bed— site for Enid not so much of sex as sleep, but none the less compelling for that. Ah, the difference between the man asleep—silent, warm, source of strength and comfort—and the man awake—abusive, demanding, damaging, and yet protective: the sleeping man impossible to abandon; the waking one always on the verge of abandoning.

Do you know all this, she wonders of Philip, her doctor, her friend Margot's husband, whom she does not particularly like, or do you keep yourself too busy? And if you don't know, how can I begin to tell you?

"I want an abortion," says Enid. Enid knows Sam. Sam is the child of the household. If deposed, he will fight, sulk, scream, threaten and finally run away. And I will be left, thinks Enid; Under-Secretary of State, abandoned, lonely and bereft, and my parents will be right, after all. My mother, with her arthritic hip, in too much pain to garden any more; my father, with his fits of paranoia, his suspicions of the milkman, the gasman, the taxman, my mother, Sam, me. The wrong man for you, they said, how many years ago? They will not have Sam in the house. I spend my Christmas with them in restless nervousness, turkey and stuffing dry in my mouth—in fear that Sam is with another woman. And knowing this, Sam does nothing to reassure me that he's not. On the contrary. "If you're going home for Christmas, I'll just have to console myself as best I can. Well, there'll be parties."

Cut my baby out, please, Doctor. I can't stand any more. Just let me get back to work. Dear God, dear

Father. I know it's murder, but it's murder in self-defense. Please accept my plea. If you were only dear Mother, not dear Father, you would surely have more compassion.

"Well," says Philip, "I can see you're upset about it. I'll send you on for a second opinion. We have to have your husband's consent, you know, before anyone can do anything for you."

20

Look, what have we here?

Margot, who should be at home slicing veal-and-ham pie for the children's tea, sits instead in Renee's living room, sipping ginger wine from Biba's, and cries and sobs, with Renee's smooth bare arms around her. Or rather, Margot reclines on an ethnic bed of Ethiopian splendor, for there are no chairs in the room, only mattresses and cushions. Margot's short little legs seem ill-suited here. She touches them under her skirt and wishes that she was altogether longer, silkier and more sensuous. Renee's room, though square and dank in actuality, looking out as it does over grey walls and boilers, is in spirit bright and beautiful. It is a room full of satin cushions, striped silkiness and multicolored fringes, scented with incense.

"What's the matter?" implores Renee. "Don't cry. I can't bear to see women cry. Madeleine wouldn't want anyone to cry."

"She had such a struggle," protests Margot, "and at the end of it all, nothing."

"It's all any of us get," observes Renee, filling up Margot's glass with ginger wine (eighty-one pence at Biba's closing-down sale). "Nothing. Well, death. If that's something."

"But some of us have a better time on the way."

"She could have had," says Renee, "if she'd wanted. So much of it with Madeleine was *wouldn't,* rather than *couldn't.* She'd only ever get angry for herself. She didn't see she had a duty to get angry on everyone else's behalf. She had no sense of sisterhood. It diminished her as a person."

"She was your friend." Margot is shocked.

"I said worse about her when she was alive, and to her face. Dial-a-Date! What a humiliation. If she hadn't gone whoring off to Cambridge after some man she'd never even seen, she'd be alive now."

"It's hard for a woman to live without a man," says Margot.

"I manage," says Renee. "A good deal better without one than with one. Are you happy with your husband?"

"I don't know," says Margot, and the truth is she doesn't. What's happiness? Or is she saying it to oblige Renee, that pretty, forceful, laughing girl of principle and moral fiber, whose youthful finger now caresses Margot's aging cheek. Happiness! Margot can't remember ever feeling she had a right to it. "I'll have to go," she says. "The children will be wanting supper."

"But what do you want?" inquires Renee. "Or don't you have any wants any more?"

"I want to stay here," says Margot, and so she does.

"Madeleine would never come to bed with me," complains Renee. "She wanted to, I know she did; she kept putting it off, and now it's too late. I don't know why she kept hankering after men. I would have made her feel warm and happy and loved. Why didn't she just buy herself a vibrator?"

"Vibrators cost money," says Margot/Madeleine, and Renee looks startled.

"You said that just like Madeleine," says Renee, and then, hopefully murmuring as she would to Madeleine, "Come to bed and you'll feel better."

Feel better? So Margot would, she knows she would; she'd feel much better. Loved and loving. She marvels. The union of like to like, she now perceives, would be so serene, so comforting, so unlike the clash of opposites which is all she has ever known: the male-female union which creates new life, but nothing much besides—or so Renee would maintain—excepting trouble.

But if her own body is so forbidden to touch, to see, to know, how much more forbidden must another woman's be? No, no, she could not, must not. To feel soft female lips against her own? There is too much danger in it. If sensuous pleasure is so easily come by, after all; if sexual fulfillment can be so gracefully, privately, gently arrived at between woman and woman; if love can be without war, without struggle, without the conflict of non-identical interests—this sly, slippery primrose path to happiness is so dangerous, so monstrous, that the very sun might hide its face in horror and the light of the world go out.

Margot hesitates. Madeleine hesitated too at this juncture, on this bed, where her longer, leaner, more contemporary legs were at least better suited. Margot looks at her own neat little feet, her thick-tighted legs, and wonders why she is wearing sandals with a broken strap.

"I can't," Margot/Madeleine says, and then, with Margot's reason surging into her, and with the spontaneity of newly perceived veracity, "I'm too ashamed."

"Ashamed? Of what?"

"Of me," says Margot. "I'm not young any more. My body is fat and flabby. I'm ashamed to let anyone see it."

Otherwise would she be the doctor's wife, content with her seersucker dressing gown? No, she'd be a whore, a courtesan; it was her ambition as a girl. She told Katriona, no one else. See how fear and shame have crippled you and made you first a nurse and then a wife? Fit to clean up, but not to live. Oh, Margot!

"If your body's good enough to receive pleasure," says Renee, didactic even on her Ethiopian bed, "it's good enough to give it. But I'll shut my eyes if you like. I'll turn out the light. This isn't war; this is peace. I'm not a man; I don't get roused by defying my own disgust. I don't have to be roused, come to that. I just decide what I want to do, to give pleasure. I'm not a man. I don't want to plunder or loot; I want to love."

But Margot is longing for the safety of her warm matrimonial bed, sagging in the middle from overuse, thus inclining her husband to herself from habit and usage, if nothing else.

"You're not going to stay, are you?" complains Renee, her pretty face delicately flushed with passion, her wide

blue eyes swimming with tears. "I've presented myself
to you all wrong. I've frightened you away, the way I
did Madeleine."

"Don't cry," says Margot sadly, "Don't cry." She knew
it was all too good to last: she is in charge again. This
child is her junior by some fifteen years. What right did
Margot even have to demand comfort from Renee, or
to be disappointed now that it is no longer forthcom-
ing?

"I get so lonely and frightened by myself," says Renee.
"It's all right while the kids are well and doing all right
at school, but if anything goes wrong with them, I feel
so alone and helpless, I really do. It was something
having Madeleine downstairs; she was very strong. And
now she's had to go and get herself killed and my
friend's gone back to her husband and I've got nobody
again. My family don't like me being gay. They won't
even talk to me, let alone help me. My husband went
and told them; he didn't have to. It's not that I'm
ashamed, but it's my business, isn't it? It was all right
for him—off at his Rugby Club night and day—but for
me it's meant to be something disgusting, making me
so dreadful that I'm not even fit to look after my own
children."

Oh, I am Renee, making the most of things, offering
love, receiving love as best I may. I am Renee, my
parent's daughter, disappointed in the world and in
myself.

"If there was something I could *do*," says Renee, her
head on Margot's bosom, like Lettice when she has a
pain. "Write or paint or sculpt, or something. But
there's not. I'm too stupid. All I can do is love. You
have such a beautiful face," she says, her little fingers
moving over Margot's surprised mouth, eyes, temples.
"You shouldn't have died and left me alone. I offered

you something and you turned away. You hurt me very much, you don't know how much."

"Never mind," says Margot/Madeleine, "never mind," and lets Renee's timorous yet insistent fingers unbutton the sturdy Marks & Spencer buttons and the sleek zips.

Does Renee, in the warm half-dark, see, feel Madeleine's face, breasts, body? Margot, her eyes shut, unclothed, warm and at peace, pleasured by Renee's familiar, practiced hands, has at any rate the confidence of the body which was Madeleine's—which, though worn and tired, believed until the end that it had some gift to offer. Margot's hands reach out to embrace, explore, and offer understanding. Or are they Madeleine's hands?

Margot the doctor's wife, mother of the doctor's children, lying with the doctor in the familiar warmth of the doctor's bed, will wait patiently for the doctor to turn to her. Yes, she would say if asked, "The doctor and I have a good sex life." And so they have. If doctors can't, who can?

But this drowsy, seductive activity, this fringed and slippery and scented room, all this is no real part of Margot's desire. She can put up with the expectation of orgasm, but not its reality. The sudden upsurge of fulfillment, so banal in retrospect, upsets her vision of herself, and what her purposes in life should be. "I must go home," she says. "I really must. I want to." And so she does.

"Will I see you again?" asks Renee, like the little girl she is. "Please, can I come to tea next week?"

"I don't think so," says Margot, wondering what she's been doing, who she's been, why she's here, how she ever had the courage to do what she has done.

"Never mind," says Renee, who seems quite cheerful again, wandering round the room naked in the confidence of her physical perfection (much as Lettice will in the privacy of her bedroom), lighting joss sticks, brewing jasmine tea. "It was a kind of celebration of Madeleine, that was all. We did it for her."

And so it was, and so they did.

21

Ordinary life!

Philip, Lettice and Laurence. Think of them, gain strength from them. Widowed Winifred, Margot's mother. The doctor's cat, pacing through the undergrowth. Veal-and-ham pie. Piles of ironing, piles of dishes. Backache. Her own face in the mirror, friendly and familiar—Margot's face.

Not so ordinary death!

Madeleine is transported once again to the undertaker's. Clarence waves her corpse goodbye, to Arthur's disapproval. "See you soon, darling," calls Clarence. "Bon voyage." Then, turning to Arthur, "What a lively lady! I hope she has fun at the undertaker's." And Arthur says dourly, "I don't know what they teach you at school nowadays, but it's certainly not respect for the dead. Help me with the shrouds, will you? You've left them lying about again." And so he has, or someone has.

Ordinary life!

"I don't think there's anything in the flat worth saving," says Margot to Lily the next day. "I think it should all go to the Salvation Army."

"No sheets or blankets? Towels, tablecloths? You know what a price they are."

"Lily," says Margot suddenly and firmly. "You can't possibly use Madeleine's sheets. It would be indecent. Jarvis would never stand for it."

"He wouldn't know," says Lily defiantly. "Look, I'm just trying to be practical and save my housekeeping money. Everyone gets so stupid about death. It always seemed to me it was perfectly all right to be the dead person, just fairly awful for the ones left behind. And I don't see that death is any excuse for waste. Well, I give up. The Salvation Army can clear the lot. Who cares, anyway?" But she does, deeply. She wants everything of Madeleine's she can get hold of, now as always.

Margot is limping again. Hilary has shut herself in Jonathan's room, and is crying. Jonathan's heel is red and sore. Jarvis's shares are dropping fast.

Madeleine lies, with her eyes open, in a rather expensive yew-wood coffin, to be paid for by Jarvis, out of money set aside for Lily's new stair carpet. Her dull eyes glitter in light reflected from God knows where.

Ordinary life. Extraordinary death.

This morning Lily is out with Jonathan. Lily takes Jonathan down to the clinic to have his poor little foot looked at. The ankle is quite swollen now, or so Lily swears. Though it looks much like his other ankle, both to Jarvis and to Margot.

This morning Margot, bending over Jonathan's foot, brushes against Jarvis by mistake, and a kind of electric shock runs through her from her head to her toe. Does he really not remember her? No. And she has so patiently worked here and waited, hardly knowing what she was doing. Plump Margot, the doctor's wife, bearing secret grudges? Oh, spite.

This morning Jarvis walks through his house and thinks of Madeleine. Here she sat, and there she talked, and now she's gone.

Death makes a firm dividing line between the present and the past. Then they were, and now they aren't, and the knife slides firmly into the home-baked cake, dividing. This side, that side, then and now. There, see, isn't that real enough for you? And you were beginning to think, weren't you, that experience slipped along in some kind of continual stream, more or less under your control, at your behest? That'll teach you. Before death, after death. Now you see them, now you don't. Life's still one long lesson, it turns out, with a slap and a cuff every now and then to help you keep your wits about you.

Jarvis prowls his elegant home. What he wanted, and yet not so. This house makes demands; it's querulous. "What next?" it asks. The old one sulked and muttered, "That's enough. That's all. Let me alone." Perhaps the old one was preferable.

Here in the bathroom is the mirror in which Madeleine once stared. Then the mirror hung from a cup hook screwed into the plaster—to the great detriment of the wall—above a crazed washbasin. Now the mirror is set neatly in blue-and-white tiles, its frame properly gilded, and Lily's neat teeth, not Madeleine's long yellowy ones, are bared in its reflection. Madeleine's mirror, all the same. Once, one morning, when she stood looking into it, her lean body outlined beneath her thin nightie, young Jarvis, twenty-nine that day, came up behind her and took her, standing up, to her surprise. He remembers now the look on her face, watching it in the mirror for his own satisfaction—the mouth parted, the eyes closed and trembling slightly beneath the lids: Madeleine lost to herself, more herself than ever before or since.

Good deeds, harsh words.

What happened next? What next? Jarvis cannot remember. They were giving a party: he remembers that. He planned to make punch over four gas rings in the basement. Madeleine said punch should not be boiled; Jarvis said it made no difference. Of such ridiculous differences are dreadful quarrels made. Then Jarvis wanted Madeleine to dress up (as she described it), and more, to wear a bracelet he had bought her. Madeleine said that was ridiculous. She didn't like going to parties; she didn't know why she was giving this one. Parties! What was the point? The only point there'd ever been was to attract other men, and all that belonged to her past. Perhaps it was different for him? Perhaps he wasn't satisfied with her? Jarvis, irritated, said what was marriage anyway? Prison? How could he have said it, with the look of her face in the mirror so freshly with him: his wife, Madeleine, still wet and slippery from Jarvis's so pleasantly and suddenly fulfilled desire?

Easily said, and easily done, by Jarvis, Poppy's son. Jarvis, with his young man's fear of commitment, and most especially to his wife, mother of his child.

Former deeds, forgotten words.

In those days the bathroom was not this confection of blue-and-white tiles, gilded fittings and carpeted floor. Envisage it then, with its big white bath, cracked basin, cream walls, dark-green paint, brown linoleum floor—

the whole dominated by a big gas geyser in chipped white enamel discolored by fumes, with a metal spout and controlled by levers, through which, if you put pennies into the meter below the basin, hot water would eventually trickle. Madeleine always bought Lifebuoy soap; the room used to smell of carbolic. So did little Hilary, as a baby, her bottom red and sore with nappy rash.

Now there is a smell of tooth powder in the room, and a movement in the mirror. Jarvis sees a face reflected there.

When the family cat dies, its owner will sometimes see its movements thereafter, but only out of the corner of his eye, and only for a day or two, a week or so. And looking will see there's nothing there but the shadow of his remembrance. Or perhaps he's obtuse and sees nothing, and it's left to a friend to say, "You've got a cat just like your old one," and for the bereaved owner to say in surprise, "No, I haven't," and the friend to say, "But I saw it there just now, sitting on the stairs, just like the old one did . . ."

Jarvis sees Madeleine's face reflected; at least he thinks he does. The mirror is steamed up, so it's hard to be sure. Steamed up? But he hasn't been running the taps—how can it be?

Jarvis turns, and sees Margot standing there. "I thought you were Madeleine," he says blankly. The light shines from behind Margot, so that Jarvis can see her shape but not her face or eyes. Thus once Madeleine turned to look at Jarvis her husband, standing there outlined in the doorway, twenty-nine, handsome, lusty, and turned back to face the mirror again with wifely docility. Oh, those were the days when the plan for our lives was less obscure; when our puppet strings pulled, and we danced, and did not struggle. Jill, said

Philip, all of sixteen, nude photography is art, and besides, I am your brother—and there she is, as God intended, in her wheelchair forever and ever, amen.

Harsh deeds, kind words.

"I'm not Madeleine," says Margot, but she advances towards him as if she were; only now Jarvis stands where Madeleine did, and she where Jarvis did, and as Jarvis once did to her, she closes up to him, and he turns away so his back is to her.

What happened next? "You shouldn't have," says Margot/Madeleine, her cheek lying against her husband's shoulder. "You shouldn't have done it."

Good deeds or harsh words? Which does she lament? Which most bound her to him?

He could swear it was Madeleine's voice, but breaking away from the arms and turning, he still sees Margot standing there. Or is it himself remembered, when he was young and never thought of death, let alone corruption?

"Come upstairs," says Margot in Jarvis's voice, and the room is heavy with cigarette smoke and the smell of spilled beer and boiled, spoiled punch. "No one will notice."

And from his own lips he hears Margot's light, young voice. "What for?"

But she knows quite well. Does she want Jarvis, or to usurp Madeleine's rightful place? Ah, both. Women, children, usurpers all. Men just sit on thrones.

And what is this? What is Margot doing? What she always meant to do. Did you think she was there to type, to help, to earn, to suit her husband and Jarvis's wife? Never. She was there to suit herself. Margot, who should be pattering away at the typewriter in middle-aged complacency, is upstairs with Jarvis, Lily's husband, underneath the fur bedspread of the spare room, as once she lay with Jarvis, Madeleine's husband, some sixteen years ago. Only now the walls are freshly papered brown and white, in a Liberty pattern with matching curtains, and not with large pink splashy flowers on a fawn ground, peeling where the roof leaks. What horror, what shame, to bring back the past—the bits of it, at least, which we so earnestly wish to forget. Dilapidation, degradation. The smell of damp plaster, dry rot, wet rot: corruption, dull-eyed, fish-eyed.

"I haven't changed," murmurs Margot, bold as brass, "don't you remember? How can you forget? Did it mean so little to you? Look," she says, baring her breasts, "don't you remember my breasts? They have pink nipples, not brown. You liked that."

Margot, in truth, has pretty breasts, plump, firm and white. Renee admired them, and Margot now has a better opinion of them. If Margot this is upon the bed, her breasts may be those of a girl, but her eyes are glazed like a dead woman's.

But her nipples, thus revealed, seem brown enough to poor Jarvis, recalling to his mind those of his wife, so that he pulls back from this obliging, frightening woman on the bed and says, "I'm sorry, I really am. I have no idea how I came to be up here . . ."

Bad deeds!

"You were drunk," she says. "You brought me up here. I was upset, I didn't know what I was doing. I was very young. I'd just had an abortion. You had no right . . ."

"What are you talking about?" he pleads. "Please, Hilary's somewhere in the house. Lily will be here soon . . ."

Harsh words.

Margot shrieks at him as Madeleine would, and did, and belabors him with her fists, as Madeleine would, and did.

"What do I care about Lily? What do you care what damage you do? You took away my life, my home, and gave them to Lily. Now you want to destroy my child as well."

But really, Jarvis looks incapable of destroying anyone or anything: a large, middle-aged, gentle man, erratically dieted, occasionally drunk, in love with his wife, with a past of erotic plundering so far behind him as to be barely remembered. Who did he sleep with long ago, how many, and why, and where? Does it matter? Did it ever? All Jarvis ever wanted was a nice home, a nice wife, loving and uncritical, and kind words. And when Madeleine quite willfully failed to provide what he wanted, what he had a right to expect, what any husband has a right to expect from a wife, he put up with it as long as he could, and then stepped aside reluctantly, almost against his will, and turned her out and took in Lily.

"It wasn't like that," Madeleine cries, in death as in life.

Oh, Jarvis, I am Madeleine. Give me permission to hate you. Approve of my malice. Acknowledge I was right and you were wrong. Then I'll be quiet. Please.

"I should have behaved better to Madeleine," says Jarvis finally, years too late. "I was unfair to her. You are quite right."

Oh, I am Jarvis, Poppy's child, and there is such a pleasure in rejecting, turning love away, abusing trust. Poppy, turning her indifferent eyes away from her husband, my stepfather, staring away out over the golf course, sipping gin, gazing blankly at her poor plain children. Poppy, smiling only at Jarvis, child of shame, child of the Great North Road, this side of Doncaster, the far side of Grantham. I am Jarvis, husband, father. I smile at Jonathan, child of comfort, and stare through Hilary, child of bare boards and leaking roof. What else can I do? It's what I feel like.

"Hilary might like to come to me," says Margot.

I am Margot, Winifred's daughter, Lettice's mother, not fit to be either. I am myself at last, naked of titles, lost to all dignity. Help me, God. I prayed to you as a child; help me now. Save me from Madeleine, save me from myself.

Does God hear? He didn't when Margot was a child, when she had her knuckles rapped for not understanding long division; she never quite lost her faith in Him, all the same. The teacher who did it fell under a bus years afterwards.

"Hilary's all right here," says Jarvis blankly. "Isn't she? Lily's very good to her."

"If she came to me, she'd be with children her own age," pleads Margot. "Young people. It's more suitable. And Laurence is her brother, after all."

Does Margot say that, or Madeleine? Certainly Margot never meant to; she hardly believes it herself. A child belongs to whoever looks after it, she'd be the first to say; who cares who conceived it? How can Laurence be Jarvis's child, any more than Jarvis was the lorry driver's child? Except, of course, in Poppy's longing, memory and imagination. Little Jarvis at the breakfast table; Ruth of the piano-legs beside him, teasing; the stockbroker at the head, disapproving, toying with his kedgeree—Jarvis was a true child of this family, not of the open road. Did any of it happen? Perhaps it was Poppy's imagining, an opium dream of the thirties; perhaps there was always only the stockbroker, the golf course, the gin, the children duly and dully begotten? Perhaps she just told Jarvis stories. He was her eldest son. He scarcely knows the truth of it any more.

Good words, harsh deeds.

Laurence sits at the doctor's table, measuring the distance from earth to moon. The doctor keeps his peace with him; therefore Laurence is the doctor's child, not Jarvis's.

Hilary sits at the architect's table, and the architect stares through her, seeing in her his own ugliness, his own unkindness to her mother. Hilary eats her Sugar Puffs; Jarvis looks the other way.

Jarvis does not hear what Margot said. He can't afford to. Margot's child his own? "Has Hilary said she wants to live with you?"

Margot, that teller of the truth, speaks lies. More her mother's child than she had thought, or more of Madeleine. "Yes," says Margot. "She isn't very happy here. She feels she has no right."

"It's her home."

"It's Lily's home," says Margot, and so it is.

"She loves Jonathan," says Jarvis.

"I could give her Laurence to love," says Margot, persisting in madness. "She's as near to him as she is to Jonathan."

Still Jarvis seems not to understand. Margot thinks she is going to faint. She is very cold. The open casement window bangs in the wind. Jarvis goes to shut it, but the double glazing is firmly in place. How long since there was a casement window there?

Madeleine's home.

Jarvis has lost the vision of himself when young, and his remembrance of her; all he sees now is a couple embraced on the old divan beneath a heap of coats, and the smell of cigarettes, spilled beer and hot punch comes seeping up the stairs, and such a sorrow fills Jarvis/Madeleine that he turns out of the room without saying a word and goes downstairs, hearing his feet clattering on the linoleumed floor, although were he to look, he would see the pale carpets nicely fitted as usual, beautifully brushed, properly swept, bringing out the faint pattern of the starry wallpaper, much as usual. Lily imagines they are worn and wishes to replace them, yet again. But they are not worn; floor coverings are her especial and expensive preoccupation. Well, Madeleine will have her coffin instead.

Jarvis remembers. Jarvis sits upon the stairs, carpeted, linoleumed, and weeps for Madeleine alive and Madeleine dead, Madeleine in the bathroom, Madeleine entering the spare room, seeing, and presently Jarvis feels the better for it.

What can anyone do? Once, in the war, a bomb fell at the bottom of the garden. Not a large one, but enough to bring down a section of the back wall of the house. Miss Maguire, household help to Mr. Karl Kominski, was sheltering at the time in the cupboard under the stairs. No one knew she was there. She was bricked up in the dark for some six days. When they found her she was speechless with shock and fright. She recovered physically, but such oddness in the head as she'd heretofore suffered from—and there was certainly a degree of it (you never saw such inefficient sweeping, such greasy washing-up)—was reinforced. Karl Kominski thereafter looked after Miss Maguire as best he could, but when his reparation money came through and he sold the house to the Katkins and went to live in Italy, where it was warm, he could no longer keep in touch with her. She had no relatives; Mr. Kominski was sorry for a fellow sufferer from the Nazis, but what could he do? What can anyone do? Jarvis weeps upon the stairs. Lily comes through the front door, holding Jonathan in her arms. "He has to go to the hospital," she says, distraught. "They think he's got blood poisoning."

"What do they mean, blood poisoning?" Jarvis is agitated.

But Lily doesn't know.

By the time Margot comes downstairs, adjusting her dress, as once she came downstairs sixteen years ago, to meet her friend Katriona's reproachful stare—poor Katriona, who as it happened had good reason to fear the results of fulfilled desire—Jarvis and Lily have gone, all else forgotten, on their way to the hospital with their child.

Good, thinks Margot, with what's left in her unforgiving, good. I hope he dies. She is certain of the thought, but not quite sure which "he" she means.

Bad deeds. Bad thoughts.

22

Home and safety!

Or so Margot rashly and falsely imagines. Her step quickens. Since leaving Adelaide Row she has been free from pain.

Ordinary Life!

There's the familiar corner house, the familiar brass plate upon the wall. Lettice polishes it daily. Good little Lettice.

Dr. P. Bailey,
Surgery: 9–11 5–7 Mon.–Fri.
Sats: emergencies only 9–12.

Margot has turned this corner how many thousands of times? Wheeled Laurence's stroller, Lettice's pram, up and over the curb; carried Laurence in the full flight of tantrum, kicking and biting, tucked under her arm, herself nervous of the neighbors' censure; carried Lettice unconscious, bleeding, fallen out of a tree, up the path and into the surgery, heavy as lead, light as a feather.

Ordinary life!

Turned the corner in stiletto heels, walking shoes, fashion boots; in her best evening dress; in her pregnancy smock; in her milk-stained shirt, running out between feeds to buy baby Lettice a comforter—in the face of Philip's wishes. That being the year comforters were unhygienic.

Margot has driven out from this drive, sitting beside Philip, in, consecutively, a Ford Anglia, a Vauxhall Cortina, a Volkswagen Van (that was in the camping days) and a Volvo Estate: sometimes bored, sometimes sulky, mostly brave, good, enduring, self-sacrificing; sitting in the back because the children loved the front, going on outings she never enjoyed except for the children's sake; staying up late to make the sandwiches, prepare the flasks of soup, gather the cushions and rugs together which would in the end only crowd her out of her own seat.

Margot has seen the blossom on the flowering cherry come and go. Lately she has seen the big elm on the far side of the street felled.

Ordinary life! Home and safety.

The doctor's cat sits on the porch roof, ears flickering in the twilight. How he gets up there no one knows. Trees crowd around the home, shading it, so flowers seldom grow, only leaves. No one has the heart to fell the trees.

This is the front door where no one is refused. The lame, the sick, the distressed, the homeless, come knocking here, and are at least in part satisfied.

Every cushion inside is familiar, its goose down, chicken feathers or foam-rubber innards known and noted; every chip on every skirting can be accounted for. That was where we moved the piano. That was where Laurence's awful friend once booted the wall in an excess of energy. That was where Philip tried to open a jar of gherkins, and broke the glass but didn't shift the lid.

One day, thinks Margot, one day there will be time to see to the trees, see to the garden, see to the skirtings, see to myself, see to everything. But by the time there is time to see to myself, what will there be left to see to? One old woman in a wheelchair, staring at photographs of her great-grandchildren? If she's lucky.

Margot goes down the side of the home, brushing past the damp rhododendron bushes which flourish flowerless in the shade, cramped up against the neighbor's fence. The cat follows Margot. How did he get down from the porch roof? No one knows, yet here he is.

Margot pushes open the back door. There's the kitchen, clean, familiar and practical. Lettice and Laurence are doing their homework.

Ordinary life!

Where's Mother been? In the arms of a lesbian lady; in the arms of her employer, whom she has named (if only he'd been listening) as her son's father. That's where Mother's been. Inside Madeleine's body, cold as ice, chilling proper response. Or Madeleine inside her, warming her up to unspeakable deeds: puppet performances, joyless and nostalgic; jerky spasm of change and acceptance.

Margot steps across the threshold and stares inimically at Lettice and Laurence. A blast of cold air comes in with her, raising the papers on the table and the hairs on their arms. Slowly their heads rise; they look back at her unsmilingly. What have they to do with her, or she with them? So she spewed them out into the world, baby fish into the stream of life: that was her compulsion, her event, not theirs. Do they catch her indifference or she theirs? Momentarily, it is mutual. Do they see her as some disagreeable, not altogether well-intentioned stranger, standing on their doorstep? Yes. Self-interest rules them. Thus they said in their tender years: If she dies, who'd look after us? Gran? An orphanage? Good. They have the color telly there. Die, Mother, we don't care. Or tenderer, angrier still: Die, Mother, you're horrible. We'll cut you up like the cat's dinner and put you in the dustbin. Thus, through fair thoughts and foul, we all achieve our independence and swim off, like the fish we are.

Ordinary life! .

The doctor's cat slips in between Margot's legs, then turns his rusty head and round green eyes to stare at her, and arches his back and yowls and spits and retreats into the dark again.

"What's the matter with the cat?" asks Lettice. "He's acting the way I feel."

"Perhaps Mum's possessed," says Laurence, "and that's why she's late home."

"Don't talk about me as she," says Margot in her nasty harsh voice. "I'm not the cat's mother."

"Do you think she could turn her head through a hundred and eighty degrees?" inquires Lettice coldly of her brother.

"I hope she doesn't try," says Laurence. "She'd only be sick with green vomit."

Their talk does not amuse their mother, nor was it intended to. She stands where she is, and sways, hollow-eyed, her left hand beating and beating against her chest.

Her children become frightened. "We were only joking," says Laurence. "You're not really possessed."

"Bastard," she says. "Little bastard."

Poor Laurence's crimson cheeks grow darker still.

"I'll fetch Dad," says Lettice. "I don't know what's got into her today."

Or as Lettice says afterwards to Andrew Monk, a boy in her class, who, though underage, possesses a motorbike, "It must have been the menopause. She's changed completely. She was like a different person."

"She ought to have estrogen therapy," says Andrew. "It makes all the difference, I believe."

Ordinary life!

Jarvis and Lily sit in the Casualty Department of the hospital and wait. Their car is parked on double yellow lines and is likely to incur a parking fine, which is now Jarvis's main concern. So far as he can see, there is nothing wrong with Jonathan, who sleeps peacefully in his father's arms. Lily, however, is convinced that Jonathan is in a coma. There is no one available to reassure her. The department is busy; having registered their presence at the reception desk, Lily and Jarvis must now wait. Nurses come and go, out of one door into another; no one bothers to attend to Jonathan. Jarvis drowses and dreams of scarlet Poppy.

Lily is frightened. Lily, who cannot remember, as a child, a girl, a woman, ever wanting her mother, now wants her mother. Ida, help me.

Ida, who married beneath her, married a butcher. Night of the long knives night after night. Until she took herself and Lily and new-born Rose off to Long Bay, Coromandel, and the Kiwi Tea House, and the truckloads of American servicemen.

From the halls of Montezuma to the shores of Tripoli, and don't forget the Kiwi Tea House, Long Bay, that little wooden shack perched on top of a sand dune, vibrating like a drum when wind and rain bounced upon its corrugated iron roof, and don't forget the tea-lady's pale little daughter Lily, first shrinking, then beckoning, behind the white sand dunes and the bleached and stinking piles of driftwood.

One moonlit winter night, here at the very edge of the world, Baby Rose wandered off into the dark, and was found next morning floating face downwards in the rock pool Lily loved the best, where the crimson sea anemones grew.

After the funeral (Lily didn't go) her father reappeared, striding lopsided over the dunes, and took Lily and Ida home.

Did Lily push the misbegotten Rose into the rock pool, to be clutched and sucked at by the crimson anemones, as the long-toothed servicemen had clutched and sucked at her? Of course not. Though had Lily thought of it, had Lily dared, Lily would have. And if the imagining is as bad as the doing, then Lily was to blame.

Well, Rose's death solved so many problems. Rose's very life was an act of hostility against her family, her birth a declaration of war upon her mother. Love me, lose everything, cried Baby Rose, stretching up her tiny arms. There are such children. Lose me, gain everything.

Lily got her father back. Alas, so did Ida, rather spoiling things. Well, two's better than three, and at least Baby Rose was out of the way, dead as a doornail, using up no more love and attention. And presently Lily could push Ida out, more or less, surpassing her mother, as daughters do. Mothers grow old.

Lily got Jarvis from Madeleine. Or almost. At least it was a good try. Now Madeleine's out of the way, dead as a doornail, and Lily's got what she always wanted: sole possession.

So why now does Lily sit upon the hospital bench in a frenzy of silent terror, calling upon Ida in her heart? Ida, forgive me, help me, don't punish me. Madeleine, forgive me, help me, don't punish me.

Jonathan's little foot slips out from beneath the blanket. It is piteously red and raw, as if sucked at by a myriad of acid tendrils. Even Jarvis can see it now. "I say," he says in surprise, "it is rather a mess."

"Do something," begs Lily of Jarvis, but Jarvis seems paralyzed by the atmosphere, the institution, his own medical ignorance and his lack of trust in Lily's panic, and in Lily's version of events.

"You have to expect to wait," says Jarvis. "This is an emergency hospital."

"But supposing he loses his foot," she implores. "Look at it!"

And indeed, Jonathan's entire foot seems to be swelling beneath their eyes. Lily wrenches her child out of Jarvis's arms and carries him over to the nurse behind the reception desk. "Please," she begs. "Look at his foot. He must see somebody at once."

The nurse looks puzzled. "It's nothing much, mother," she says. "I'm afraid you're going to have to wait for half an hour or so. The doctors are busy. We have all the intensive-care units in operation. Please sit down and wait quietly. The little boy is sleeping nicely; he isn't in pain."

But Jonathan tosses and moans in Lily's arms. The nurse is clearly lying.

Oh, I am Lily. Jonathan's mother, as I've never felt it before. The world in conspiracy against me. Is this what it's like to be a mother? Was this what you felt like, Ida, when you found Baby Rose missing from her bed, and there were no neighbors, no one to help, and you ran the length of the lonely beach, up and down, up and down, looking, and when the dawn came, what did you find? Poor Mother, poor Ida, poor Baby Rose. I'm sorry. So sorry. Poor me.

Lily cries. Jarvis pats her hand. "It's all right, Lily," he says. "Jonathan's all right. He just needs some kind of injection."

"It's Madeleine," says Lily. "She's doing it to him. I know she is."

"We none of us behaved very well," says Jarvis. Madeleine, I'm sorry.

Good behavior? What's that? Not an activity much reckoned by those in the grip of incestuous passion, certainly. To those not involved, good behavior may well be not leaving your wife for your partner's young secretary. (But how great the temptation, the renewal of youth!) Nor may it be going to bed, after long and romantic delays, with your boss's married partner. (But what vigorous young woman, erotically inclined towards her father, can resist a married man?)

"Lily's been turned out of her flat by a mad landlady," says Jarvis to Madeleine one evening. "She'll have to come here and use the spare room. It's no use getting hysterical. You've always told me sexual jealousy was degrading; now's the time to practice what you preach. Besides, she's pregnant."

Does Lily tremble as she approaches Madeleine's territory? Does she hesitate as she goes up the linoleumed
stairs to the spare room, with the ugly red roses on the
peeling fawn wallpaper?

No. That wallpaper will have to go, is what Lily thinks.
And Jarvis is mine, and mine alone, she thinks—if she
thinks—by virtue of my love for him. "The next few
days won't be pleasant," she tells her best friend Alice,
who sits open-mouthed and marveling. "But I've got to
do it. His wife is so thick-skinned and insensitive, she
just won't budge otherwise."

Madeleine budges. Madeleine takes some good towels
and the best tablecloths with her, grabbing what she
can, breaking a few windows as she goes, spilling ink
into Lily's suitcases—and all in front of poor little Hilary.

Madeleine's quite mad, Jarvis and Lily agree. Poor
Lily, Jarvis comforts her. What she has to put up with!

Later there's the restraining order, to stop Madeleine
pushing, punching and snatching Lily as Lily walks up
Madeleine's path to Madeleine's front door. Well,
Madeleine shouldn't have left. All the lawyers agree. It
is Lily's path, Lily's front door.

Oh, punishment!

Lily rocks to and fro with Jonathan against her pretty
brown-tipped breast. Nurses go to and fro, not bother-
ing. Jarvis takes Lily's hand. She shakes it off. "If I
didn't behave very well," she says evilly, "I'm paying
for it now, aren't I?"

"How do you mean?"

"I'm landed with Hilary," says Lily. It's an easier
thought than that she's going to lose Jonathan.

"I thought you wanted her," says Jarvis, baffled.

"I didn't ever want her; I just wanted to be better than Madeleine at bringing her up," cries Lily into the antiseptic silence. Jarvis does not reply. Jonathan's foot throbs. He moans and tosses.

"You're so useless," says Lily to Jarvis, "I'm never going to have another child—not with you as father."

Lily's own first pregnancy, the cause of her moving into the spare room, evaporated after two nights spent with Jarvis beneath the peeling, splodgy roses. Whether the bleeding started as the result of his ardor or because the pregnancy had only existed in her imagination, Lily never knew. She had dreadful period pains that month, anyway.

Jonathan, child brought to fruition, moans. He is in pain. Oh, punishment! Madeleine, I'm sorry. Ida, forgive me. I'll write to you tomorrow. All this, for what? For Jarvis?

To have a husband is nothing. To be a wife is nothing. Sex is an idle pastime. To be a mother is all that counts. Lily recognizes it now, and the shock of the discovery numbs her for a moment to the anxiety and distress which accompanies the state of motherhood. Then it surges back. Jonathan, little Jonathan, don't die. What will become of me if you do? I will have nothing. I will be nothing. Jarvis, you don't count.

Oh, punishment!

23

Philip, puzzled, regards his drumming, lapping, scowling wife.

"Is it the menopause?" inquires Lettice, taking her revenge upon Margot, remembering her mother's callousness of the previous morning, how she savagely stripped the blood-spotted sheets from the bed. Be as unkind as you like, Mother. See, I grow up and you grow old. If I start bleeding, you'll have to stop.

"Do go away, Lettice," says Philip.

Laurence has already gone, sidling out after the cat into the dark, to seek out friends and the more ordinary aspect of life in households not for the time being, at any rate) in the throes of that black, convulsive tumult of discontent and resentment which will overwhelm the most calm and pleasant home from time to time, so that the plants wilt, the children stay out, and the cat leaves home—until it's some other family's turn, and ordinary life returns.

"But I'm doing my homework," protests Lettice.

"Do it upstairs," says Philip, and Lettice capitulates. "I should try estrogen therapy," she says as she leaves, not so much pert, as terrified. Her mother's hands seem unfamiliar: taut and tense, and curved almost into claws. Mother, I'm sorry. What would I do without you?

Oh, punishment!

"Margot," says Philip, when Lettice has gone, in the soft voice he used during their courtship, and regards her—how? Lovingly, soulfully, or in the manner of some deceitful spaniel, droopy eyes, licking his lips after the lamb chop, cowering under the kitchen table, trying to avoid retribution?

Margot, peering at her husband through a mania of suspicion and resentment, clearly thinks it is the latter. "Oh," she says, "it's you, is it?" as if she were some rich and famous lady, and he a debt collector or a despised ex-husband who dared to approach her at a party at which she was having a good time.

"You're behaving very oddly, Margot," he remarks mildly.

"Me?" She is outraged. "You're trying to drive me mad. But you're the one who's mad."

It is quite normal in any marital quarrel for both parties to consider the other mad—more, to be incensed at the insult of an accusation which both are quite happily making about the other. But Margot seems to have drummed this quarrel up out of nothing. Philip says as much, and declines to take offense. His very mildness inflates her fury. "Go back to your surgery," says the doctor's wife. "Go on sticking your hands up the lady patients." At which the doctor blinks.

"That's the only reason you're a doctor," says the doctor's wife, "so you can stick your hands up young girls and get them to undress for you." Still the doctor just smiles, as if about to prescribe a tranquilizer. "You killed my baby," says the doctor's wife. "How many other abortions have you done?" But nothing seems to move the doctor. He smiles.

"Answer me," she shrieks.

"Do be quiet, Margot," he murmurs. "Don't upset the children. I know you're very upset yourself."

The words are quiet and reasonable, but is there pleasure in his eyes, as he watches, from the cool heights of his aloofness, his wife's distressed and murderous writhings? Yes. Or at any rate, she sees it there, through glazed eyes which in their lifetime have seen little else but the disagreeable underside of things: the mold and mess behind the refrigerator, the rot under the floorboards, the mice droppings at the back of the cupboard, the malice behind kind words.

Oh, punishment!

"You don't care about the children," whispers Margot/Madeleine in her dusty dead voice. "You don't care about me. The only person you ever cared for was your sister Jill, and you killed her. As good as. First you stripped her, then you killed her. That's what you do to women. Or want to."

The doctor frowns. His face stiffens; the cracks in his façade deepen. She has made him angry now. He looks what he knows he is—his sister's murderer—an old, old man, his true face, his true nature, at last revealed. It is a skeletal face, grinning animosity. His father's face; his own as well.

Oh, punishment!

Margot smiles in triumph. She sees him now for what he is. "I never loved you," she says.

"Then why did you marry me?"

"Because I was pregnant."

"I loved you," he says.

Ah, love. So long ago, and in the past, in both their true voices. A great grief overwhelms Margot. "Thank you," says Margot/Madeleine, harshly thrusting back grief with anger. "And your deigning to love me is supposed to compensate for a lifetime of servitude? What a con it all is. I love you; you wash my socks."

The room is very cold. The doctor's wife bites and bites her yellow hand with her long teeth, as if to stop herself speaking the words her mouth utters.

"Can there be anything left for you to say?" he says. "Anything left to hurt me and damage you? Take your time."

"It's all been worth nothing," she says. "My life wasted," and she believes it.

"You have more than most women," he reiterates. "A house, a garden, a husband. We have a car, two children—"

"I have two children; you have one." And her long jaws clamp into her hand, too late to stop the words.

Philip laughs. "Which of them isn't mine?"

"Laurence."

He laughs again.

Blood flows from the wound in her hand. "I hate this home, this prison. I hate you," she shrieks.

He shivers. So his sister Jill once spoke to him. Why is it so cold? The back door is open, wasting the central heating. Her strong, bleeding hands move towards his throat; they will clearly kill him if they can. He catches them in his own. She screams. It is a strange, distant sound, as if there was not enough breath left in her body to give it proper strength.

"Margot," says the doctor in desperation, "you are not Madeleine. You are my wife. Madeleine is dead. This is some kind of hysteria. Please stop it."

Margot's hands lose their strength. Her breath, coming in gasps, gradually quietens. She looks at him with her own eyes; her hands are familiar once again—small, powerless, unblemished.

"All I can say," says the doctor, "is that if having Hilary here means so much to you, by all means, go ahead."

Oh, I am the doctor. I have seen the past resurrect itself in the lives of my patients. I thought I was immune, but I am not. The dead rise up and speak against us with our own voices.

He looks at his wife sadly and warily.

The doctor's wife is puzzled: she had forgotten all about Hilary, the sense of her own grievances drowning all ordinary, everyday compassion. Why does the doctor mention her now? He smiles. The habit of acceptance, of subservience, is strong. She forgets the past; her wrongs are swept away in the relief of his forgiveness; she smiles; she stretches out her small plump hand and touches his cold, bony fingers, allowing them their secrets. She is the doctor's wife again, mother of the doctor's children, feeder of the doctor's cat. Habit triumphs, or is it love? What's love?

Presently the cat creeps back, and Lettice with her homework, and Laurence from his friends. The doctor's wife makes cocoa.

Yes, says Lettice. I'll move over, I suppose, and make room for Hilary. If I have to. Yes, says Laurence. I did it once for Lettice. I'll do it again for Hilary. If I have to.

Making room!

In the outpatient department, still on the shiny plastic sofa, Lily sits clasping Jonathan, who now lies completely still. His eyes are partly open, and as far as Lily can see, they are glazed over. She is in a frenzy of grief; she looks like some wild old woman; her hair in the harsh neon light has the greyness of age, not of artifice. So Ida looked once. Lily believes that Jonathan is dead. Jarvis has gone looking for a doctor. Jonathan moans; it is not all over yet.

"Lily."

Lily looks up. There's the familiar clatter, and here comes Hilary, loping in her ungainly fashion down the glaring length of the waiting room.

"Lily, what's the matter with Jonathan? You didn't tell me you were here. I thought you were out."

Hilary speaks reproachfully, more like mother than child, and takes Jonathan from his mother without so much as a by-your-leave, and shakes him automatically to bring life and sense back into him. "He should be in bed," she cries. "Look at him. He's exhausted."

And Jonathan, no different from any other half-asleep child who does not care for his surroundings, grizzles feebly, and then, waking up sufficiently to perceive their full horror, buries his head in Hilary's puffy bosom and begins to bawl, crimson in the face. Every now and then he lifts his head from the enveloping flesh to gain more breath to make more noise.

The noise is indeed astounding. A doctor comes running. He is a fierce, dark-eyed young man of Mediterranean complexion, with a silky beard. "What's the matter with this child?" he demands. "Why is he making this dreadful noise?"

"It's his foot," says Lily.

The doctor picks up the foot and inspects it disdainfully. "It's only a little blister," he says. And so it is. "Any child who can make a noise like that is perfectly healthy." And it is true that thereafter Jonathan, having learned that it is better to protest than to endure, will set up such a volume of noise to get his own way that the people in Nos. 9, 13 and 11 Adelaide Row sometimes debate whether or not to call the Society for the Prevention of Cruelty to Children and report his callous mother.

Making room!

Lily takes Jonathan home. Jarvis follows. Hilary lumbers behind, limping where she has turned her foot in her absurd platform heels in her hurry to get to the hospital and protect Jonathan from his past and her own.

"You're lucky," says Jarvis, "that you didn't break your ankle." Lucky Hilary!

Jarvis has a parking ticket; he will have to pay a £6 fine. He does not mind. He has gotten off lightly and knows it. Lucky Jarvis.

Hilary squeezes into the back of the car. She has been hurrying. Lily wishes that Hilary used a deodorant. Madeleine disapproved of them. Smell is natural, Madeleine would say; only people who are afraid of sex are afraid of smelling. Well, Lily will soon bring Hilary round to better, nicer ways of living. Lily thinks.

"I took the guinea pig round to the doctor's house," says Hilary. "And they asked me if I'd like to stay. I said I would. Well, it's nearer school. Would you mind?"

"It's as you want," says Jarvis with a touch, the merest touch, of sadness. But enough. "If you'd be happy there," says Lily, dazzled by her good fortune.

"I could come to you on weekends," says Hilary kindly. "The same as usual. And look after Jonathan."

"I'll make over the spare room into a proper bedroom for you," says Lily. "After all, it's your house as well as mine. You were there before I ever was." Stepping back, chastened, making room. Understanding what she's done.

"If Jonathan wakes in the night," says Lily, "I'll go to him myself. I am his mother."

Lucky Lily, to have a child to go to, who wakes in the night. Lucky Lily, to have a child to go to. Lucky Lily, to have a child. Lucky Lily.

Lucky Lily—thinks what remains of Madeleine, without envy and without regret. Lucky Lily. You are my sister too. Keep your child. Just don't keep mine. Good night, goodbye.

There is, after all, quite a respectable gathering around the grave as the coffin is lowered on its canvas holders into a hole which is tactfully lined with sheets of plastic green grass. Not a worm in sight. Such burials in mother earth, decently clothed, come expensive. Jarvis does not mind. The new stair carpet and the new roof will have to wait awhile. He has told Lily so and she accepts it. "I worry about the paper in the spare room," says she, "that's all. I don't want the roof to leak and the paper start peeling; I want it to be nice for Hilary at weekends." And so she does. Nice Lily. "Well," she says, "it's not for nothing I come from the Antipodes. As for the roof, I'll get up there and mend it myself." And so Lily does. Good Lily.

Hilary eventually chooses new wallpaper for her room at Adelaide Row. A twenties revival: splodgy red roses on a fawn ground. It is not to Lily's liking, but she allows Hilary her choice. Kind Lily.

The doctor is at Madeleine's graveside, and the doctor's wife, and the doctor's children, Laurence, Lettice and Hilary. Renee is there with her friend Bonny, back from her husband for the fourth time. Renee smiles at Margot, and Margot smiles back. Each to her own taste.

It is not a particularly tearful or dismal funeral. The cemetery is at Ruislip, in North London, a green and leafy place. The wind blows fresh and strong; the sun even shines.

Lily is glad she came. Though she finds the décor and the plastic music of the chapel distasteful, and the presiding clergyman, though pleasant enough, quite hopeless when it comes to comprehending the sorrows of strangers—as how could he not be? At least the coffin is longer than Baby Rose's must have been.

Lily has had to bring Jonathan with her; she cannot find a baby-sitter. He totters off confidently to play hide-and-seek amongst the tombstones. Thousands of them, stretching off far beyond the limits of his vision. His foot is completely healed except for a small drying blister, which on Margot's instructions Lily is leaving uncovered.

Margot has handed in her notice; she will not be working with Jarvis any more. Nor will Jarvis replace her. Business is contracting to such an extent that it is hardly sensible to do so, and Lily is pleased to observe that he can be so realistic and sensible about his affairs.

Mr. Quincey is there, smelling strongly of tooth powder. Renee relented sufficiently to tell him the time and place of the funeral. Standing there watching the gold wood box lowered into the bright green fronds, he feels, if not part of the family, at least part of a greater humanity, and the living part of it at that.

Good night, Madeleine. Goodbye. Thank you.

24

Recognition, realization!

> *"To his nest the eagle flies*
> *O'er the hill the sunlight dies . . ."*

sings Hilary a week later, walking through wet streets. The damp air, or the aura of tears in which she has been living, has undone the work of the hairdresser, and her shorn hair now curls tenderly around her face.

> *"Hush, my darling, have no fear.*
> *For thy mother watches near."*

Oh, I am Hilary, daughter of a once-living mother, mother of children yet unknown. I shall never eat Sugar Puffs again. (How closely, inextricably, intertwine the sacred and the profane.) My mother's death has set me free. My life, her death—that's the sum of what she gave me. Dying was the best thing she could do for me: this was her best and final gift.

Hilary turns into the doctor's gate, goes down the side of the doctor's house. The doctor's cat uncurls, gets up, pads after her as if he'd always done it, always would, and follows her through the kitchen door.

Recognition, realization.

The guinea pig stares at Hilary, unblinking, through the meshes of his cage.

"You'll have to clean the cage out, Hilary," says Margot. "He's beginning to smell. I'm not going to do it. I have quite enough to do."

Hilary sits at tea between Laurence and Lettice and nods politely as Laurence tells her about the changing weather patterns of the Sahara—though how long such civility will last, who's to say?

Hilary's hands are like Laurence's, thinks Margot tonight; they are red, cold, knobbly-knuckled, strong.

When Philip comes in from surgery and sits at the head of the table, there they are again—serving the salad, dissecting the ham with the efficiency of indifference.

Recognition, realization.

Margot sits in shock. Where was Madeleine sixteen years ago when Margot was with Jarvis—in the shadow of the peeling pink roses? Where was Philip? Did he come looking for his Margot through the haze of boiling punch and candlelight, and find Madeleine instead? In the garden, in the bathroom, on the dark stairs where Jarvis so lately sat and wept—in heaven, hell, anywhere? Before or after Madeleine discovered Jarvis and the dumpy nurse entwined? Her shock, his disappointment? Which? Or both?

Hilary is home. Next to Laurence, her half-brother, and next to him, her father, gazing at her, and not through her.

"I can't imagine you with long hair," says Philip. "Madeleine's was always short."

Margot goes to fetch the mayonnaise. Then she gets up and fetches the mango chutney, which she's forgotten to put on the table.

Enid comes on Wednesday for the last time, setting Margot free to help Philip with his taxes. She is moving to a little flat the other side of London. "I can't have the baby *and* Sam," she says. "I just don't have the time. I'd rather have the baby. It offers me a future, and Sam doesn't—just more of the same. He doesn't seem capable of change. He can only go on looking at things in the same old way."

"What about your job?" asks Margot.

"I'll manage both somehow," says Enid, and no doubt she will. She has been crying. It is not easy thus to change the patterns of the past, to forgo the reassuring pleasures of servitude, to face the unknown. Don't think it doesn't hurt. The first sea animals crawling up onto dry land must have had an agonizing time: struggling for breath, burning in the primeval sun.

"I don't know what it's all about," says Laurence to his mother, lifting his head from the O-level astronomy textbook. "Do you? You can find out any number of facts, but they don't seem to get you anywhere. And we're all so infinitesimal ... First you're born and then you die. Why?"

"I can only suppose," says Margot, "that we are here to consider the ways of the Creator, and be amazed."

Does Margot speak with her own voice, or does it still have the resonance that came with Madeleine's death—an afternote, like the aftertaste of a good claret, gravelly, with the flavor of churchyards? Margot thinks perhaps it does. Her eyes, she sometimes thinks, are less shallow, less buttony, less doll-like than they used to be. Or is that just age, creeping on, and the pain of experience recognized at last?

> I am Margot the doctor's wife, no longer young. I shall be happier now that I have acknowledged grief, and loss, and the damage done to me by time, and other people, and events—and the damage that I did. I am Laurence's mother, and I can tell him nothing; none of us learn from another's experience; and besides, he is male and I am female. He is the doctor's son. Hilary is the doctor's daughter. I am Margot and Madeleine in one, and always was. She was my sister, after all, and she was right: her child was mine, and mine was hers.

Madeleine lies in the cemetery; in three months the earth will have settled and Jarvis's money will provide a stone to take its place amongst the thousands already there. There her mortal remains will lie, where the wind blows down from Hampstead Heights.

As Laurence said, somewhat desperately, at the funeral, "Did you know that in the last Ice Age the glaciers stopped at Hendon Central? Hampstead Heath is the scree. That's why nothing much has ever grown there, and it's been left open ground." He cried all the same, briefly and painfully, for a total stranger, Hilary's mother.

"Oh, my sisters," whispers the memory of Madeleine to the still troubled air, "and my brothers too, soon you will be dead. Is this the way you want to live?"

Which at least seemed to create some kind of consensus, for or against, because after that there was nothing but the wind to ruffle the grasses and disturb the little gay pots of dried flowers on the more recent graves, and whatever trouble there was dispersed, and there was peace.

About the Author

FAY WELDON was born in England, but was brought up in New Zealand and went to St. Andrew's University in Scotland, where she studied economics and psychology. Thereafter she had a series of "odd jobs and hard times" until the mid-sixties, when she started writing. She is the author of three novels (*The Fat Woman's Joke, Down Among the Women* and *Female Friends*), and several plays, for both the theater and television (for the latter, several of the first episodes of *Upstairs, Downstairs*).

Ms. Weldon has three children and lives in London.

Fay Weldon
at her delightful, devilish best
!

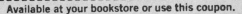